BIBLIOPHILIA

Also by Michael Griffith

Spikes

BIBLIOPHILIA

A Novella and Stories

MICHAEL GRIFFITH

Arcade Publishing • New York

FIRST EDITION

Library of Congress Cataloging-in-Publication Data

Griffith, Michael, 1965–
    Bibliophilia : a novella and stories / Michael Griffith. —1st ed.
    p. cm.
    ISBN 1-55970-676-7
     1. Women librarians—Fiction. 2. College librarians—Fiction.
    3. Academic libraries—Fiction. 4. College students—Sexual
    behavior—Fiction. I. Title.

PS3557.R48928B53 2003
813'.6—dc21   2003045323

Published in the United States by Arcade Publishing, Inc., New York
Distributed by AOL Time Warner Book Group

Visit our Web site at www.arcadepub.com

10 9 8 7 6 5 4 3 2 1

Designed by API

EB

PRINTED IN THE UNITED STATES OF AMERICA

For Nicola

Contents

BIBLIOPHILIA

Bibliophilia

Now I may wither into truth.

— W. B. Yeats

1.

Myrtle is making her rounds. On silent shoes she patrols the fourth-floor stacks, stalking offenders. She turns down the main literature aisle, eyes the stepstools in endless rank alongside the gunmetal shelves. Up the row, two stools are missing — *in use*. At 11 A.M. on a fall Saturday, in a remote corner of (she gauges how far ahead) Germanic poetry and fiction: unlikely to be any early-bird scholar. No, it's filth she'll find, again — the only ardency here, as usual, is the low and loinsome kind. She accelerates her pace a little, giving a weary wink to the Puritans as she passes: *I'll nip it in the bud,* she promises the good Doctor Mather, the Reverend Wigglesworth, staunch Mrs. Bradstreet in her bonnet and bun. *This place is a church, not a cathouse.*

But it's no wonder that the students go after one another in here like dogs mad with rut. There's something in the character of the place that encourages it: the plush chairs, the hotelish carpeting, the druggy buzz of the lighting; those stools, reminiscent of the bathroom — stools on which you might climb to fetch down hemorrhoid salve or the toilet brush; the open stacks themselves (*access,* that faintly ribald word). All these create an air of false, dangerous intimacy. It starts small. Every day she sees students roaming with their shoes off, flossing their teeth, sharing smuggled smoothies or nachos, exchanging massages in the smoking lounge. She confiscates pets: fish, lizards, a pair of white rats she saw cavorting in the hood of a man's sweatshirt as he strolled the stacks. Last week a grad student tried to claim that the tabby lapping tuna in her carrel was a seeing-eye cat, and when Myrtle gently pointed out that the student wasn't blind, the response was huffy: "I never said it was *my* seeing-eye cat." She rouses snorers on the couches, confiscates radios and six-packs and marijuana pipes made from soft-drink cans. And she sees countless young legs slung over chair arms: that vulgarly sexual widening of the thigh, the faint blue lattice of veins. From there, just one small step . . .

Now Myrtle hears a sigh, a loud and throaty mewling. With two fingers she damps the clapper of the bell she carries; she keeps up her steady creep. And then — *This is not a drill* — she catches sight, through a gap in the curtain of books, of a shocking white hip canted forward, and with the next step spots the . . . the mound of Venus, with its absurd auburn nimbus, and there's a male face *lapping* at it. All this is at eye level, impossibly high, and Myrtle realizes they must be using the stools as some sort of sordid pedestal. Her stomach seizes up — this is not covert, zipless, fretful; it is flagrant nudity and pubic tangle and writhing statuary. The brazenness of it — the nerve. Myrtle is forty-nine years old, a Mistress of Library Science, a woman of the world. She's no prude. She hates this duty, truth be told. It's just that there will be no *lapping,* for God's sake, on her watch; there Myrtle most emphatically draws the line.

Her duty is to hold firm, even if it means a scene. Myrtle despises scenes, which are for those who lack self-control. A rule: Only fools show themselves in public — as for pudendum, the same for soul. She wishes these shiny young people would keep their ids and orifices to themselves: diddle one another silly in private, if they want, but keep the library a preserve for the book and its dusty devotees. Is that too much to ask? The books, safe in their cellophane condoms, set a fine and celibate example, but no one heeds. No one heeds.

She slows, averts her eyes from the gyrations *d'amour.* Why has her boss, Mort Bozeman, assigned her the sex watch? He seems not to understand that a woman of a certain age, having passed (thank God) her change in life . . . that such a person, having put the foolishness of breeding behind her, should not be forced into service as a deputy sheriff of nookie. Why must she see these open mouths, clashing pelvises, dewy genitals? What will she say to this pair, cunnilinging away like minor Greek gods on a makeshift plinth that's library property, paid for by the taxpayers of the great state of Louisiana? I, Myrtle thinks, am a woman of dignity. This is beneath me.

Then she hears an avid whisper, and at once her mood changes. The voice, panting like some porn star — "Oh, Rex, you *stud*" — is familiar. It belongs to Lili, Mort Bozeman's seventeen-year-old daughter. Modest Lili of the knee socks, the *What Would Jesus Do?* charm. Lili the cheerleader, who had to ask Daddy if she could don the microskirt and Scotch-plaid bloomers of the parochial school she's true to. Lili the candy striper, Lili of the velvet hair ribbons. These squeals, that scarp of hip, that taut alabaster skin: they belong — despite the girl's careful sham of innocence — to that little vamp Lili.

Myrtle is a woman of stern self-restraint; she is a woman of character. And yet, as she pivots around the metal stanchion and enters the trysting place, she can feel a grin teasing at the corners of her mouth. Behind her teeth, her tongue flits joyously. She swings her bell high.

2.

Alone, Seti mans the circulation desk. He tries to give this a heroic ring, like *Alone, Seti wields his mighty scimitar to smite the foes of Ra,* but to no avail. The pharaohs and satraps would never have ventured across oceans and centuries to scan ID cards and stamp books in a university library. They would never have surrendered to the cheap seductions of cable television or cupcakes in clear plastic . . . or these milky southern girls in their bows and jumpers. What is wrong with him? With resignation he watches another gaggle of sorority sisters leave — all in bright, clingy leggings, braless under sweatshirts, long hair piled negligently atop their heads and held in place with clips, a hairstyle known locally as The Morning After. His eyes ache as each girl, in turn, gives the turnstile a little sideward nudge with a perfect hip and squeezes through. He savors a fleeting whiff of the cinnamon gum they're all snapping. "Happy reading, young ladies!" Seti sings out, but as usual they ignore him. It is the curse and the joy of Saturday mornings that he sees them like this: these coiffed and meticulously made-up creatures who once a week — at the one place and time they *know* they can't encounter desirable boys (who scorn the library anyway and are now sleeping off beer binges) — slink through the stacks au naturel, their faces bare, babes on the slum. They're irresistible like this, with their blotchy chins and their abundant hair stacked in Medusal coils and harboring, he sees when they bend to rummage for ID, an occasional pill of sweater or bedclothes. They give off a doughy aroma of sleep, and occasionally their cheeks still carry pillow creases, and it's too much to take. An hour into this morning's shift, Seti's knuckles are scarred with the inky remnants of due dates and he's terribly footsore and he's begun, again, to doubt his destiny.

Seti lives in a crime-ridden slum pinched between campus and the levee. Gentrification is beginning to nibble at its edges, mainly in the form of student condos and iron-gated apartment complexes. His neighborhood is overrun with lean and hungry cats, scruffy things with bobtails and lopsided whiskers and paws like frayed cuffs. They vie for scraps at the Dumpsters, loll on greasy wooden flats behind the Vietnamese restaurant unfancily named Eat Place, nap on the hoods of the wheelless Detroit behemoths — Cadillacs, Lincolns, Oldsmobiles — that line the streets. These low-slung felines are Seti's only link, here, to the glories of his ancestry, and he feeds them. It started as a small, sentimental tribute to the cats of ancient Egypt, who were sealed into the pharaohs' crypts along with tidy heaps of dead mice to sustain them in the afterlife. One day Seti slipped some freezer-burned sausage links, a legacy from the tenant before him, to a bony tabby he found on his stoop — simple as that. But word soon spread, and now he is greeted each afternoon by alley cats of every description. Seti stands among them with a platter, forking out the slick ghosts of fish, and in gratitude, these down-on-their-luck gods rub his legs; they sharpen their teeth on his shoes. This is as good as it gets, here: the love of those raw tongues in a dooryard filled with blowing trash. Though it's September, there are milky Styrofoam cups, brown-streaked and friable with age, crammed into the fence-mesh of the radiator shop next door to spell out MERRY XMAS.

Not long ago, Seti's fate seemed clear, simple — but for the last three years he has been in the United States. Here destiny is not thrust upon you: "No, you have the freedom," as Seti's sarcastic friend Ms. Myrtle puts it, "to muck up your life any way you like. The choice of what to fail at is yours." She means to comfort him, assuage his doubts ("Sure I understand," she teases. "Who *wouldn't* dread an existence with actual meaning?") — but far from home, far from the reminders of duty, Seti finds himself horribly tempted by America . . . and not just by its air of sexy indolence. He can't help musing, day after day, about what job he might have if he lived here. He might be the farmer who pours heads of garlic from a gunnysack into the slatted wooden bins at the produce market; a Civil War reenactor with a butternut uniform, a yellow dog, a metal detector, and a wheelbarrow-full of minié balls; the woman who sits in a lawn chair at roadside, her lap swarmed by Puppeez 4 Sale; an aproned man on TV moved almost to tears by his miracle broaster or granola roller; a professional pressure-washer, stripping this wet world of its mildew. He envisions himself as a construction worker propped against a stump, eating lunch from a miniature silver barn; a minor-league hockey player on steel blades, the ice (ice!) slipping underfoot; a rare-books librarian snapping on a pair of latex gloves.

Wirewalker, art potter, glider pilot, trimmer of holiday hams: all the glittering possibilities. He keeps a list he will never show anyone, in a spiral notebook emblazoned with the picture of a can of Spam. His guilty secret, his pink block of meat, his *America*.

Yet Seti must not yield. He has come — has been sent here — to study hydrology, to learn how Egypt might shepherd its most precious resource. The Suez and Ismailiyah canals and the Aswan High Dam have helped, but not enough, not anymore. How to irrigate crops more efficiently? How to make drinking water available in the As Sahra al Libiyah, the vast desert highlands of the West? These issues are far more important than his occupational whims, more important than well-walked wires, well-trimmed chops, well-carpentered rumpus rooms in decadent America — Seti must keep that in mind. Back home he excelled at his studies, weathered countless tests, and was elected by his government and his God to assume this responsibility. Seti and his family are thoroughly westernized, but he retains belief enough to keep in mind that the word *Islam* means "surrender to God's will." It means it, he understands, in the imperative: *Surrender or else.* He cannot let the lures of wearing the U.S. postal carrier's summer uniform (including pith helmet and stretch socks), or designing bright vinyl flags for porches, or replacing the letters on movie marquees with an angled magnetic pole . . . he cannot let these divert him from his devoir, his sacred duty. Following the path *should* be easy. Temptation is laughable, is the way of weaklings. Seti is an Egyptian, bound by promise and duty and affection. *He who sets foot in the water of the Nile,* goes the old proverb, *will always return.*

And he's grateful to his parents, to the government; it's not like he wasn't given a voice. He was allowed, for example, to pick his institution. "Anywhere in the world. This will be the first of many fateful choices, Mahfouz," said the minister of labor, who kept rubbing his pince-nez with a brilliant white handkerchief: "Choose well." Oh, how Seti had wanted to enter the minister's lofty world. That white linen cloth with its monogram. Those oval lenses, that tortoiseshell nosepiece. This office with its sandstone balcony overlooking a garden of date palms and crocuses, the broad desk on which you could, in a pinch, set down a helicopter. The green baize blotter, the rosebud inkpot. He knew better than to be desirous of *things*, of mere trappings, but still . . . perhaps he was, that early on, in trouble.

Yet he'd forged ahead eagerly. That he would choose the United States was never in question: Seti was born on the day of the Camp David accords in 1979, and an enlarged photograph of Sadat and Begin and Carter smiling and holding their linked hands high had, throughout his childhood, pride of place above his bed. And where better than south Louisiana, nearly the dampest place in the States? He remembers poring over an atlas in the government library at Al Zaqaziq — an oversized volume with a cracked leather cover, its pages edged with gold and inked in fantastic pastels, the place names recorded in the exotic alphabet of the West — and discovering this green boot, *La Louisiane,* encroached on from the south by countless sloughs, gulfs, bights, bays, and bayous. The inviting blue of water was everywhere; Louisiana's wadis were always wet. *There,* Seti said to himself, solemnly tapping the page, and he liked the sound so much that he spoke the word aloud, in English, over and over: "There. There. There."

At the airport his parents alternately wept and beamed, and when Seti's father, looking for refuge from emotion in his rudimentary English, honked loudly and said, "Honor us, son, you are the bright lamp hope of our nation," it seemed only slightly ridiculous, and that just because of the mucus clinging to his father's good and golden nose. Seti bowed, for perhaps the first time in his life, and hugged them (taking shameful care not to graze with a cheek his father's slick mustaches), and then his mother pulled out a pince-nez just like the one whose legend he'd been building in the preceding weeks. She cast her eyes down so as not to see her adult son, her leaving son, her son grown *distingué* at a stroke. Seti snugged the lorgnon over his nose and bowed again and turned and strode, tears streaming, down the walkway to the airplane.

Flying over southeastern Louisiana, the knotty skeins of brown or bluish water unraveling among bursts of jungle green, Seti pressed his forehead to the windowpane and gaped. Never had he seen such a color. During the descent his fellow passengers chewed honey-encrusted peanuts or dozed or read romances, but Seti shivered and gaped at the wide emerald swaths of lawn, the banana trees flapping in the heat, the clumps of live oak like broccoli florets of a hue so dark and rich that it could not, must not, be real. The bounty, he thought helplessly. And then he found himself — greenhorn in a green world, green behind the ears (was that how it went?) and, after the long flights, a little green around the gills — headed down the escalator to baggage claim, and from there, through glass doors that disappeared before you could touch and dirty them, into the landscape of his chlorophylly dreams. The humidity rushed to meet him, wrapping itself around his neck like a smothering towel or a python or . . . Seti had no way to say, having left behind not only his parents and his past but also his language, even his way of thinking. Already at that moment, he sees in retrospect, the moist Gulf air had seized his throat and begun to choke the Egypt out of him.

Now, three years later, he is only three months from finishing his baccalaureate degree. The district *muhafiz* is eager to have him back for a couple years of apprenticeship under a more experienced hydrologist, and only then will Seti become eligible for advanced study abroad. His father's heart has weakened, and his mother, whose knowledge of medicine seems iffy, thinks it can be set right by Seti's return. His time here is running out. Crane operator; shrimper; Dadaist; pool man. Peanut vendor; tree surgeon; blackjack dealer; sculptor of ice swans for weddings. No, none of these. Water engineer. Yes: hydrologist to a parched land. Dutiful son who must his progenitor's heart unclog, who must water the land of the dusty fellahin. He thinks of the blinkered water buffaloes turning tight, blind, endless circles as they move the waterwheels, the *sakiyeh,* in the heat.

3.

One thing must be absolutely clear. Myrtle is a woman of dignity. She knows whereof she speaks, dignity-wise, has more than a nodding acquaintance with that yearned-for quality. For twenty-two years she was a law librarian. She stood behind a walnut counter downtown and saved, without ado, the hides of hotshot lawyers. Or without much ado; a woman, underpaid and underappreciated, needs just a *hint* of ado. Subtle, inconspicuous ado, that is, ado of a kind (it should go without saying) that doesn't undermine dignity.

Myrtle always kept the countertop free of clutter, bare of personal effects, polished to a fierce sheen. It was chest-high, like a garment tugged up tight for protection: a breastplate, a cuirass. She refused all blotters, gewgaws, jokey calendars, which would only tame and shrink that rich brown expanse. What's more dramatic than an empty stage lit brightly?

Often the youngest, most arrogant lawyers — like husbands who on car trips refuse to ask directions, preferring lostness to any least hint of dependence — would be ashamed to seek her help. They'd slink in, hands in pockets or in prematurely thinning hair, staring holes in their wingtips, their crisp pantcuffs. These callow boys she'd string along most cruelly, disappearing for minutes at a time in a pantomime of search, leaving them to be haunted by their reflections: no shoes could be shiny enough to keep their eyes for long from the hypnotic gleam of the walnut counter. She'd drink a leisurely cup of coffee in the back, watch from a hidden nook as her supplicant twitched and fumed and dreamed up, for his supervising partner, an excuse for failure. That's something the law schools teach well, of course: magniloquent weaseling. She would let the youngster steep in his shame for a few minutes, and then, at last, she'd make her entrance, clutching a massive book — one finger pinched discreetly between the pages to mark her place. She never betrayed any emotion, any hurry, allowed herself only the blankest expression. Then, with a flourish of hands, Myrtle would spin the volume 180 degrees and drop it so it landed with a crack like gunfire. Amid a mist of book-dust, the undeserving little pissant would find before him the obscure but perfect precedent. She'd tap her index finger on the page: *This wouldn't happen to be on point, now would it, dear?*

Once he left, Myrtle would permit herself a brief and modest smile. Then she'd reach under the desk for her solvent, give two quick spritzes, and — having donned her gray velvet polishing mitt — lovingly restore the woodgrain's shine. It happened a thousand times, a hundred thousand. Those were wonderful days.

Myrtle is the possessor of a graduate degree, an immovable iron helmet of hair, an air that brooks no nonsense. But she isn't a caricature, isn't a prim crone in sensible shoes or a petty hardass or a lean, sexless bureaucrat with an iron-gray bun. Cartoonishness and dignity do not mix. She doesn't wear half-glasses on a leash; her ankles have never swollen a single time; she's never once lifted an index finger to her mouth and narrowed her eyes to shush someone. She doesn't spend her weekends lamenting the demise of the card catalog (though, okay, a little, maybe she pines just a jot for that musty, tactile, blond-wood *glory,* that row of massive rectangles atop spindly legs, like a showroom full of Cadillacs parked on nightstands). Truth be told, she doesn't read much, off the job: maybe *Smithsonian,* the newspaper engagements and obituaries, home-gadget catalogs. And having no spectacles means — obviously — that she couldn't very well fling them off, shake loose her glowing hair, and, an insta-vixen, jump some lucky jasper's bones in the bookmobile.

Those are myths; Myrtle has no patience with myths. She is, instead, someone who believes deeply in what she does — did. She practiced a noble profession. Through all those years at Gedge & McGillis, Myrtle worked to develop the stately, incorruptible air of a judge. She never let personal animus interfere with her duties. Despite the temptation, she never lost the paperwork for, say, that pink-faced scumbag Wills, who entertained his colleagues with a stream of Latin gibberish she wasn't supposed to follow, but the point of which was to smuggle in a few lecherous winks and the word *fellatio,* or a phrase like "doggie-stylus ad feminam cum rug-burnum." Such things were — when in Rome, speak Roman — infra dig. Myrtle wore drab clothes, muted makeup, minimal jewelry; her voice was low and calm; her heart was a steady thing she kept safe in her chest. No affairs, not even flirtation.

Sober as a judge. The analogy was exact. They had, after all, essentially the same job: keeping attorneys in line, books in order, preserving respect for the just and proper. No accident, Myrtle believes, that silence is enforced in libraries as in courtrooms. It's a matter of . . . dignity.

A judge must be judicial at all times, so Myrtle sweeps through daily life, too, in invisible robes. When tempted in the grocery line by sugary treats or tabloids — or if inclined to punish a neighbor kid for trampling her lilies — she merely poses herself a question: *Would Learned Hand buy a Blow Pop? Would Felix Frankfurter paw through the trashzines to see if Harrison Ford looks puffy? Would Oliver Wendell Holmes whomp a brat with a hand trowel?* The elderly gentlemen have always guided her well.

The answer to these hypotheticals could never be clearer than now, in the case at hand: Frankfurter and Holmes and Learned Hand would never stoop to *this.* They'd never find themselves exiled in middle age to the state university's library, with its tattooed nitwits and stained carpet and misspelled graffiti and gray, mucusy gum stuck in every cranny. With its deplorable open stacks (the first step toward anarchy). They'd never work in such a garish fluorescent hive, with no oak wainscoting, not a single green banker's lamp or ficus tree or Persian rug in sight. They'd never handle books like the one Myrtle came across last week, in which some shining hope for our future had drawn, on the endpaper, a detailed and intricately labeled sketch of Gertrude Stein's vulva. *A snatch is a snatch is a snatch,* he'd scrawled underneath.

And God knows that, being possessed of dignity to an extraordinary degree, up to their gills, their eyeballs, they'd never — after more than two decades of flawless work behind the glowing walnut bier of The Law — be replaced by a computer program, and they would *under no circumstances* be pressed into service as sex cops, junior grade. They would not spend their days walking a book-lined beat, carrying a massive flashlight and a dinner bell gone glandular, creeping through aisles on fools' errands, peering through chinks in the unmoving stacks for flashes of throbbing flesh, keeping an ear out for any squeals or coos that couldn't be accounted for by the delights of solitary reading. *They would not.*

4.

This morning the international students are out in force, and they've expanded upon their usual beachhead in the periodicals room. Seti's ragtag troops — with their funny shoes and drapy garments that exude cooking smells, their veils and dots and turbans and dashikis — rule the field; the stacks are their foothold in this country, their musty dominion. But briefly, briefly: on football Saturdays the library closes at noon, at which point it becomes impossible to wade through the tailgaters outside. The *normal* people, pie-eyed white men with their faces and barrel bellies painted purple; wives with cheeks discreetly inked and with earlobes distended by huge earrings, GO in the left, TIGERS in the right; boys in golf carts equipped with horns that blare out the fight song as they chase skate punks through the streets, pelting them with hushpuppies or sausage balls; girls applying face glitter by the light of a pickup's chrome wheel wells.

In here, though, native-born kids are nowhere to be seen, except for the smattering of sorority girls — and Seti seldom sees them *working*. Mostly they rove in chattering packs, rummaging through rucksacks and laughing out loud. Yet this morning they seem intent on some task at hand. They arrive in ones or twos, stop at the desk to check which study room they've reserved, then march upstairs. If curiosity gets the best of you, you'll find them on the fourth floor, immured in their glass-walled cubicle, sitting at the table around a tower of plastic party cups ringed by inkwells of nail polish; they're decorating sorority totems for tonight's game. It's a twisted genre portrait: the china painters, their tongues tender buttons of concentration, wielding tiny brushes in a fog of acetone: "Go Tigers! Rip the Tide!" If you linger outside the window, straightening the books on a reshelving cart (books that happen to be unstraight, that cry out for straightening), they'll glare until you leave.

To them, Seti is a dark-skinned serving boy. It gives him a guilty thrill to think of the rest of the world encamped here in the library, an invasion army, ready to beard these lazy Americans in their den. This morning the poor and tired masses are doing their huddling over computer screens in the reference room, poring over microfiche downstairs, casing the moth-eaten boxes of government documents kept behind crude fencing in the sub-basement, in Compact Shelving. A few are in Periodicals, reading newspapers. The aliens: his people. Patiently unlocking the secrets of the West right out in the open while the skinheads and militia crazies shoot pop bottles off fenceposts or are splayed across moldy basement couches, vetting TV cartoons for race-mixing and faggotry.

A little after ten-thirty, Mr. Bozeman strides through the doors and toward the desk. "Alles in Ordnung?" he asks. He clearly thinks this the height of wit: a Ukrainian-American speaking Kraut to a son of Egypt.

"Ten-four, goody buddy," says Seti. Always give them what they want. Anyway, why is Mr. Bozeman in the office on a Saturday?

"Have you seen Lili?"

He has; he has. Darling Lili, the girl of his dreams. Lili the lovely, the diligent. How many teenagers arrive at the university library, clutching a bouquet of schoolbooks, on a weekend?

"Good day, Miss Lili," Seti had called as she swept past the desk. She was wearing a red tube dress and untied sneakers. Her hair was pulled back into pigtails.

She stopped, turned, walked over. "You crack me up, Seti. You're like from a different planet. Where did you get those *duds?* It's Saturday. Chill out a little." She set down her books, leaned over the counter. Then she reached for his throat, loosened the knot of his tie; she untwisted the lapel of his suitcoat. Seti imagined the cords of her calves as she stood on tiptoes to minister to him. It was nearly enough to make him faint.

"Hey," she said. "Mind if I borrow those coolio glasses for an hour or so? Today's a big day." Seti, as always around her, was tongue-tied. He could not speak as, grazing his skin with her fingers, she removed the pince-nez his mother had given him. Lili left a light wake of lavender mixed with, what, sour apple? She planted the glasses at the end of her long, straight nose and raised her chin. "Shhhhh," she hissed suddenly, and Seti nearly jumped back: What did I say, *Habibi?* What have I done? "Speech is silver, silence golden," she barked. This was one of her father's mantras, and she delivered it with fierce and scary accuracy. She tapped her nose and said, "Sure it's okay?"

Seti thought for an instant about the minister of labor, about the trouble his mother had taken to have these lenses ground, this nosepiece handcrafted. What would she think if she knew he'd lent them to a painted American girl as a plaything? But Lili had not spun and left without an answer, content with having posed the question. She must have known that he couldn't deny her anything, yet she was doing him the favor of standing there, waiting for his consent. A big day, a good girl. She gifted him with an incandescent smile, peered down that wonderful aquiline nose at him again, and wagged a finger.

At long last, his chance. His time. "You may, Miss Lili. Certainly you may. For me also this is a red leper day." A what? Relax. Speak English. "For me also this is a day of great size. I have a favor and kindness to ask of you."

"Whatcha need?" asked Lili, her chin still high. Her throat was perfection, a crystal champagne flute. She grabbed both pigtails and twisted them as though trying to adjust a TV antenna, but she couldn't home in on his desperate signal. *I would like to request the honor . . .*

"I would like to regress the hunter . . ." His tongue knotted itself again, and he could feel his eyes beginning to bulge. A professor strode toward the desk with a teetering stack of books in her arms. Now or never. "I would like . . . to request the honor . . . Miss Lili . . . of talking to you later today." Cop-out. Again.

"Great. I'll have something to tell you, too, I think. I'll drop by on the way out. Thanks a bunch, Seti. *Mr.* Seti," she'd laughed as she plucked up her books and flounced toward the stairwell.

Mr. Bozeman, it turned out, needed him to convey a message. "I'm running late," he said, "for an important appointment, and I'll meet her back here at closing. I know she has plenty of work to occupy her until then. Could you track her down? You know her spots better than I do. I'll have someone from reference cover the desk."

Two minutes later, Seti was bounding up the steps and trying to devise the patter that would make her love him. He would say that she was as sweet as pistachio brittle, as candied caraway seeds; she was as beautiful as the season's first thunderhead. This time if she produced photos of her dog, a black furball named Dewey, he would not merely moon and goggle at her like some halfwit until she asked in horror whether they *ate* Scotties back home. Instead he would segue suavely into the story of the rabbits and fowl he kept, as a boy, on his parents' rooftop. From there he would move to extolling Egypt's charms. He would describe the baroque pigeon-houses — whitewashed or gaily painted architectural marvels, some outfitted with minarets or flying buttresses — that people built to attract a source of fertilizer for their crops; he would speak of the wizened old men in caftans who hawked bodybuilding magazines on the street, terrifying Seti with their crooked fingers and cloudy eyes. *You are my pale goddess,* he would say. *If I may make so bold: the way that dress clings to your form restores one's faith in a benevolent God.*

Maybe this will be the day when he can say these things, when he can get past his knocking knees and burrowing eyes and tangled tongue. When, emboldened by the sight of his glasses riding her nose, he can penetrate her torrent of bright American palaver. *Yes, my dear Lili, but leaving aside the Red Hot Chili Dogs and body-piercing and Mr. Leghorn Foghorn . . . I must soon return to my homeland, a glorious place, and would you come with me?* He'll settle, of course, for the first date he has planned, but a man can dream, can't he? In America, a man is allowed to dream. Tugboat captain; water-slide operator; harbormaster; lifeguard; pool man. Barrel-rider: yes, he can see himself bobbing just below Niagara Falls, throwing open the hatch to drink in the mist and the applause. And Lili there too, waving a handkerchief, tears of relief glistening on her cheeks — this last the most sought-after water of all, the highest water Seti can aspire to. Nearby there is a hot tub still in full roil, a heart-shaped bed that bears the fresh imprint of their bodies. A man can dream: lover of Lili.

But where is she? Seti suspects she may be with Rex, whom he saw slip in a few minutes after Lili. Rex is a sophomore, smooth of skin and oily of manner. He has a dime-sized soul patch of an unnatural yellow, a silver charm in his earlobe; he was carrying no books when he passed. Seti would hate to repeat the scene of a few weeks ago, when he happened upon them in one of the nooks that used to be smokers' lounges. He couldn't bear to see Lili's feet in Rex's lap again, him massaging her arches and twirling her WWJD anklet and saying, "What would Jesus do, baby? Jesus was *cool*; Jesus was *rock-and-reel*. Hay-soose would *get busy*. You know I'm right."

Seti pauses on the fourth-floor landing to steady his breathing, to tauten his tie. Maybe she will seize the lump at his throat again, loosen it again, right in front of Rex. *That* would show him.

5.

It was eleven o'clock on her first morning at LSU, back in June, and she was taking a break with a young student-worker. His name was Sadie, she thought he'd said. Sexy Sadie: the boy *was* pretty, in an exotic, sun-burnished way, and his shyness, what she insisted on thinking of as his sphinxlike reserve, was appealing as well. His unusual spectacles — what were they called, the ones that balance on the nose? — made him look like a smoldering-eyed colonial clerk from a novel about the British Empire. The daughter of the gruff regimental commander had better watch out for her heart, and her maidenhead. Myrtle was appalled at herself for thinking this way even idly, transiently, but being fired had loosed her from her moorings. She has been plagued these last two weeks by the fear that she ought to have led a life more like the one she foresaw in youth: wide travel, strong drink, hot sex. She stole a glance at where the boy's Adam's apple and collar met and tried to convince herself that this peek, this taking note of the contrast of hues — bronzed Egyptian skin versus bleached Egyptian cotton — fell under the rubric of aesthetic appreciation. But that would be a lawyerly dodge, and she'd left such casuistry behind forever when one of the partners at G&M, apparently driven loony by years of euphemism, tried to mollify her by saying she hadn't been sacked but instead *decruited*. No, it was best to call things by their proper names: hot pants, nether stirrings, lust. And lust was for the young, Myrtle reminded herself. In the aged it was a sign of weakness, of wishful thinking. It was a denial of the sad fact: adulthood is just another name for decline. You flip your tassel and then maybe swing by the altar before toddling off toward the grave, and the best you can do is drag your feet for a few decades. Eros against Thanatos isn't a fair fight, and once you know the bout is fixed, how to take the old slap-and-tickle seriously anymore? You do what you can, in the face of such knowledge, to maintain your equanimity, your dignity. You hold your tongue and keep your distance. You do not linger on the blemishless skin of the children you work alongside. You do not notice the little dimples imprinted on their noses when they remove their spectacles for cleaning.

Seti buffed his pince-nez just as the minister of labor had, with a spotless handkerchief embossed with initials. (Seti's, alas, had been bought in bulk at a thrift shop off campus, and the florid lilac monogram it bore was that of some poor schlep who'd had to hock his snotrags . . . but the principle held, insofar as principles could be made to hold in this place.) He and Myrtle stood next to a pebbled bench in front of the building and looked out over the bike racks at the hirsute palm trunks, the dark tent of oaks, the root-riven concrete paths through the quad. Myrtle had been musing about why the chief had called her: He didn't know her, she said, from — an atom's howl-scat? She was a . . . had she said pig in a pork? A pickin' up oak? A peg in a pope? This being south Louisiana, it could refer to anything, from cannibal hog to staked pontiff.

Myrtle had questioned everyone she could. Friends told her this new job was a gift horse, and its teeth were its own business — why be a pony dentist when pony dentists never prosper? The lady at the bakery gave Myrtle a free petit-four, either as lagniappe or to shut her up. Her hairdresser nodded sagely, said, "Man pur-poses, and God imposes," then leapt into juicy gossip involving a local politician who, at a whorehouse bust, had been found cowering in an upstairs closet *in diapers*. Her husband speculated that one of the attorneys she'd bailed out must have called in a favor, but that wasn't plausible. Several partners at G&M were capable of generosity, in a pinch, but they'd never forgo the credit. Altruism is for fools and children; lawyers jones for good PR like junkies crave smack.

Myrtle had twice come to the library to introduce herself, but Mort wasn't there on either occasion; in both cases she "*just* missed him." He was never available by phone, and he seemed to have a well-tuned instinct for when she wouldn't be home to receive his return call: "Sorry I missed you, Ms. Rusk!" he'd boom at her machine. "I shall look forward to making your acquaintance. This is Mort Bozeman, by the way, *jefe de la biblioteca*. That sounds like an Old West comic from when we were kids, doesn't it? 'Mort Bozeman, Jefe de la Biblioteca.' I'd carry a six-gun in one holster and one of those mean-looking date stamps in the other, and miscreants would quiver in their boots. Oh ho ho. Oh ho ho ho. Well, good-bye then, Ms. Rusk." How was she supposed to take this? How did he know her age, even approximately? What made him think that she hailed from a time and place that might have given birth to something called "Mort Bozeman, Jefe de la Biblioteca"? What made him think that "Oh ho ho" was an acceptable way to laugh?

She'd interrogated her soon-to-be colleagues, even enlisted the aid of a teenage neighbor to check him out on the Internet. She'd been able to amass a small dossier.

Mort Bozeman was born and reared in New Orleans. Few things on earth were so inimical to dignity as life in the Big Sleazy. Besides the traditional decadence — sex parts on parade, feats of alcoholism, an army of ill-dressed hustlers and eccentrics swarming the streets on the make — there were the . . . well, the atmospherics. Long ago, Myrtle's mother had instructed her: "A man sweats; women of the uncultured classes perspire; ladies *glow*." In New Orleans such notions were more than usually ridiculous. Every woman or man, duchess or stevedore, was drenched in sweat ten months of the year. On visits, Myrtle was always disturbed that she could smell everyone's hands. They perched in laps, held straps or poles, raked scalps, fished food out of greasy sacks, flew over spit-slicked valves. In the streetcar she was overwhelmed by the yeasty odor of palms; they all glistened, stank sweetly of bread. In New Orleans the perfume of tropical flowers mingled, even in the grandest neighborhoods, with the stench of river scum and rot. Order was unimaginable: no feat of housekeeping could beat back the vermin, the fungi, the mephitic air. Even the rich had peeling paint, green-tinged ceilings, scufflings in the walls. Nothing and no one was spotless.

Dignity is always and everywhere an illusion, but in such a climate it's an unsustainable one. The people opt for the dubious consolations of the flesh. Those bready hands rove one another's juts and clefts; sweat intermingles; the damp and tangled sheets look like thunderheads; the floors creak and the ceilings craze.

Which, Myrtle scolded herself, would account for Mort Bozeman's *birth*, at most — get hold of yourself. It's just that she's scrambling to find something to account for, or at least vaguely to presage, the good professor's academic career. Mort Bozeman (a widower, fifty-two; one child, Lili, eighteen this autumn) began as one of those quasi-Catholic scholars who devote themselves to some nutty blind alley of the sacred, in his case to representations, in Renaissance portraiture, of Mary fondling the rosy little pikielulu of the Christ child — showing off his miraculous God-given fleshliness, his having taken on a form in every way frail and human: *For God so loved the world that he gave his only begotten son, and outfitted him with a goofy nub just like yours.* Mort Bozeman's dissertation was entitled *Her Hand on the Staff of Life: Genital Display in Renaissance Portraiture of the Son of Man.* For a stretch there the Italians, especially, depicted Jesus with swaddling clothes always slightly disarranged, and Mary's hand was either subtly aiding our view of the lordly equipage or was brandishing it in praise. According to Myrtle's informant on the subject (a bitter lost-book cataloguer named Brenly, not wholly reliable), the only feelers about publishing the manuscript came not from the Oxford University Press but from fetishists' magazines called *Diddle* and *Onan the Barbarian,* whose editors stumbled across a tiny item in *Harper's* about Bozeman's research, a squib that was cruelly headlined "Beating the Bishop, Praising the King." Promotion was not forthcoming ("Skin mags don't count as refereed journals," Brenly laughed), and Mort was eventually exiled to the library, where for almost twenty years now he'd been serving as director of circulation and, lately, dean. He still taught an art-history class every semester, and for that reason (one supposed) spent much of his time away from the office. When he *was* in, Mort was often closeted away drafting answers to the smartass complaints kids shoved into the box at the side of the circ desk. "Can you people spare us some goddamn toilet paper for a change?" and "I'd check out way more books if you pooled the fine money and had a keg blowout at the end of every semester. Isn't this university supposed to be for the *students?*" were answered with sober, sesquipedalian essays that might run on for four or five hundred words: "The word *keg,* you may be interested to know, derives from a measure of how many sturgeon could be fitted into a small oaken cask. How's that for a pretty kettle of fish?"

"Mr. Boss-man," said Seti musingly. "Mr. Boss-man is an unusual fellow. I am not sure — you would have to —" He abruptly fell silent, and Myrtle saw what had snared the boy's attention: down the way there was a red-haired giant galumphing toward them, wearing a bright peach shirt and pale yellow pants. Students did double takes as he passed, his face buried in a book; he was all over the path. He would veer toward a flower bed or lightpost or knot of bystanders for twenty strides or so before, with a fleeting glance upward, correcting his course. As he drew closer, Myrtle could see that he wore an Amish beard, a shiny white belt. He looked like a Dreamsicle, but one that would scorn modern conveniences.

"Get a load of that guy," said Myrtle. "He's like a leprechaun on steroids."

The man stumbled through a sorority conclave, a sidewalk chalk drawing, and a hacky sack circle, leaving a wake of bewildered faces and obscene gestures. About thirty feet away now, he paused and, without looking away from his book, raised one foot. Then he swung the toe of his right wingtip outward and began scratching the inside of his left ankle with the heel.

Until then Myrtle thought it had to be a put-on. Over the years she'd known plenty of tax lawyers who'd cultivated some idiosyncrasy — a bow tie, a waxed mustache, a cane passed down from a Confederate general or made from the stretched and cured phallus of a bull — to pretend not to be run-of-the-mill bloodsuckers. True, she'd never seen anyone cultivate the look of an Amish push-pop, but she supposed you had to work harder at being weird in academe; the competition was stiffer.

Yet any man who would scratch an itch that way, among gaping students whisking past him on the way to class, had to be the genuine article. He was a freak, and therefore deserving of a freak's respect. Early in her tenure at the law firm, Myrtle had made it a point to file her rough edges, root out her eccentricities. Her job was to be invisible, laconic, efficient, wise. She banished much of her personality, traded it for repute, for *fair name* and *good odor,* which were the best an underling could aspire to. She swapped her quirks and irreverences for dignity, and she'd come to revere that quality — even, in her careful way, to love it — but she was painfully aware, sometimes, that she lived in a kind of sarcophagus. The dignified, like the dead, aren't allowed high spirits.

Maybe Jesus felt it as a loss when his mother could no longer be shown innocently polishing the godhead. Surely he, too — fully human and all — *liked* being touched, until his dignity would no longer bear it.

In youth — her dirty secret — Myrtle had been wild, rude, reckless. She ate peyote in the desert, spoke in tongues at a camp meeting and was rewarded afterward with a wet, wormy kiss from a circuit-riding preacher; she mounted her boyfriend while he drove eighty miles an hour through the Chisos, her skirt snapping loudly around their ears. Her prom date, just for kicks (and to let the townspeople know that she didn't mind their sneers and insults — floozy, slut, mattressback, the rest), was a quarter-ton hog, freshly scrubbed, on a leash made out of a velvet bathrobe sash. At eighteen she hitched a ride to Guatemala with a man flexible enough, he showed her, to suck his own cock. But then she grew up, left Texas. She married Milt, stolid Milt. She became a librarian at the law. She settled in, settled down, settled under. Her thighs and jawline widened, and her world narrowed.

Yet after all these years Myrtle bore a vestigial admiration for people who managed to ignore or flout or explode the proprieties. And this goofus in yellow highwaters, still abstractedly digging at his ankle with his clownish shoe, clearly didn't give a damn what people thought about him. His self-absorption had a winsome purity about it. Here was a man who knew what to do with an itch.

The titan leprechaun resumed his ramble. His beard, against the backdrop of trees, was a vivid red, like that of the contortionist who drove her to Guatemala. Suddenly she remembered the flash of Butch's pubic hair, his blue-white hips, in the jungly *plein air*. She recalled his amiable challenge: "What do I need you for, anyway? If you can do yourself, sugar, life gets pretty simple." Myrtle remembered her younger, lither, cleverer self as she pulled off her blouse, shucked her shorts. "What you *need*," she'd told him, "is a little complication. The short circuit gets a bit dreary, doesn't it?" Butch had been sitting on a camp stool, nude, watching her approach. He closed his eyes. She'd licked his eyelids, each in its turn, and then she sank slowly into his lap. Butch arched his hips, and the stool creaked. In the trees Myrtle heard the high chitter of wildlife. She joined in.

This reverie was a moment of weakness, not to be indulged — and it was uncharacteristic of Myrtle, who never allowed herself to catalog her losses. It's just that everything had gone topsy-turvy so quickly. After twenty-two years of impeccable work at Gedge & McGillis, she'd been dumped in favor of some ridiculous *computer,* and immediately, providentially, there'd been a call from Mort Bozeman. She'd taken no time off. Only twelve days before, she'd been sniffing the lemony sheen of the desk she'd ruled all those years. Now, suddenly, she was here, in front of this squat, ugly edifice, watching a comical reader wend his way among the nubile children. One of those children was alongside her, still ruminatively massaging his glasses. He had black hair, a white shirt, a long and glowing neck. It made her wonder how things might have turned out differently, and she couldn't afford that. Coming up on fifty; childless; steaming downstream, having left her fun thirty years astern. Stop it.

With every step the clumsy giant edged closer to the bike racks on his left, and Myrtle was about to call out a warning — he was only ten or twelve feet away — when his knee clipped a wheel rim and he went down hard.

Seti calmly folded his handkerchief and replaced his pince-nez. He stooped to retrieve the book, which was wedged between the metal slats of the rack, and stepped forward.

"Dagnab it, Mahfouz," said the redhead. "Who put this blasted rack in the middle of the path? It's a menace."

"Ms. Myrtle," said Seti, "meet Mr. Boss-man. Mr. Boss-man, meet Ms. Myrtle."

Mort propped himself onto one elbow; there was a little love bite on his forehead, and his pants were soiled and scarred. He extended his right hand upward, and as they shook, Myrtle could feel in her palm the tickle of gravel and blood. "Ah, my dear Ms.

Rusk," he said. "*Enchanté.* Step into my office, would you? You're just the woman I wanted to see. You're going on special assignment."

Seti and Myrtle pulled him to his feet, and he sprinted off to bathe his wounds. "See you in a twinkling," he called over his shoulder.

"You're kidding me," said Myrtle when he was gone.

Seti merely smiled, turned toward the door, and offered her his arm.

6.

Ten minutes later, Mort Bozeman — wearing on his forehead a small round bandage that looked like a witch's wen — waved Myrtle into his office. He was all business now. He closed the door, pointed to a chair, shoved a well-worn Xerox into her hands and thumped it once. It was from something called the *Quarterly Journal of Library Security.* Myrtle glanced up, and he nodded encouragingly.

"I have a few questions first," she said.

"All will in due time be made clear," said Mort, slipping into guru mode. There were specks of gravel in his beard that marred the effect . . . well, or maybe they enhanced it; Myrtle had little experience with gurus, and it might be that gravel in your beard was a sign of freedom from petty bourgeois concerns like a gravel-free beard. He nodded again at the soiled copy, and she began reading.

The article was a screed — alternately indignant and despairing in tone, alternately purple and purpler in prose — about the spreading epidemic of sex in American college libraries. It cited trumped-up statistics (for instance, 11 percent of the books in a sample at one suburban Philadelphia university were marred by "stains of suspicious origin" . . . which Myrtle presumed to mean that someone in reshelving there had a Twinkie habit), and the author struck a steady tone of hysteria as he railed against "eructations of Eros." Mort had jaggedly underlined the most spectacular anecdote, an account of "outrages against decency" at UCLA, where three nude undergraduates allegedly slathered molten cheese over one another in a special collections room. The story was surely apocryphal, some kind of joke, but one calculated to shiver the timbers of any library dean: "Physical damages amounted to only fifty dollars," the article concluded, "but a rare Shakespeare folio narrowly, by a margin of inches, evaded sullying by a stray dollop, and who can put a price on the injury to an institution's reputation when three students are hauled off in manacles, orange dreck dripping from their privates? What sort of future does this foretell? What randy beast slouches toward our stacks to be born, or at least sired?"

The rant was accompanied by a sidebar about the ten most notorious college libraries for sexual hijinks: LSU was ranked seventh.

"Do you see what a disaster this is?" Mort asked when Myrtle finished. The laugh in her throat was squelched only by the question of what this might have to do with her special assignment. Did he want her to don lab gloves and vet books for stuck-together pages, deciding as she went whether the culprit was doughnut glaze or not? Did he think he'd hired some kind of love-chemist?

"What if the media get hold of this?" Mort continued. "Bloodsuckers. Jackals, as I know all too well. We've got to respond immediately and decisively, so that if the news ever leaks out, we can point to measures already taken. Dramatic measures. Searchlights; body-heat sensors; giant posters of syphilitic lesions; full-body condoms, if that's what it takes. Dogs . . . or no, cancel the dogs; the little reprobates might figure out a way to enlist the poor animals in their pleasures." Now — moved, it seemed, by a vision of man's best friend corrupted into lechery, mutt into slut — he lifted his fist, lowered his voice to the fit pitch for speechifying. "We've got to make it clear, Myrtle, that we're for the free flow of ideas, not the free flow of bodily juices. Pardon my French." Mort sounded like Elmer Gantry, or maybe Johnnie

Cochran. The wordplay, though, came from another source, Myrtle thought. The article's author had ripped into a UCLA official who downplayed the cheese scandal, calling it "an innocent *fromage-à-trois*. They're kids; they're limber and hungry and can still get away with eating fatty foods — I'll bet it wasn't even half-skim." Mort's rallying cry was born, it seemed clear, of pun envy. What kind of man was capable of *pun envy?* Did he honestly think that the stacks were acrawl with dog molesters, or that the way to take care of the problem without attracting attention was to install klieg lights and hang posters of VD sores? Even his taste in sexually transmitted diseases was old-fashioned; had no one told Mort of the discovery of penicillin? Myrtle discreetly covered her smile. The man needed help.

"This is no joking matter, Ms. Rusk, as you must know from your reading . . . unless I've misjudged you terribly. We have a crisis here."

Given Mort's sour experience, Myrtle could understand his worry about attracting press attention. She'd be media-shy, too, though she doubted that even the arcana hunters of *Harper's* would cast a net wide enough to include the *Quarterly Journal of Library Security*. The notion of naked adolescents leaving their spoor among the books did distress her — she thought Eros should do its eructing, if eruct it must, on its own time and in its own place — but she didn't see anything that could be done. This was what happened when you succumbed to the siren song of Free Access, that silliest of democratic ideals. Books got misshelved or scrawled in; furniture got destroyed; slime trails were worn into the carpets; clothes got shed and cheese got spread. What do you expect when you let young people run wild? You reap what you sow.

And it was hopeless to try to stop them. Kids were going to find dark, quiet places to couple. She'd done it herself, way back when, in what seemed now like a previous life. Even so, there had been rules. Sure, she rattled a cage or two; she spent a good bit of time under ropy-muscled ranch hands. But Myrtle had never done it on the faded felt pool table at Ike's Bend-in-the-Road-House or under the dryer at her mother's favorite beauty parlor or on the cigarette-scarred coffee table at home while her dad, in sock feet, snoozed through *Gunsmoke*. Back then sex was dirty, furtive. It was *the nasty,* and Myrtle liked it that way.

She fought off the image of the Texas sky as seen from the bed of Levon Broome's pickup in April of 1967. No cheese, but there'd been the odor of souring chum from the bait bucket alongside them; at the height of things Myrtle had feared the pail might slosh over. And then there was the fallout shelter beneath Bobby Sudduth's backyard, amid the attar of a shattered jar of peach preserves tipped from its shelf by their exertions. Bobby's cat slithered in through the cracked door to run its raspy tongue along her side and meow. What was wrong with her today? Hush! Enough.

"Do you follow me?" asked Mort, seeming pleased by Myrtle's grimace.

"Mmmm," she said. Levon's pickup had been smoky red, an old International Harvester, and above the tailgate was a huge expanse of blue. Beside them, in the pail, fish guts had churned and roiled like in a piranha movie. For days after, her back had worn wide pink stripes from the corrugations of the truckbed. Grimace and moue; moue and grimace.

This didn't seem to suffice. "You *did* understand what was being described?"

"I'm a grown woman," said Myrtle. "I grasped it. Human fondue."

Mort winced, then forged ahead. "I don't want *my* daughter exposed to such tomfoolery, and I'm sure you don't either. The library is a haven. Do you have children, Ms. Rusk?"

Myrtle cleared her throat. Softly she said, "No."

Mort strode to his tabletop tranquillity garden in the corner and raked frantically with what appeared to be a tarnished dinner fork. The stones made a sound like a grinding transmission. "Ever since the oil bust in the mid-eighties," he explained, "our funding has been iffy, and I can't afford to take chances with the legislature. We can't be on any sex lists. It's in loco parentis or bust. The Capitol boys don't like book-learning in the first place. If they see evidence that it turns the kids kinky, we've acquired our last volume." He paused, pressed his index finger to the Band-Aid on his forehead. Myrtle expected to hear the whir and click of a jukebox in mid-change, then the beginning of a new speech. The man looked animatronic.

"I know, I know," she preempted. "I follow. You of all people can't afford it."

"What?" said Mort. "How dare . . . ?"

She interrupted. "I asked around. I know what came of your book. And you're right. One whisper along those lines and you'd be a national bogeyman, the poster boy for why higher education is dangerous and shouldn't be funded."

Mort looked relieved. "Exactly. The Whoremaster of Liberal Academe. The right-wingers would claw at my hair looking for the Mark of the Beast. I was writing about something holy, not sordid. Those paintings are to marvel at the miracle that Jesus took on a form *fully* human, with all our frailties and fleshliness. But I get credit for being some kind of leering pervert. I knew you'd grasp the problem, Myrtle. You came highly recommended as a foe of unvirtue. The state's purse strings are clenched tight, and so must be our thighs." He did a quick pantomime of what was presumably clamp-thighed virtue, though it looked a lot like constipation, too. "But we do have recourse," he said. "We do have recourse." He set down his fork and strode back to the desk.

There, Mort Bozeman wagged his head enthusiastically, dripping a crumb of beard gravel onto the blotter. His eyes glittered. "This," he announced, "is our answer." From a drawer he pulled an enormous black metal bludgeon, about two feet long. He had to grip it with both hands to keep it steady. "You're the only . . . well, you're the only person here of my generation, the only one who knows that books and foodstuffs make poor bedfellows, if you get my drift, and I want you in charge. You are our champion. You, my dear Myrtle, shall be the guardian of our virtue. And here" — he smacked the cudgel against his palm — "is our chastity belt."

It would be wrong to say that Myrtle was taken by surprise.

She was a woman accustomed to peeling away excesses of rheto-
ric, after all, and ever since she caught her first glimpse of the
phrase "eructations of Eros," ever since she heard the first steam-
shovel rasp of Mort's fork among the stones, she'd had the sinking feeling that she was to be installed as the Archenemy of Love.
Her reputation, born of her precious dignity and raised like a
child, or a bet, for more than twenty years — now it had come to
this. She was to be a quaint old triticism, a cliché, was to become
the stereotype that for decades had vexed and haunted librarians
the way veiny noses and a bent for drink plagued Irish cops. The
sexless functionary. The prude, the bluenose. That joy-spurning
old biddy, the Puritan at the Circulation Desk, always making the
sign of the cross by lifting a wizened finger to sere, thin, loveless
lips. The straitlaced Christian thing between her legs sewn up, or
grown over. Abandon all hope, ye who think to enter here. Old
Miss Berryhill rides again.

7.

For three decades after World War II (and maybe still, maybe forever), Myrtle's hometown library had been ruled by the Iron
Maiden, a perpetually middle-aged shrew named Ivy Berryhill
who had seemed to Myrtle the brittlest husk of womanhood imaginable. Miss Berryhill wore her never-cut gray-yellow hair thickly
braided and crossed and recrossed over the top of her head. The
braids looked like ship's hawsers, ropes as broad as a longshore-
man's arm and as strong. The only changes in her appearance over
the years seemed to be the addition of ever more plaits and coils
and a tiny shift, perhaps (there were those, boosters of her myth,
who would dispute this), in the ratio of gray to yellow. She was
Medusa tightly corseted, her serpenty tresses tamed and snugged
in with two dozen hairpins. Her forehead was stretched taut, and
every blink or scowl looked like it might set off a chain reaction of
popping pins. Miss Berryhill wore sack dresses that appeared to

have been made of bedspreads thriftily resurrected; she took austere pleasure in sucking lemon-menthol candies that swathed her in an aura of medicine chest, lightly sweetened. She was lean and hard-edged, a battle-ax in button-up shoes, and she had the longest, yellowest, most spatulate fingers Myrtle had ever seen, as if made — natural selection at work — for the task of violent shushing, at which Miss Berryhill was singularly gifted.

Of all the people Myrtle had ever known, Ivy Berryhill was the one she least expected to become. She recalled the time Miss Berryhill had come upon a couple of kids kissing behind the gigantic globe in the alcove. She'd dragged them outside, those talons wrapped tightly around their elbows — sheepish girl on her left, sullen boy on her right — and once the doors swung closed she'd uncorked a speech, audible even through the glass, about germs and wickedness.

Myrtle was fifteen then. Working at the library was the most respectable — or perhaps the only respectable — excuse for a girl her age to be out late. Her parents were inattentive at best, didn't much care where she went or what she did. But even a rummy like her father, a tranquilizer fiend like her mother . . . well, there were rules to play by, proprieties to be observed, at least in public. So she'd taken the job as a blind, a feint, a merkin, and she and her boyfriends had laughed about it as she shucked frocks and ribbons after her shift. For them she did a spot-on impression of Miss Berryhill that involved fumbling with padlocked underdrawers and rehearsing moans of pleasure in the tone of voice you might use if you spotted the butcher's thumb on the scales.

Yet she'd fallen in love with the place, despite herself. Those brown slotted poles through which the newspapers were threaded, for example: somehow they lent even that dreary pastime — her father's gray rattle of cough behind his gray rattle of newsprint at breakfast — they lent even newspaper-reading the romance of the gondolier. And she loved the way the papers hung on their long, low racks when not in use, like kitchen curtains framing a view. There were high transom windows along two sides of the building, and on comfortable days it was Myrtle's job to open them, using a long iron stick with a knob on the end with which to catch the eyehook, which was bright from the frictions of thirty years. There were the blond-wood catalog the size and color of hay bales, and each drawer's cards, gray-smudged on top by flipping fingers, were mounted on a tin spindle. And the map alcove, and the children's room, sealed off from the main hall by leaded glass, the room where old Chief Brant, wheezing inside a horse costume that reeked of mothballs (poor Chuck Burke, another library aide, usually stooped behind him, grumblingly, to be Patch the Pony's back half — one time the chief asked Myrtle to fill in, but Miss Berryhill, thank God, didn't think it proper for a young lady to join a grown man inside a hot, lumpy costume and play a horse's ass), showed a filmstrip to schoolchildren about the fatal lures of candy in sedans. The climactic moment involved a drawing of a sinister man in a fedora, his head half-shadowed in the window of a black sedan from the 1930s, hands cupped and overflowing with taffy and sourballs and lollipops.

"Nei-ei-ei-gh, neigh, from strangers stay away," whinnied Chief Brant, pouring it on.

"Oh, for Christ's sake," hissed the pony's butt.

Best of all were the tall, cramped reference stacks behind the counter, open only to adepts, to the priestesses and their acolytes. Myrtle had loved the way her superiors walked briskly back, surveyed the shelves (which were unsullied by any label or sign that might be visible to the patron), then tipped out the wanted book with a forefinger, the most casual magic. She'd loved the spinning rack of ink stamps, each wooden bulb shaped to fit the hand and nestled, at its slender neck, into a curved metal cradle; on morning shifts it had been her task to work her way around the little carousel, turning tumblers to mark a new due date. And then there was the back room, where Myrtle did most of her work: shellacking books. She used a hot pen — a wood-burning tool — on a roll of white paper laid over the spine. She burned on the call number, then dressed the wound with shellac, which had a pleasant, cleanly odor. Overnight she'd lay the books, butterflied open, on the tables to dry; they looked like birds drawn by children.

Then they'd get their second coat, and she'd gather the discarded dust jackets for bulletin-board displays.

And now Myrtle, the fun-girl who'd snorted at Miss Berryhill and her scalp-stretching plaits and brocade dresses . . . now Myrtle was to be cast as the gray lady of the stacks, hunting down pleasure and treading it into the dirt. It took every last reserve of dignity not to cry, not to sigh, but to hold her face in a rigid pose of something that might look like normalcy.

Oh, but that was a lie, wasn't it? The worst part was that in some secret, terrible way she *liked* the prospect. It might even be, for all her sniffings and protests, that the stereotype — Ivy Berryhill, writ large by legend — had been part of the lure, after Myrtle's oversexed youth, of the bookish life. Maybe she'd been moving toward this all along, for thirty years now, at the silent, stealthy creep that would now become her most valuable weapon. Could she have wanted for all these years to be dull and gray and neuter? Was that why she'd married mousy Milt, a man whose only vices were eggnog out of season and a revolting fascination with his nail parings (which for years he's stowed in a lacquered box, as though he'll have to account for every last sliver at Judgment Day)? Way back when, she let herself imagine that beneath the scoop-neck undershirts and unbreakable pocket combs lay a swashbuckler, a man who would sweep her into his arms and set out on voyages of discovery and plunder among the stars. He'd been an astronomy grad student, full of big (or, well, *modestly* big) talk about quasars and cosmology and dark matter, about the booty that would spill out when he and his colleagues cracked open the black night sky. But had she heard even then the faint whisper of failure? Had he been the apotheosis of the stable and the pleasantly second-rate, her knight in shining double knits? Had she known that after all the interstellar gases had settled and the quasars had fired and gone, Milt would end up tending the parish park system's planetarium, a graceless cinderblock box in a clearing hacked out of the swamps to the east of town, that he would play host there to an endless procession of schoolkids, seeing fewer celestial objects each year as the buses became more numerous and the cityscape swelled and brightened and his eyes flattened and hardened? Had she divined that the day would come when, the years and the clippings having accumulated, she'd buy him one Christmas a bigger vessel — a kind of ossuary starter kit, a gray strongbox with a key — in which to accommodate his treasure trove? Those wispy yellow ruins: minuscule arcs, parentheses, tiny eyebrows quizzically arched, the little boomerangs a child might crack loose from the core of a sand dollar. Had she somehow realized she'd one day accept a hug for such a purchase and then watch as her husband — till death do us part — cheerfully decanted old into new and shed his puffy Rudolph socks and pulled out the clipper on his keychain to put her gift to good use?

Of course he'd never been anything like a freebooter. He wasn't going to swive her on a campstool in the jungle. He might drive a Cutlass (low mileage, minty odor of its one elderly owner), but he wouldn't swing one. Astronomy was about laying your eyes on things, not laying your hands on them. You sat still and peered into an enormous lens. And the sought-after visions weren't even of present, palpable things. The stars were phantoms, afterimages, glowing trails marking fires that might have ceased to burn centuries, even millennia ago.

Myrtle and Milt had begun in hope, like all young couples. But when she didn't become pregnant after years of grim and dogged trying, when she was forced to confront her . . . barrenness, is what her mother called it, she had to wonder whether it was her fault. Was her stretch of floozyhood responsible? If you taunted and thwarted fertility the way she had through her teen years, did fertility finally get fed up and exact revenge? Myrtle knew better, she thought, but maybe it had to do with being treated, that time, for chlamydia; maybe it had to do with cosmic payback. She couldn't confide in Missionary Milt, who knew only the prim Myrtle who'd fended him off through a formal courtship, even feigned inexperience on their wedding night. And Milt, for his part, seemed unfazed by the news that they wouldn't be having any kids. He never mentioned it, just smiled his thin, distracted smile and kissed her on the cheek and headed to the observatory day after day, year after year. As for sex, his work was done, and that seemed a relief. For the past ten years they'd made love no more than twice a year, and then mostly to work off some quiet mutual seething. They kept their noises to themselves and washed up just after, side by side at their dual sinks, passing the wrung washcloth without a word. They lived alongside one another cheerfully. They were companions capable of quiet tenderness (he might steer a fallen eyelash off her cheek with a fingernail, give her a pat on the hip when he came to bed; she massaged liniment into his calves after a day spent lifting squirming first-graders to the telescope sight), and they were unfailingly polite to one another. Theirs was a life without surprises, almost without change. And Myrtle had grown, over the years, to depend for every shred of her identity on her work at Gedge & McGillis, and now that was gone, and she was an old woman, past her grand climacteric and barren for all time, and ruddy and wrinkled and increasingly sour, and now here she was, in Mort Bozeman's office, about to be given a giant menacing-stick.

What had made Mort call her? Myrtle began to scent the faint tang of destiny; it smelled like book shellac. Maybe this was where being a librarian led, just as Milt had ripened into astronomy. Once he'd dreamed of a plum academic post in one of the great observatories, but when he saw he couldn't win, he'd sued for his separate peace, a small lens all his own. He ushered bored brats through the basics and wiped noses and served refreshments so that when the buses finally crackled out of the lot, leaving a white mist of oyster shell, he might steal an hour or two each evening in the pursuit of flashing evanescences long gone: the scintillant stars, his faded potential.

Yes, Myrtle was treading near the oldest, most awful stereotype — the one to which she'd reduced Miss Berryhill. Did even the Iron Maiden take down her hair at night and let some lissome prince climb up? Was there a rope-charmer — in her mind's eye she saw her new Egyptian friend, Seti, wearing a rose cape and pointed slippers, but she quickly dismissed the thought — who could, with an air of his flute, make those dense yellow coils rise and dance? Myrtle had never thought to wonder. That knotty weft of hair had been so formidable, like a work of architecture. She would have thought it as likely that they dismantled the library at night and rebuilt it every morning. But there had been that time — remember? — when she'd seen a woman she thought must be Miss Berryhill's sister, maybe fifteen years younger, at a stock-car race near Ozona. The woman had been handing a lug wrench to a swarthy Mexican with a Fu Manchu, and her head was tilted back in a laugh, and she had gorgeous golden hair tied back at her shoulders with a gypsy scarf.

But the time for Mexicans with blunt mustaches, for flutists in burnooses, had passed now, passed for good. It was time to pack it in, to submit to the rough justice of stereotype, which provided, after all, a certain protection; you didn't have to wonder anymore what people thought of you. Miss Berryhill had lived on her own terms — or no, not that, but she adopted the world's terms so ferociously as to win a kind of freedom. Myrtle was ready to take the role she'd ridiculed for all these years. She didn't relish being a figure of fun, but do you kick destiny in its teeth just to preserve your air of unpredictability? What do you need, after a certain age, with an air of unpredictability? Do you shrink from duty just to go against type, to preserve the illusion that you're more than what you appear, a stern and lumpy frump who will leave no legacy in this world?

Yes, when everything else is taken, you can fall back on stereotype. She had suffered more lustful thoughts today — that boy with his shy fire; even this chat with Mort had a sexual frisson about it — than in the preceding fifteen years together, and that was dangerous. To begin wearing short skirts and decolleté blouses and dangly earrings would be a midlife crisis, would make her a joke. She was not a joke, is not a joke. She will not be a joke. There comes a point when the thing may as well be sewn up.

Meanwhile, Mort Bozeman was blathering on, still holding out the black club. "Will you help me, Ms. Rusk? Will you help me throw the sex-changers out of the temple?" He frowned. Best stick to the script, as improvisation can go awry. "Will you help? May I count on you, Myrtle?"

Dear God, had it come to this?

8.

A dozen years ago, just after they bought their house, Myrtle and Milt had liked to lounge on the patio, drinking bottles of beer and stargazing. Milt's tripod was set up next to the barbecue grill, but they rarely resorted to it. She wanted to rest her feet, and he had enough lens-fiddling in his work life; evening was the time of the naked foot, the naked eye. Milt would rattle off heavenly bodies in order of brightness, a hit parade in gibberish: *Deneb, Becrux, Fomalhaut . . . and down two this week, to number twenty-one, Pollux.* She found obscurely touching the way he would lift his beer, close one eye to sight down his wrist, and point, as if that ungainly rig, forefinger and waggling bottle — seen at a bad angle and in dim relief against the roofline of the garage, the leaves of the Chinese tallow — might make it clear to her which pinprick he had in mind. "Okay, hon, number nineteen is Deneb. It's right there, upper right of the Summer Triangle. It's at least five hundred parsecs away, but it's colossal. Its name means 'tail,' so the people who study it, ha, are Tail-Chasers. It'll explode before too long, they say."

"Tail-chasers," repeated Myrtle. "Explode."

That *before too long* would turn out, upon further questioning, to be millions or maybe gazillions of years. Myrtle's time frame wasn't quite so massive. The mosquitoes and the weltlike stripes on her legs from the lounge chair, in combination with her dwindling beer and swelling bladder, would drive her inside within the half hour. But she did take pleasure in their ritual. *Their* flagstones, *their* chairs, *their* grill, *their* beers, *their* stars. Their house.

That fall, while she was away at a librarians' conference, Milt repainted their bedroom ceiling as a replica of the night sky. A tenth-anniversary surprise, he said, a token of his love, and so he had included the five hundred brightest celestial objects that could be seen from their backyard on their wedding night. This had been a staggeringly and pointlessly complicated undertaking. They hadn't lived in the house back then, of course, so he couldn't use a photograph, and he hadn't freehanded it, either, like a sane person would. He could have introduced new constellations — Zither, Pineal Gland, Vas Deferens — and she would never have objected, or for that matter even noticed, but Milt was a man for whom there could be no surer expression of love than scrupulous photorealism.

Instead, as their neighbor, that Daughters of the Confederacy retard Sarah Sue Phemister, would put it, he went the whole nine hogs. He got hold of a new Caltech computer model, plugged in the date and their precise latitude and longitude — down to the second, the split second — and winnowed the field of stars according to their luminosity. He then adapted for the dimensions of the bedroom and created a grid and, ultimately, a wax-paper template marked with grease pencil. He erected scaffolding and went to work, meticulously razoring out holes to accommodate the stars. He bought fluorescent paint and diluted it as necessary, using a calculator and beakers that allowed him to measure to the centiliter. It took him three sixteen-hour days.

Myrtle's friends and neighbors were abuzz, agog, atwitter, above all ameddlesome. (*She* hadn't told them, God knows. Over the weekend someone had spotted Michelangelgoof in the yard with phosphorescent paint all over him — he was trying to wash his hair in a bucket of turpentine, which misadventure killed her plumbago and, nearly, a thirsty schipperke from across the street — and had asked what he was up to. That was all it took. Suddenly Milt and Myrtle were, as Sarah Sue crowed, "the talk of the toast.") For weeks Myrtle had to endure the grilling, the gushing. It's like one of those romance books, they said, so precious and sweet, just like a novel: *For Her He Hung the Stars*. And this bodice-ripper's improbable hero, the man with a rose between his teeth and pecs with which he might flex out "Je t'adore" in Morse code, a lover whom the stars would never dare to cross, was . . . Milt? Milt Rusk? Were these people nuts?

Myrtle *had* been touched. She couldn't deny that. The project was insane, sure, like a meat sculpture of a peace lily or a portrait of Jesus made out of bottle caps — but it was beautiful, too, in its way, and it *had* sparked several weeks of goodish lovemaking at first, there under the softly radiant stars, in a fog of passion and possibly paint fumes. It was nice to have a firmament all your own, and she appreciated the amount of work that had gone into it — she *did*.

But eventually the afterglow jokes got a bit tired, and the neighbors' oohs and ahhs began to rankle. "Oh," said stout Roberta Rhein, the mother of two grown children, a woman twenty-five years Myrtle's senior, a keg in muumuus who was heretofore known to the Rusks mostly for the richness of her red-velvet cake, "oh, to make love in a bed of stars. I suspect we'll know in about nine months what that slyboots was about. You're so lucky. My Walter doesn't have a passionate bone in his body — hardly has a bone in his body at all anymore, if you get my drift." Myrtle got used to getting drifts, drifts and drifts of drifts. She heard it all; being the object of such a gesture made her somehow public property, everybody's intimate. Could they not keep their cysts and veins and dysfunctions to themselves?

So when at last the newspaper came calling, wanting to install Milt in the paramours' hall of fame, alongside Casanova and Cary Grant and what's-his-name, the English prince who shucked his throne to marry that American divorcee with all the moles on her face, well, surely that would have been too much for *anyone*. Myrtle shooed the reporter and photographer by telling them that Milt's modesty absolutely forbade such publicity. The *gesto appassionato* was in its very nature private. To sound it about would ruin it, would be (she knew this would do the trick) a *sin against romance*. She was sorry they'd wasted their time, sorry too that she couldn't invite them in to see the fabled bedroom and have a cup of coffee. If they wanted coffee, maybe they should swing by Roberta Rhein's house; she always had a fresh pot brewing, and her red-velvet cake was to die for. Now *that* would make a nice article. So red, you know, that eating it made you feel like a vampire. It was of a moistness positively newsworthy. A scoop — better get on it. Bye now, and thanks for stopping by.

Certainly she couldn't voice her misgivings, her irritations — what kind of sourpuss, what harridan, what stone *bitch* would fail to appreciate such a paragon of husbandhood? But Milt grew no suaver, no less inept. His accent stayed prairie-flat and irksome, and he didn't learn even one word of Italian, unless "Boyardee" counted; he was the same sweet-tempered, distracted goober he'd always been. He never shaved under his nose properly, and his frequent sneezes were like howitzer blasts. This was a man who remained capable of leaving for work wearing two different *shoes* . . . you couldn't tell Myrtle that *that* happened to Valentino, or Porfirio Rubirosa.

And beneath the marital bed that lockbox of his nail parings, his scurf — the prudent man's mounting riches. Now there was a story for the papers. Come *back*, boys!

But she'd be a villain now, heartless, to gripe that he didn't fold towels into the proper fraction (crisp thirds) or that he left the broiler on once a week (his beloved cheese toast, which he baked to soot). Okay, so there was a ragged arc of hairs under his nose; so he didn't capitulate to the fashion of wearing *pairs* of shoes; so his calves were balding, his kidneys spreading. These petty sins, stacked end to end and compounded for all eternity, would never reach the stars.

The whole enterprise — *hanging the stars for her* — came to seem coercive, in a half-accidental way that was characteristic of Milt. Mooting his shortcomings: that's what it was about. The detail of the hair-washing set her to wondering. Had he purposely chosen the front lawn for this bit of slapstick theater, in order to take their little squabbles and unrests to the court of public opinion? In recent years she might now and again have complained about his impracticality, his obliviousness, might have barked the occasional querulous remark. Was this his revenge? Could he be, Lord forbid, *working a jury?* She half believed this was the case — why else had she failed to tell him about the reporter who'd come sniffing around? But no, no. It couldn't have been as conscious as that; Milt had *never* been as conscious as that. Besides, what jackass would try to make his case for husbandly perfection by bathing in the open, before God and the civic association, in a bucket of turpentine mixed with baby shampoo? No, she knew he hadn't *intended* to make her feel bad. Her spate of self-loathing and cosmos-loathing wasn't his fault. Milt loved her, and he knew he was in small ways a disappointment to her, and he set out to make it right, spectacularly right, right all at once and for good.

She thought back to their wedding night, when Milt dawdled through south Texas on the way to the coast. He'd postponed consummation to stop in a dark country cemetery and snap a few shots of the emptiness above. She'd been impatient, had refused to get out of the car, had even shut her window to mute his exclamations of joy, his ecstasy of identification (though she'd relished it countless times before, as a sign of his Capacity for Wonder). He'd clambered onto the rental car's roof and stood there, his feet making loud dents; she'd thought he might fall through. Pock, pock, flash, pock, pock, flash — the noise overhead was a cheap radio-show imitation of thunder, the flash cube like feeble lightning. She'd been envisioning a real storm, Zeus concealing himself as a mild-mannered astronomer for the courtship, then making himself back into a hurled, headlong bolt of lust on the wedding night. She had been so impressed by Milt's restraint, by the way he said, "We'd better leave it at that, my dear, before we get too hot and bothered and I get moved to ravishing." *Moved to ravishing* — that was his phrase, and they'd gathered up the blanket and telescope and headed back to the car. It had been a nice change of pace, at the time. She'd found his old-style manners quaint. But it was rapidly becoming clear that the man couldn't, when called upon, ravish his way out of a paper sack. "Myrt!" he shouted. There was the double pock of a weight shift. "Look, sweet! Look how bright

Venus is!" This lumberer, this man overhead: heavy-footed stargazer — husband.

But still, but still . . . Men of a mild disposition, the soft and biddable boys who kept always to the bright side, smiling through every humiliation the world could dish out: such men seemed to have a reserve of blind cunning, the one thing that kept them from haplessness. And it was that cunning — in Milt's case a near genius for passive aggression — that was the source of his sexiness, what tatters of it remained. This was the kink and complication that saved him. Otherwise he'd be merely a drear, a dope, a doofus: the Good Spouse. She resented his unconscious guile — it meant that you could never point to any overt meanness, never identify any malign intent, and so you, being straightforward, preferring your nastiness aboveboard, seemed always in the wrong — but she found it irresistible. She loved him for it.

Which left her sleepless in the aquarium glow of the bedroom, her little rectangle of the cosmos, feeling guilty and sour and alone. At her side Milt — sainted painter of the Sistine boudoir — slept the sleep of the just. She knew already that the late flurry of lovemaking wouldn't come to anything. The black night, the empty galaxies. This was it, the two of them under glowing paint. The history of the universe is a story of heat dispersing, of loss, of creeping entropy. Our lives are all aftermath.

She lay there seething, stars above her like winking eyes, and she wanted, one by one, to put them out. And there was no one, would never be anyone, who'd care to hear her point out the facts, to tell her sober side: that in Baton Rouge (she'd gone to the trouble of looking it up, a bit of spiteful research she'd never admit to) it had *rained hammer-handles* on their wedding night, and that therefore you couldn't have seen anything from their future backyard but, during lightning, maybe the leaden belly of a cloud. No one else mourned her plumbago, and there was no one to make sympathetic noises about the permanent creases Milt's scaffold had left in her Persian carpet, no one to whom Myrtle might confide that, over the long haul, maybe black wasn't the *most appropriate* color to paint your bedroom. The once or twice when she ventured even a mild sarcasm, friends looked at her like she was grousing about Paris's pedicure or something. So she shut up and kept it to herself; she endured their creepy intimacies and their songs of praise.

But that wasn't even the worst of it. It got more twisted, more strange. What had happened to the days when emotions were simple and discrete, like keys on a ring or fish on a stringer? Once she had been able to turn tumblers with them, display them with a thumb looped through their gaping, inert mouths. Now love and hate had fused together, and guilt and pride could not be uncoupled.

She couldn't stop thinking, and enviously, of the solitary pleasure Milt had taken — while she'd been trapped in a Cincinnati hotel, checking out the newest innovations in hanging files and highlighter pens, he fussed and fiddled with lumens and with grades of phosphorescent paint. He unscrolled and taped his template. He mixed and whistled. He lay on his back, wiped the brush on his shirtfront. Why hadn't he shared his plan with her? Why hadn't they done the work together? Really, there was something masturbatory about it. It came to seem less an expression of love than a proxy for it. For Milt, married love was a series of projects around the house, was keeping the sidewalks edged and the azaleas mulched; love was keeping his foot calluses neatly pumiced. Of course she couldn't kvetch to neighbors about her "perfect man," who had undertaken "the most romantic thing *ever*" . . . but it seemed too fastidious, too polite and careful, to be anything like the loves she had known. She felt left out.

These days the bottoms of Milt's feet look like yellow cauliflowers; she gets a chill every time he brushes her with them in his sleep. He sleeps on his stomach, and the night sky glows above her, an ever dimmer and dingier version of July 1977, when she was young. There are chips and flecks near Altair that look like portals into pure luminosity, and at the northwest corner a spot of water damage has swelled to a tumorous bulge . . . the universe, trying to expand in the only way left to it. Beyond the stars, rats die of thirst in the rafters.

9.

Fifteen minutes till break, and nothing to occupy Seti except his worries. Almost an hour since Lili borrowed his glasses, and no sign yet of her or Rex. His errand for Mort came to naught. He couldn't find them, though he haunted all their usual places until he feared the woman in reference who was covering for him would think him a malingering dog. Where are they?

Once again Seti anxiously reviews the scene he saw in the lounge. Lili's foot propped between Rex's thighs. Rex's thumbs palpating, his crucifix earring swaying in time with the effort, mouth running as usual. Corrupting her; despoiling her. Grooming her with his forked tongue. Anointing her feet with his snake oil. Just what are these *rock-'n'-reel* and *bumping uglies?* They are the key to understanding Rex's plea, or sermonette, or whatever it was. Immediately afterward Seti had sprinted downstairs, whispering the phrases to fix them in memory, and cracked open the big slang dictionary in the reference room. He saw to his surprise and alarm that "rock and roll" derived from an African-American term for sexual congress, but that was generations ago, keep in mind, before the white people stole it, like everything else, and tamed it down to mean only loud guitar music; and anyway it had nothing to do with "rock and reel," which was distinctly what Rex had said. "Reel" would belong to the idiom of angling, or perhaps the cinema. Yes, sure, Americans and their movies; that made sense. "Bumping uglies" sounded like something from a Mafia film: *Don Corleone, do you want I should bump his uglies?* But Rex was talking about religion, he gathered, about Jesus. Jesus had been a fisherman, right? (Or maybe some of his disciples had been; Christianity was Western through and through, chock full of middle management — priests, vergers, vicars, canons, monsignors, popes. The first thing the Son of Venture Capital did was to tap twelve Executive VPs. daVinci painted *The Last Board Meeting*.)

As Seti stood, puzzled, over the canted wooden lectern that held the dictionary, Myrtle happened by.

"Need help?" she asked. For a moment he didn't respond. "Not that I'll know it if it came into the lexicon since 1970. In America, slang's just another way for the kids to remind elders that our time has passed. Uncool is the first step toward dead. Square, then old, then ashes. Anyway . . ."

Seti brushed a hundred or so pages forward to obscure his tracks, gave a brisk bow. "Thank you for the offer, Ms. Myrtle," he lied with an ease that distressed him. "I was looking for between the rock and the hard place. No problem. And please permit me to say that you are not old, Ms. Myrtle. Your cinders remain hot."

Myrtle glanced away, but too late to conceal the flush in her cheeks. "It's been a long time since anybody told me I had hot cinders, Seti. You're a charmer . . . but your math's not so great. Anyway, I hope you get out from between your rock and your hard place. I've got to chase down some journal orders. Are we still on for coffee?"

"I shall see you at two. Salaam."

"Salaam your ownself," she said over her shoulder.

He couldn't ask her, couldn't. True, she is virtually his only friend here, and kind, and indulgent in her way; she would accompany him to a shabby Lebanese café that serves resiny coffee somewhat like that of home. She has become devoted to phyllo-dough pastries dusted with pistachio, and she'll nibble at them and refill Seti's cup from the earthen urn Mr. Shaheen leaves on the table and listen to him talk about his homeland. But to say to her, "I am lovelorn, Ms. Myrtle, rent in twain by love, and I must know what are uglies and how they bump" — impossible, beyond impossible. She is a priestess, and above such sweaty vanities.

So he lets it go. Rex and Lili were discussing the filmic arts, specifically Christian fishing movies — fine, okay, that must be it. Seti dimly remembers catching a few moments of a New Testament rock musical on late-night TV, and Jesus was wearing a yellow slicker like the old salt on the packages of fish sticks Seti feeds the cats. Yes, and singing a tune called "Fishers of Men" as He walked on water — or, actually, did a splashy disco dance on it. And, too, there is that piscine emblem Christians affix to their cars. Fish and Jesus go together. So it was innocent, after all: Lili's feet had been aching, and Seti would never want her denied any comfort, even from the likes of Rex.

What business is it of his, anyway? He'd listened in like some common, cringing spy. There is no reason to let Lili, her beauty aside — her unpolished big toenail, he'd noticed that day, had at its center a crescent of white like a Moorish moon, and her heel bore a faint amber tinge . . . from the tannins in her shoe leather, most likely, but to Seti it looked like the dust of Cairo streets, and he would have loved to whisk it away with a brush and unguents — there is no reason to let her reduce him to some sort of moony-eyed *majnoon,* a fool, an unman.

But now, today, the worry is reignited — it's been an hour and ten minutes, and Lili can't concentrate for that long, and Rex probably can't *read,* and Seti has to admit, a week late, that there's something maybe not quite totally persuasive about the Jesus-fish link he came up with — and it occurs to him that he could ask his friend Doug the Stoner to translate. Doug the Stoner does not judge. If only Doug the Stoner were in town.

They met during Seti's first summer in Baton Rouge, three years before. Overnight there'd been a torrential downpour, and Seti woke up to write his parents an ecstatic letter about the thrum of rain on the roof as he slept, the eerie water-shadows projected through his patio door and writhing on the bedroom wall, the flashbulbs of lightning, the grumble and pop of thunder. The trees' dark leafage shuddered and rolled in the wind, and when the thunder got close, his windowsills rattled in sympathy, as though cherishing the memory of being live wood lashed in a storm.

When the letter was finished, Seti tucked it into an envelope and opened his spiral notebook. He reviewed the list, at this point limited — the notebook was near-new — to the wet callings: well dowser; snorkeling guide; professional beachcomber; wave-machine operator at the water park. He tremblingly added "underwater demolitions," then closed the book and flung his pen and prayed for forgiveness, for guidance. He'd justified the purchase of the notebook as a way to burn off his temptations, to set them down on paper and thereby banish them — fleeting silliness — from his head. Thus the Spam logo: what could be more laughable, less alluring, than salted pork shoulder in a sleeve of gelatin? And in a can, and that can opened with a scrolled key that looked like an Egyptian amulet, like the *ankh* that should promote immortality rather than atherosclerosis; and the meat bearing the impress not of an animal's skin and sinew but of the tin tomb (with its thick Frankenstein seam) into which it had been stuffed. But recently a Samoan boy, another Third World lonelyheart whom he encountered at an International Center meet-and-greet, had introduced Seti to something called Hawaiian *musubi*, a sushi made of Spam with pickled plum and seaweed, and it was delicious. Was there no end to the sirens in this place, trying to sing him to watery doom? Even the lowliest things had their hooks into him.

Seti felt filthy, so he kicked the book into a corner and savagely showered and fiercely dressed and stoutheartedly headed to the library for work, never once thinking about wave-making or underwater demolition. Never once, never once, never once.

But when he swung open his door, he discovered that there was water lapping at the threshold. He could see a woman in the middle of the street, and she was in up to her hips, slogging with her head and shoulders pressed forward as if burrowing into high wind. His first response was a flare of jealousy. Wastrel Nature, bestowing its embarrassment of riches. At home, tax rates were once based on the level of the Nile — high in years of exceptional flood, low during drought — and Seti had never seen such munificence; the Nile these days, sapped by dams and diversion canals, had grown sluggish and stingy. The rich richer, the fat fatter, the wet wetter. America, land of absurd overplenty.

But the woman's housedress was floating around her like a floral-print lily pad, and her head was swiveling back and forth, on the lookout. The old Lincolns were in up to their fins. Down the block a shirtless black man was tearing at a roll of tape with his teeth, trying to seal his trunk. Maybe this wasn't munificence after all. Seti could see the Vietnamese women across the way haplessly sweeping brown bilge out of their kitchens and watching it rush back in. One of them was laying down a dike made from burlap sacks of rice. Two husbands sat in a low crook of crape myrtle out front, smoking and chattering and knocking fuchsia blooms into the swill.

In a dim way this made Seti feel better. Americans tended to take abundance in all things as their birthright, and often the costs of wealth were pitifully small. It was right that there be no firm line between plenty and surfeit. It was right that there be some adversity to face, some bill called due. Here was Seti's chance to lead. He built a bank of towels inside his door in case the rain resumed, packed a change of shoes and trousers into his backpack, and waded to the bus stop — he had to get to the library, which would doubtless remain open, a reminder in these troubled times of what was truly important, a beacon of hope. But when he turned onto the main street of his neighborhood, what he saw astonished him.

Bobbing in the wash were two dozen inflatable dinghies, kayaks, kiddie rings bearing the heads of ducks and dragons and superheroes, and Styrofoam pool-recliners with built-in drink holders. A few of the vessels were sloppily tied together with plastic rope. But this was no dismal flotilla of refugees, forsaken by God and ferrying their sodden valuables to high ground and new hope; these were, unmistakably, pleasure craft. Several people had boom boxes on board, with tunes blasting. Students were tossing cigarette lighters and cans of beer back and forth. It was 10:30 A.M.

Seti pushed on to Milo's Kash-and-Karry, which was set on a concrete hummock high enough to keep it dry inside. On the store's door was a notice: NO BEER LEFT. NADA. ZILCH. BUPKUS. DON'T EVEN ASK. NO BATTERIES NO STERNO NO ICE — NO DICE.

At the bus stop just past Milo's, a woman reclined in a tractor-tire inner tube tethered to the smoked-glass shelter. She was wearing a bikini, and her toes were painted with purple polish. Seti averted his eyes. "Pardon me, miss," he said, "but have you seen the campus bus come by?"

"No bus today, guy," she said. "Classes are canceled. You might have noticed, Mother Nature gave us a day off. Want a brew?" She gestured with her thumb to the Styrofoam cooler bobbing beside her.

"No, thank you," said Seti.

A four-wheel-drive pickup with oversized tires rattled over the railroad tracks and splashed heavily into the floodwater — the end of a log-flume ride. The resulting surge soaked Seti's crotch (despite his attempt to time a subtle little tiptoe-jump for when the wave arrived), and the girl's tube nearly capsized. "This is a no-wake zone, motherfucker!" she yelled. Yet the yell was somehow amiable, and the driver flashed her a smile, lifted the bill of his baseball cap. Down the way, rafters made a raucous game of throwing crumpled cans into the truckbed as he crept past.

Seti looked up to see someone pushing across the street toward him and the bikini girl. It was a young man wearing chest waders. There were Rollerblades slung around his neck, and he was attached by a shoulder harness to a small rickshawish thing with overinflated tires; it floated along behind him. The waders were comically large, like the bottom half of a clown costume.

"Hey, Cecilia," he said to the bikini girl. "Bad day to tan, dude. The UV sucks."

"Hey, Doug. I'm laying in a little base. Overcast is good for that. When the sun breaks through I'll be *primed*. You got to take what it gives you, you know?"

"I hear you." Doug readjusted the straps of his rickshaw, which appeared to be filled with a pile of heavy gray tape. He would have been handsome but for a complexion like a baking potato.

Seti could see his friends the cats atop Milo's Dumpster in

amazing numbers, almost haunch to haunch, looking out at the water; they looked like mismatched gargoyles riding a parapet.

"You got a long wait for the bus, chief," said Doug, turning to Seti. "I mean 'chief' like, you know, *dude,* not chief like you're an Indian, I mean Native American, in case you are," Doug continued. "In which case I owe you an apology, 'cause we palefaces seriously screwed you over. Hey, I'm Doug the Stoner."

"It is a pleasure to meet you, Doug the Stoner. I am Seti. I am of Egypt." Seti extended his hand politely, and Doug the Stoner lightly slapped it front and back, then extended his thumb and pinkie and oscillated his fist from side to side. He seemed not to notice that Seti's attempt to mimic the gesture looked like a palsy.

Most of Seti's conversations here were brief, superficial, stillborn, like his chat with Cecilia, which had reached its crisis point just as Doug arrived. Seti could only have stood by for a few more seconds waiting for courage, that sad figment, to kick in, then muttered good-bye and waded back home, haunted for weeks by her creamy belly with its winking little sideways omphalos, her plummy toes with their silver rings. It would never have occurred to him to discuss tanning oils and sun-protection factors with her, as Doug was now effortlessly doing, much less to sweep a finger across the shiny bow of Cecilia's collarbone to test her lotion's fastness and then to plant that finger in his mouth and say, "Pure coconut, baby. You be careful now." Seti's only source of social pleasure was eavesdropping. He was awkward, laconic — *foreign* — and Americans tended to leave him alone. But Doug either didn't read the signs or blew blithely through them: "You look like a man with a plan for a tan, Seti," he said. "What do you think? Cecilia here wants to be a Hawaiian Tropic girl. Any advice?"

Seti didn't think anything, didn't say anything either, but he beamed at Doug, glad to have an excuse to keep standing there and taking in the uncanny scene. These people knew how to wring delight from life, how to make a gray day and ugly water — water full of fast-food flotsam, water that exuded, now that Seti had been in it for a while, a distinct stench of sewage — into a kind of street carnival. He could memorize Cecilia's muscular stomach, the curved staves of her ribs, the three tiny blond wisps below her navel; he could marvel at the boisterousness down the way — canoe races seemed, now, to have broken out — and at Doug, whose pleasant, open, lumpy face wore a ceaseless smile. Why was he lugging a rickshaw full of tape?

"Cat got your tongue, Seti? You think she's got the makings of a Hawaiian Tropic girl or not?"

What was a Hawaiian Tropic girl? "She is beautiful," Seti said. That was bold, frank, a start. But he pressed his luck, or rather his luck pressed itself. "They eat sushi there," he continued, "made of Spam. In Hawaii. All Polynesia, to be the truth. It is savory."

Doug laughed. Cecilia laughed, too, and when there seemed to be no meanness in it, Seti laughed as well. They laughed together. There was a tiny white halo overhead. The sun was trying to burn through a frayed spot in the clouds, and for Cecilia's sake, Seti rooted for it. He even joined in the cheers when the canoes tore past. Everyone seemed to be rooting for the one with a recumbent nude painted on its side, just above the waterline, so Seti too urged the naked woman along. It was strange to hear his voice mingling with others again. Their shouts echoed oddly, exaggeratedly, over the water. It was like being in a funhouse, and for a moment he enjoyed it.

But then he caught the distorted sound of his own laugh, the bray of a donkey, the screak of a crow, arrogant, preposterous — American. His moral compass had gone haywire. This was a disaster, after all. Just around the corner, not two hundred yards away, the Vietnamese women — refugees once already — were fighting a losing battle, trying to beat back the tide with their threadbare brooms. Their husbands roosted in a tree, cursing the slipshod god who let this happen. Those families' few sticks of furniture were going to be waterlogged, and good rice plumped in vain. And still the highboy trucks were prowling the streets, making waves — *wave-making*, came the terrible aperçu, *underwater demolition.* Could all this be punishment from Allah for *his* wickedness, *his* weakness? Was Seti to blame? No, no, best not to think that way. It was the trucks that were churning up higher water yet. Thoughtless; heedless. They couldn't pin this on him. This is a no-wake zone, motherfuckers, thought Seti indignantly. Can you not see we suffer here?

And where were the African-Americans? Half the people in the neighborhood were black, but except for Seti this party seemed lily-white. These were students — kids on the way to snug suburban futures and celebrating the unneed of knowledge, which they'd spend five or six years in college beating back, sleeping through, drowning in skunky beer; impermanent residents who could afford the extra twenty-five a month for upstairs and who, heeding parents' or weathercast's warnings, had moved their cars to higher ground the night before. Or they were tourists, day-trippers from higher ground (and virtually anywhere in town was higher than this). Sure enough, Seti could see several dozen sport-utility vehicles parked around the built-up railbed. They looked like they'd been scattered by a runaway locomotive.

He had sunk to a new low. He was standing in shit-filled water and his moral compass was broken and his privates were wet and he was ogling the comely Cecilia, a *mara*, a loose woman intent on cooking herself, and he had cheered on a bulbous painted nude who cleaved the water with her mount of pubic, and he'd touted the tastiness of Spam, and what under the *shams* was wrong with him? Worse yet, in some sick way he liked it all, reveled in it. The water tugged at his trouser legs, and his nether parts prickled pleasantly, and his feet were slowly sinking. He felt moist and serene, like a crocodile. He had been infected.

Last century, he'd learned recently, people thought disease was caused by the humid air here, which harbored *malades horribles* — and that, the professor said, had been a quaint superstition, like believing in witches or magic beans or Marxism. So much of education consists in learning how foolish people used to be, when they lived in chaos and error. *We are past that now, praise be.*

It was easy enough for people in this country, Seti thought, to cherish the idea of manifest destiny, to believe evolution followed a straightish line from amphibian to ape through Apache to *American*. It's flattering to think oneself the culmination of history. But what about nations that reached their highest flourish three thousand years ago? What about their sons and daughters? Were they merely breathing fossils, holdovers from a dead era when mud people built giant crypts and worshiped the dead and used too much kohl mascara? They'd had the bad taste to endure beyond their allotted time, and America kindly suffered them to keep living, like the elderly in their shuffleboard villages or the coelacanths in their black depths. To live as burdens, oddities . . . and as caretakers of history, which was now just another tourist destination. Were Egyptians supposed to live out their days as pyramid guides and camel keepers and technical advisers to tomb digs or mummy movies? How appalling the United States was, yet how resistless its charms. Seti wondered whether the old fancy had it right after all: maybe Louisiana was full of malign vapors. Maybe he'd been invaded by them. This moral indolence, this lethargy, this growing feeling of giddiness — there was no explanation but that Louisiana had insinuated some poison into his blood.

Two kayakers eggbeatered past, and when Doug the Stoner and Cecilia put in on the side of the red one, Seti found himself whooping, too. What was wrong with him? He should get out of these wet clothes, get home, offer aid to the stricken, pray for pardon. But he was lonely, and in no mood to look askance at a potential friend, even one called Doug the Stoner who was, when Seti looked to see, gulping down the last of a beer and crushing the can against his acne-scarred forehead. He dropped the can, along with the bikini girl's, into his wagon, saying, "Thanks, Cece. That's supplemental income, much appreciated. May you brown evenly and well, my child."

Then he turned back to Seti. "These are lean times, my Egyptian friend. There appears to be a beer famine at Milo's." Doug gestured toward the sign on the door, and it occurred to Seti to wonder why they had no dice left. Were these students setting up casinos in their dinghies, floating craps games? Had the decadence gone so far as that? "But it's nearly eleven, and the bars will be opening. Cecilia's got to turn her mind to serious tanning, so we'll let her be. What say we get some suds?"

Seti was confused. Was Doug suggesting that they bathe together? "I have no need of soap just now," he said, though a shower was his dearest wish.

"No, no, I mean beer." Doug pointed across the street, to the neighborhood tavern.

"I do not drink beer."

"Just come and sit, then. It's dry inside, and they have dollar Pabst, and stale pretzels for free. Come on. Be a pal."

At that moment Seti felt, pathetically, a rush of joy like the one that afflicted him when he met the minister of labor and watched him, across that helipad desk, wipe his lenses. *Mustafa,* chosen.

Be a pal.

The scene in the bar looked like an orgy just getting cranked up, or anyway like Seti's fevered imagining of such. Five minutes past opening, and the place was packed with buzzing college kids in dishabille, many of the boys dressed only in boxer shorts, laughing girls tugging down T-shirts to cover their bottoms. Every ten seconds, somewhere in the room, one could see a young girl reach back to pinch the elastic of her up-riding underwear. There was a horde of ogling bouncers at the door, armed with mops, wringing people out or making them strip. Seti slipped into a bathroom stall and changed into his dry clothes. When he returned, Doug had shed his waders and tossed them atop the giant pile of pants and shoes beside the door. He'd unhooked his rickshaw and persuaded the bouncers to let him display it at the front with a cardboard sign: "Duct-Tape Billfolds and Handbags. Great Gifts. Five Bucks." Scrawled at the bottom in red was an addendum: "They Float." Doug was wearing a surf-shop T-shirt and a shiny green bathing suit. He motioned Seti to the bar.

Seti had never been inside a pub before. It looked like a seraglio gone to seed, with brittle straw blinds instead of muslin curtains, neon beer ads instead of braziers. Women were squeezing water out of their hair, comparing sub-waistline tattoos. There were men wandering about wearing makeshift breechclouts fashioned from T-shirts; they looked like infants, or savages, or infant savages. Rap music was thumping from a corner jukebox, and nearby a few couples were grinding their pelvises together. He and Doug took wobbly stools at the bar, behind which swirled a garish wall of daiquiris in windowed blenders. Seti was given, after a season of whispers and chuckles between Doug and the bartender, a nonalcoholic drink named after a little girl with auburn pincurls whom he'd once seen in a TV matinee. The glass was topped with two soggy, oversweet cherries that were an obscene saturated red, and Seti did not want to know how the concoction earned its name. He took in the blinking bar signs, the nearly nude students, the O's of the girls' mouths when they tipped their bottles up for a sip.

Doug talked. He talked and talked and talked. "I don't want you getting the wrong idea, Seti. I'm not a stoner. Well, I am a stoner, but I wasn't always a stoner. There were two Dougs in my group in high school, about the same build, same bowl cut, same hair color. The real difference between us was that . . . well, it would have been my acne except that he had it as bad as I did. Which is a blessing. It saved both of us, I guess, from being called Zit Doug, or Pizzaface Doug, or Krakatoa Doug. The truth is that he was walleyed as hell. But he was a good guy, and it seemed kind of vicious to call him Walleye Doug, because he was sensitive about it — I mean, hell, how could he not be; it was like he had eyes coming out both sides of his head, like a hammerhead shark — and I had a *Hemp Rules* T-shirt, so I became Doug the Stoner, you know. And when your name is Doug the Stoner, it brings some responsibilities. You may not like it, at first, but eventually you mellow into the role. You step up. Truth in advertising, man. It was my duty. You know about duty, don't you, man?"

The rest of it was a blur to him: stoner walleye hammerhead zit. But did Seti know about duty? Yes, Seti did. He nodded vigorously, then bit a cherry off the plastic sword on which it was impaled.

Doug told him that he traveled by Rollerblade and hitchhiking between Tampa and Houston, staying here a month, there a month, hitting the beach when possible and along the way selling his wallets and bags. The rickshaw marked him as a harmless eccentric (how many homicidal drifters pulled a collapsible homemade cart adapted from an old Radio Flyer red wagon and piled high with tape products?), so folks tended to pick him up to hear his story, and he'd developed a reputation among truckers as decent company, so it wasn't hard to get from town to town. Doug too was a nomad, an outsider, and cut off from these students, too, by his ugliness and his age — only now did it occur to Seti that he was thirty or so, not twenty, that the scars on his face were not ephemeral acne but its permanent tracks. "Yeah," Doug said at one point, "if I were a TV actor they'd only let me play drug dealers. The white suits would be cool, though. Say what you will about dealers, they've got sharp threads."

No one said anything to them, no one looked at them. It was as though they existed inside a bubble of foreignness. The girls cavorted and jiggled, the boys flexed; Doug the Stoner kept talking. The bar grew crowded.

And then they were suddenly surrounded by a coven of beauties shouting out orders for frozen drinks. Seti tried not to notice the freckled shoulders, the crescents of underbuttock, the creamy tops of breasts. He tried not to stare at the fraying peach bra-strap nearest him, at the worn plastic hook and eyelet midway between her shoulder blades. Desperate, he rubbed his fingertips together, let his eyes roam upward, to safety, to the ceiling . . . but it, too, was festooned with bras, dozens of them, limp and smoke-damaged, interspersed with written-on dollar bills.

Precious Allah, forgive me, forgive me.

And then the girls, pursing their lips to suck at straws, sidled away. Doug turned to Seti with a sad smile. His ruined cheeks glowed in the neon. "Water, water everywhere," he said, and slugged down the last of his second can of Pabst. "But not a drop to drink."

Since then Doug and Seti have been friends, of a sort. Doug has introduced him to the other campus legends: Marley-san, the Jamaican jerk barbecue guy from Japan, with his converted ice-cream cart and his Rasta wig-and-hat combination; Lorenzo, the man with the whistle and the tall fur shako who directs traffic from a bus-stop bench; Levi, who sells shrimp and velvet wall hangings from underneath the tin canopy of an abandoned garage; Sybil, the taciturn accordionist; Byron, the elfin dude with the aged green tweed jacket and the thick glasses who carries a sketchbook everywhere; Wino Ike, a former lawyer in a rumpled seersucker suit who earned his name by looking like the swollen-faced alter ego of Eisenhower; the skateboarding skinheads who hang out behind Blockbuster Video, kids whose only politics, for all their warlike piercing and dyeing, turn out to be wanting the world to be a hassleless free-skate.

Seti among the outcasts: cats, crazies, beefeaters, sketch artists, presidents gone bad. And his friend, Doug the Stoner.

But Doug isn't in town now. He's in Florida, enjoying the September lull and living off the proceeds from his new line, with hand-painted "art-deco" curlicues (nail polish, dude, the secret is nail polish) and sterile-gauze dividers. Wino Ike and Sketch Byron aren't fit sources for advice. You don't get your erotic tips from men who cut their stench by carrying urinal mints in their coat pockets. Sure, Seti will ask Doug when he gets a chance. But in the meantime, break is approaching, and he must look for Lili.

10.

Myrtle took the billyclub into her hands. It was sleek metal, black, stout as a fencepost, and she felt a shudder run up the seldom-used muscles on the backs of her upper arms (she'd been getting a bit floppy there, old-womanish) and down alongside her breasts.

Meanwhile, Mort was singing raptures. "This isn't the biggest one," he said, reaching in to brush the casing with his fingertips, "but it will strike fear in the hearts and loins of our libertines. Spare the rod, spoil the child."

Mort explained that the club doubled as a flashlight. "This one's an eight-cell, takes eight D batteries. They sell ten-cells, even twelve, and some of the new ones have a weak cattle prod in the butt end" — he paused, too wistfully for Myrtle's comfort — "but that seemed on the verge of excessive, a mite too Latin-American-dictator for our purposes."

Myrtle was aghast. "I'm supposed to *knock* the students apart? With a flashlight? Why do you think the legislature would like *that* newspaper story any better?"

Mort came out of his trance for a minute. "No, of course, no. I apologize. I gave the wrong impression. What I have in mind is merely gunboat diplomacy. A woman of your bearing, your moral stature, your experience, and with heavy artillery bolted to her decks, pardon the expression . . ." The USS *Myrtle*.

His eyes caught on the flashlight as she wrung it in her hands, and the trance resumed. He insisted on showing her how to press the on button — another chance to run his hands over the thing. When he yielded it again, she could see his avid fingerprints up and down the barrel; he'd fogged it like a windshield.

Mort pushed on. Myrtle would need to learn how to wield this technological marvel, to which end he was sending her to bouncer school. "We can't have you handling a weapon," he said, "without proper training. Neither conscience nor our insurance policy would allow that. Don't come back till you can kick some patootie. Figurative patootie, I mean to say."

Myrtle worked, now, for the kind of man who would sic a menopausal woman with a cold steel mace on kids making out in study carrels. She worked for the kind of man who could use the phrase "figurative patootie." She worked for a man whose idea of restraint was to stay, for the moment, one merciful step short of Pinochet or Papa Doc. Mort grinned and, narrowly missing her breast, reached in to give the flashlight one last parting caress.

Mort's weird passion aside, though, she rather liked the heft of the thing. She thwacked it into her palm a couple of times, the sap with which she would fight the rising saps of youth. After all these years, a blunt object of her own. Her arm was already beginning to ache from holding it, but it made her feel powerful. It made her feel bold. Myrtle tried on this new image: bogeywoman, figure of fear. Maybe she *wasn't* averse to kicking a patootie or two, if circumstances warranted.

She looked around the office, something she'd felt too dazed and harried to do before. The side walls were lined floor to ceiling with shelves, along which were ranged color-coded folders recording every fine levied, every acquisition, every interlibrary loan. At the room's far end was the tabletop Zen garden, above which hung two Madonna-and-child prints: one from the fifteenth century, all pink cheeks and lambencies (the mother used one arched finger to keep the blanket from obscuring her boy's rosy wing-wang), and one from the mid-twentieth (with Mary's head purplish and splotchy and possibly upside down and the child looking like a chihuahua peeking from the pocket of her ratty bathrobe, but, happily, no wing-wang in sight).

Behind Mort's desk was a metal-mesh cabinet, retread from an old pharmacy or gun shop, which housed the several hundred volumes that were designated as too dangerous, too prone to inflame aberrant lusts, to be housed in the open stacks. These affronts to public morality were picked, Myrtle had heard, by Mort's own hand, judged by his eye. Even the calligraphy sign taped to the cabinet, "Restricted Shelving," bore flourishes Myrtle could recognize as belonging to Mort and Mort alone. Also in the cabinet was the ledger in which he recorded the names of those with nerve enough to check out such items.

He required a brief personal interview, or at least a brief personal stare-down, and his routine never varied, it was said: He emerged with his ledger and his tarnished key on a jailer's ring and his evil eye. Once the required signature was given, he'd take out a chlorined handkerchief and scrub the ceremonial pen for several seconds — long enough for it to register with the borrower that this wasn't neatness but decontamination. Then Mort would waggle the open ledger back and forth under his nose, as though some angle or tilt would yield hard evidence (but what?) of the impure motives he suspected. After that he stepped into the back, unbolted the cabinet, pulled the book in question, and returned to say, "Three hours. Do not leave the library. Big Brother is watching."

The story was told (by the circulation-desk students) as malicious comedy, but Myrtle couldn't help recognizing the similarity between Mort's Ritual of the Dirty Book and hers, back at Gedge & McGillis, of the Apt Precedent. Was his billyclub fetish all that different, finally, from her obsession with a shiny desktop? Here was a man partaking of the modest pleasures at hand, keeping order in his little corner of the morass. She couldn't help liking him again, a hint.

But the access of friendliness faded when she recalled the conclusion of Mort's playlet. After the borrower finally left with his swag, Mort would chuckle and jangle his smutkeeper's keys and say, "Got to put the fear of God into them, you know. The Saltpeter Principle at work."

Myrtle hated puns. Stuff and nonsense, cleverness that wasn't worth a damn. Puns were low and lazy, belonged only on billboards, T-shirts, bumper stickers, and on the façades of salons and kennels and boutiques she would never patronize. They were an offense committed only by the smug, and the attendant wink and elbow-wag were inimical to dignity.

And how was this pun to be interpreted? Kids today could have no idea what Mort was talking about, *saltpeter* having left the lexicon about the time *whalebone corset* and *chastity belt* did. Seti, who'd reported this to Myrtle, did so by way of asking what saltpeter was. He'd looked it up, and wanted Myrtle to explain what Mort was saying about gunpowder or meat-reddener (for some reason he seemed keen to know if saltpeter was used in Spam). The OED had reported it was the element in gunpowder that made it "exalt the air" and propel the shot. Seti was afraid it had a kinky connotation. He'd asked a girl in reference for help, and she'd fixed him with a baleful stare and handed him the university's sexual harassment guidelines. Back at his post, Seti had earnestly vetted this brochure for news about saltpeter, without success.

Furthermore, what did Mort's line have to do with the Peter Principle? There had to be more there than just the lame pun. Language, as Mort well knew, was required to *mean* something. What would a Saltpeter Principle entail?

When Myrtle finally — or maybe only five seconds of silence had passed, possibly seven, while she twirled the light in her palm and let her eyes rove the room — when Myrtle after five or seven seconds conceived a hypothesis, she seemed its awful exemplar . . . after every high there comes, instanter, the crash. Nothing so short-lived as joy, she thought, and then: Oh my, had this been *joy?* One never knew until it was gone.

Her hypothesis: The Saltpeter Principle holds that you don't *rise* to your level of incompetence after all. You wane to it. You subside, droop, wilt, wither. At some point, maybe in your thirties or forties, you lose your hard-on for life. (Perhaps there was something to carrying this whupping stick. Myrtle felt *equipped,* and the vernacular came easily.) You ebb, you shrink — the years fly by. You no longer allure; you deter. Before you die, you must be shriveled of your sins.

And then she herself had punned, out of the blue, and there seemed no turning back from this new course. Age, misery, unhope, all the rest of the tatty furniture of her life — it didn't seem so intolerable. In fact she was feeling frisky, on the edge of jaunty. Noticing that joy had fled brought on its echo or aftershock — look there, you're still capable of joy! — which was nearly as good as the thing itself. To learn, at this age, to be a happy hypocrite . . . what could be better? But her energies needed a channel. Eyes on the prize.

Yes. Loosening morals, widening legs and gyres. Mere anarchy was being loosed on the library, last stronghold of order, maybe the only part of the world worth saving. A preserve; *her* preserve. Her palm prickled from the blows of the club, and she felt her cheeks flushing, saw Mort eyeing her with approval. She was on the cusp of a newness, a by-God risorgimento. Her arm muscles were hardening, and a career as a cast-iron bitch loomed ahead. She had a big, noisy weapon all her own, and she reminded herself of its potency with another palm-thwack. What she felt . . . what she suddenly felt was something she hadn't experienced in years. That prickle under her ears and between the shoulder blades, the spine aligning itself, breasts lifting and separating, the smile beginning to spread. Lord have mercy, Myrtle felt *sexy*.

She tried to tune back in to Mort, but he'd lapsed into an account of shopping for the flashlight in security-guard catalogs. Were there really rent-a-cops out there packing shoulder bazookas and wearing camo face paint? By the way, he added, if her club was too heavy to carry, he'd seen nice-looking ammo belts, in a variety of designer colors . . .

Myrtle's eyes drifted over the shelves behind him. She'd seen Mort's blacklist at the circ desk — looking it over was a popular diversion there, a parlor game for the staff — and many of his choices were predictable: photo books of prostitutes, whether in Storyville or the Reeperbahn or the slums of New Delhi; arty outdoor shots of semi-clad children in poses of concentration, staring up the lens as if to dare you to call this exploitation (she'd poked about in a chain store that didn't have Mort's qualms); Mapplethorpe's black-and-white homoeroticons, with their unsettling resemblance to Ansel Adams's hymns to the crags and rills of the West; a book about Vito Acconci, who during Myrtle's college years installed a ramp in a Manhattan gallery and lurked beneath it, staring up skirts and masturbating while fantasizing over loudspeakers — the catcall elevated to art.

Then Myrtle caught sight of Mort's own book, and she couldn't suppress a twinge of empathy: What must it be like to be accused of lewdness and blasphemy, and then — years later — to have to confess to the crime, more or less, in order to stave off the public prurience that was what played you false in the first place? Mort's accusers had been ahead of a curve he'd failed to see. Time and rampant lust had made them half right, and that fraction growing ever larger. The context had changed, the world had. His book wasn't filth before — or that wasn't quite right, maybe; even if you granted his pure motives, what did they avail against a riptide? The harder you pull, the more savagely it tugs you under — his book *may* not have been filth before, but now it was, and he'd had to file it here among the strokers. What must it feel like for him, she thought, to see it pinched between such rakes and blades — Henry Miller, Céline, Rabelais? Maybe he soothed himself by thinking of this as protective custody, to keep anyone from complaining about the book to higher-ups. Either way, having it here was an admission of what must be a painful kind.

"I'm not against amatory expression, in its place," Mort was insisting now. "Don't get me wrong. We all have our private delectations." He seemed taken aback by the look he found on Myrtle's face. "Present company excepted, to be sure. Present company excepted. It's just that . . ."

Myrtle felt for him. The Diviner of Motives, Chatelaine of Art. She let her eyes rove a shelf of mostly fiction, much of it from the 1960s and '70s, books that had been pathbreaking and/or notorious in their youth: the first and cuntiest two books in the *Rabbit* tetralogy, *The Sot-Weed Factor,* Kathy Acker, *Spanking the Maid, Down the Whore's Mouth: A Bukowski Reader.* And a book she recognized from her own college shelf, Stanley Elkin's *Searches and Seizures* (ah, "The Making of Ashenden," in which a suitor in search of a heroic deed to sway his intended is confronted by a young bear in estrus and realizes that to save his life and prove his mettle he must mount her, in a way no taxidermist would dare — a novella Myrtle's boyfriend at the time had referred to as "Screwin' the Bruin").

There were others sprinkled in: Colette's *Collected, The Arabian Nights,* the raunchy Brothers Grimm, *Fanny Hill,* a copy of *Madame Bovary* with its spine defaced to read *Madame Ovary,* and several dozen volumes Myrtle couldn't make out. Just below was a separate gay-and-lesbian shelf, she presumed, surprisingly large — Myrtle's eyes caught on *Rubyfruit Jungle* and Dorothy

Allison at one end, an armload of Oscar Wilde at the other, and between them nothing she recognized.

Then she turned her attention to the bottom shelf. It had, by contrast to those above, a bordello laxness about it, an air of disorder. It was a jumble. Books lolled on their sides and backs, in promiscuous clumps. Were they aspiring verbotens trying out for the squad, or was this a private stash? Myrtle strained to make out titles. The Marquis de Sade's *120 Days of Sodom,* okay. Naughty Nicholson Baker, with his tics and tockholes, check. A book she'd heard about on the radio that featured pictures of farm animals — pigs, heifers, guinea hens — shot in the lurid gloss and with the cheesy accouterments of pornography: absolutely, but how had it come to be in the library's holdings? Why the untidy stack of books that, to judge from their titles, had to do with circus sideshows? What, pray tell, was *Vigiliae Mortuorum* — some kind of embalm-your-own-loved-ones guide, perhaps — and why was it keeping company with Anaïs Nin? There were erotic parodies of children's books, their narrow spines hard to decipher: was that *Tintin in Bangkok? Curious George Gets His Nut?* And what reason could Mort have for locking away a paperback she'd seen in every grocery checkout: *Holding the Bag: How I Beat Self-Pity,* the inspirational memoir of a starlet who made her way back — back, at least, to TV movies and afterschool specials — from a colostomy?

And then, by itself at the far right, she spotted the *Psychopathia Sexualis.* It was riddled with red fluorescent tabs — hundreds of them, on every side, so lavishly stuffed that the book gaped open. It looked like a pincushion, like a scarlet-quilled porcupine. It had the sodden look of a skin magazine peeled up from a storm grate by a ten-year-old. It looked like a book read hard and put up wet. (Damn this impulse to pun. You gave in once, and then it owned you.)

Ten minutes before, this would have seemed to Myrtle a revelation, and Mort would have been unmasked as just another debauchee, just another *man.* But one benefit of embracing your own hypocrisy, it seemed, was that it freed you to be indulgent of others'. She'd started with the assumption that Mort was chaste, out of priestliness or the herpes (who knew?) or because, well, just who would get it on with an oversized Amish jester? But it occurred to her now that she'd been amending that notion as he talked. Abstemious he might be, but not *vestal*. There was his daughter, for one thing; Myrtle had been reluctant to conjure a mental picture of the event, but Lili must have been maculately conceived. There was the randy way he handled the flashlight, the dewy prints he left. There was this note-swollen copy of the *Psychopathia Sexualis*. And what had he said a minute ago about "private delectations"?

Also, it had to be admitted — joy, even its shadow, tended to give the old generosity of spirit a boost — he was pretty well built for a jester, wasn't he? A couple times as he railed and ranted, she'd thought she caught sight, through the button-gaps in his shirt, of an actual abdominal muscle. An ab on a pentagenarian, when it could no longer be the accidental by-product of good genes or an active lifestyle. Once you got him out of those duds, he might turn out to be a hellion. He was certainly *well-read* in the dark arts, from the looks of it . . . and his Kikuyu hair might be fun to fondle, especially for someone accustomed, as Myrtle was, to the waxy sparsities of Milt's.

Good Lord, was there anything lower than fantasizing about Mort Bozeman? She couldn't believe how violently her opinion of him kept vacillating, back and forth and back. Why had her self-control gone haywire this morning? She was a person of a certain age, of a certain . . . shut up already. No pep talk needed; no need to lean on her trusty crutch. Now was not the time to come on to him. Never was the time to come on to him. He was her boss, and the nature of their partnership, just sealed and now being solemnized with the passing of the symbolic lead pipe, was a battle against illicit sex. Erotic reveries were hardly the order of the day.

What about this guide to sex-crazies, though, a book so sick they had to leave its title in Latin? How did he account for that? Know thine enemy, sure, but there was knowing and then there was *knowing*. "Ralph Luckett knows Muriel the hash girl *in the biblical sense,* so I hear," her father used to say, crackling his square of newspaper for emphasis, thinking Myrtle couldn't follow. Follow, hell — Myrtle could *lead.* She got it fine: Begat and begat and begat.

But how closely did you have to inspect thine enemy? Did knowledge require that you insert a semi-adhesive tab into thine enemy's every joint and crevice until it looked like a badly shuffled deck of cards? Mort seemed to be conducting something like the fat man's reconnaissance of the lamb chop. *Fat man licks his fingers, coughs up a glistening bone. "That's a lamb chop, all right," he says. "Good thing we caught it early."*

And then it struck Myrtle — how could it not have before? — that maybe Mort had made the whole thing up. Of course! How could her hard nose have gone so suddenly soft? The Xeroxed article was a canard, the sex epidemic a lie. The only dangers here were safely shut away in Mort's cabinet. The situation was in hand; there was no situation. The pun should have given it away first thing. It was all for the sake of the pun. That ridiculous dairy saga — UCLA's special collections probably consisted of Fatty Arbuckle's stained girdles and Esther Williams's bathing caps rather than a Shakespeare folio. Besides, what embattled library dean would say such a thing? And where — come on, now — where did the alleged children melt their alleged cheese? Did they smuggle in a fondue pot as well? She hated to be a killjoy . . . well, it was turning out that she didn't hate it, that there might be a joy in killing joys, a tidy little kickback for repossessing the ones folks couldn't afford. Still, somebody had to be the one to collect past-due accounts, to ask the hard questions about fondue pots and such. Someone had to be the adult; this was Myrtle's charge and writ.

She pulled her focus back from the caged books — Mort had for several minutes been an orange foreground blob — and was dismayed to find that she'd been punctuating her mental litany with flashlight-slaps, like a street tough. Worse yet, Mort wasn't talking anymore. He was sitting on the corner of the desk, three feet away, wearing an inscrutable smile. How long had she tuned out? Five seconds, ten, a minute, an hour?

"Any questions?" Mort asked, still smiling, giving nothing away. "I can see you have questions."

She did. They'd been there all along. She'd never been gulled. Myrtle was a woman of hard nose and dignity, of dignity and hard nose. She rested the blackjack on her lap — it felt like a turnstile she couldn't push through — and began the questioning.

How had they come up with a ranking, she wanted to know. Guesswork? Rumor? "I'm pretty sure," she said, "this guy didn't hide in every college library in turn and make an actual count of sex acts." That would make him the biggest pervert of all, a grown man with his hand on a pocket clicker while he crouched under the dictionary stand and watched the kids go at it: *Thirteen, fourteen — come on, now, we're two blowjobs shy of a hotbed.*

She kept on: She didn't mean to suggest that Mort was in on it, of course. The fraud or joke would be laid to the part (she bore down on the legal language to bleed it of any unentendred entendres) . . . would be laid to the part of the previous part, the man with the clicker, that is, or rather the man who would have had to have a clicker to do his research the right way but who patently hadn't, not in every American college, at any rate, that being physically impossible as well as morally degenerate — the right way being a very, very wrong way, if Mort followed. Anyway, was there evidence? Could the list be based on some screwball formula that correlated LSU's party-school rank with an index of the number and wattage of fluorescent tubes in the library (it *was* rather dim in here, Mort would have to concede) and with area sales of condoms? Could the list be the product of urban legend or puritan hysteria? Could it all be a *joke?*

Mort smiled on, pleased either by her aggressiveness or by the rare invitation to spell out depravities. "These are excellent questions. I was told you were good, and you are. You do not disappoint. As I said, the perception of trouble counts for as much as trouble itself, but the fact is that we have a problem, and you have every right to know how deep and vile is the root you will be, will be, the root you will be" — metaphor failed him — "uprooting. In recent months we've had an epidemic: not the usual, relatively innocuous things — boys surfing forbidden areas of the Internet, a tearoom or two in the comfort stations." Innocuous? Wasn't a tearoom a place in New York with samovars and borscht? Were these junior reprobates *teeing* — Myrtle's mother's word for what a later generation would promote up the alphabet to "peeing" — on one another for fun? Even "comfort station" sounded dirty in the context. Bathrooms were not places for people to comfort one another, in that or any other way. They were a place for silent, private voiding. Myrtle always felt ashamed if she had to resort to a public loo. If one had to venture there, one swabbed the seat and, seated, drew one's feet tight underneath for invisibility. One handled all fixtures with a hand swathed in paper pinched soundlessly off the roll; before proceeding, one set in the bowl a layer of tissue for soundproofing. One did not give oneself away.

Mort, warming to the task, kept ticking his way down the blotter. "We've had a cavalcade of deviants. One male student was crawling under carrels, taking pictures of coeds' tootsies. Eventually we caught him with a fistful of photos: sandals, toe cleavage, and so on. On some, presumably photos of feet he'd crawled close enough to sniff, he'd written wine-tasting notes: *Fruity, despite the Dr. Scholl's,* that kind of thing. He's been banished. Another young man, trolling pornography on the Web, was observed *licking the screen.* Barred. There was a grad student who stretched out in her carrel with a Persian dictionary and began pleasuring herself with battery power while giving a simultaneous translation of the action, if you follow me. Exiled. Another young woman set up a piercing parlor in the basement, in an alcove behind broken microform readers. We caught her because someone heard muffled screams and thought we were running a torture chamber down there.

"Myrtle, what I'm driving at is that these kids aren't like us, I mean they aren't like we were. At that age we were babes in the woods, *nicht wahr?* We didn't know one end from the other." He seemed to have drifted into deep waters, so he paused and muttered a "so to speak" and went to gouge at his litterbox for a minute. He wandered back. "The times are loose; our discipline must be tight. In the last six months we've had no fewer than thirteen reports of fornicating couples in the stacks. In every case we've arrived too late to catch them. You will end that unlucky skein. My first thought was surveillance, but it's impracticable. It would require an outlay of public funds, for one thing, and that would be tough to explain. And who would surveil the surveilers? It would take a second person to watch the security guard watch the bank of screens, and a third person to watch the second watch the first, and no matter how far you go, there's someone at the end of the line who can get his merries without fear of being seen. No, the only solution is community policing. The solution is you. We're glad to have you aboard. You do us proud service. Don't forget your training tomorrow."

Mort gave one last longing glance toward the flashlight, which lay safe on the fortress of her lap, untouchable. He nibbled at the tuft of beard just below his mouth. Myrtle stood and dropped the flashlight into her satchel. The weapon rested heavily among her tissues and butterscotches and the embroidered sleeve in which she kept her reading glasses, and she had to lean hard to the left so as not to be unbalanced by it.

These kids aren't like us. You do us a proud service. Myrtle avoided Mort's eyes as she shook his big, dry hand. She was a soldier on special mission, and memory could do no good, serve no purpose; best to be rid of it, to be aware only of the task at hand.

Gallantly humped she her burden through the door. "It will be done," she said.

11.

Oh, Lili, how low love lays us. Now he has become a thief for her, a common thief.

Or no, more accurate to say that Seti has become a common *borrower* — the book will be back in Mort's cabinet inside fifteen minutes. Moreover, it is *her* book rather than the library's, bought with *her* baby-sitting money. A useful moral distinction, that. More important yet, Allah all but *told* him to retrieve it. So: not thief, not borrower, nothing dodgy and sinning but instead a liberator, a setter-right of wrongs. That's more like it; there's no need to feel guilty. Seti has joined the long line of Ptolemies, warrior-librarians, men adept with both the quill and the *husam,* who in ancient days tended the cuneiform treasures of Alexandria. His is a just cause (and he needs only, say, *twelve* minutes, he won't push it, most of your heroes who get their rear ends in a sling — a phrase of Myrtle's — end up that way, rear-end-slung, because they don't know when to quit).

Seti needs the book as proof of his devotion. A week ago, Lili confided — well, it was more a rant than a confidence, but he was the one she chose to share it with — that Mort had seized something of hers, a book she'd bought on the Internet, and it was just a movie-star biography, and it was *hers,* after all, not his to annex for the library, and if Seti could manage to get it back she'd be *eternally grateful.* Seti made lavish sympathetic noises, but he knew that was as far as he would go. He was no criminal, and he'd spent a long time gaining Mr. B's trust; besides, the jailer ring stayed locked in the desk at all times.

So a few minutes ago, when — worried about the dwindling time between now and next Saturday (the day Seti has arranged for the life-changing date that, thanks to his fumbling this morning, Lili doesn't know about yet), between now and noon (when Lili will be whisked home by her father, not to return until Monday at the earliest), and anxious too about the ever-lengthening time since Rex set off in search of her — Seti went into Mort's office to check on the status of a reordered book and saw the keys atop the blotter, in the open, he did not snatch them up. His first impulse was to leave the ring where it was and close the office door and keep watch for marauders until twelve, then to collect Mort's praise for his defense of the battlements.

But one grew tired, eventually, of being a good boy when the bad seemed always to prosper. At length it occurred to him that Mort's oversight was perhaps a gift from Allah, a nudge in the right direction — an attempt to buck up his flagging faith. Only three months remain. If he is going to win Lili's heart, if he intends to so bedazzle her that she'll wait for him through her last term of high school and then her freshman year of college, it is time to get a move on.

And heart-winning, he realized, might require pushing the box, thinking outside the envelope. It was not for the fainted heart.

Was all this correct, this flurry of slangs? Seti's usual next step would have been to jot down the recalcitrant phrases and check his beloved dictionary, forty feet away, an excursion he could make without losing sight of the circulation desk and thus without being a truant or slacker. No one could complain of him.

But heart-winning required someone bold, someone chained neither to desk nor to petty laws of usage. Love was not for the poultry-hearted; it was not for the Lili-livered. This once, the dons and deans — those priests and professors up on their high whores at Oxford, telling the common man what to say — could kiss his oven-loving ass, could flyingly fuck up the moon. It was time, past time, for Seti to *go off script*. It was time for him to *get busy*.

The life span of a euphoria is necessarily brief. One soon recognizes self-determination for the bootless lie it is — Allah or Destiny holds the pen, so one is always on script, even when off script. It took only a moment for doubt to take hold, and for traitorous memory to start piling up phrases to look up later: *Why would one's ass love an oven?* But by then the surge had carried Seti through Mort's door and closed it behind him, and that was enough.

As he fitted the key into the lock, he felt a surge of power — Allah, no doubt, availing himself of the static charge in Mort's carpet. The shock meant that this was the right thing to do, but get the book back in a jiffy. Seti found that he was getting better at reading the signs.

Once Lili sees the book, she will at last and instantly understand the depth of his passion. She will burst into tears (how could she have overlooked him for so long?) and fly to him to be enfolded, and Rex will only be able to shake his sleek, ottery head and stand aside, tugging at an earring; then — from a heretofore hidden reserve of nobility — the bested rival will summon up a grin and a good-bye handshake for each of them. The yellow delta on his chin will bow to the better man.

And of course Lili won't want her fiancé compromised by having burgled for her, so on their way into the sunset they will stop to replace the book *exactly as it was* in Mort's restricted cabinet — bottom shelf, eighth from the left, spine down. Later, Seti will go to Mr. Bozeman and firmly, in the interest of fairness, his case bolstered by his new status as son-in-law apparent, argue that *Cocksman with a Pencil-Thin Mustache: Errol Flynn Uncensored* be restored to its rightful owner.

Okay, he's getting ahead of himself; but surely even a brief reunion with the book (which really does have to be back in the cabinet pronto — it's eleven already, and Mr. Bozeman said he'd be back by noon) will be enough to persuade Lili to accept Seti's invitation to New Orleans. The immediate goal: First Date. The longest journey begins with a single plunge into the abyss.

Building up to asking her out has taken a year, so far. He has dithered, one couldn't deny that, but he hasn't *only* dithered. There have been impediments to think through: he is twenty-one, she not quite eighteen; he lacks both car and cool; he will be returning to North Africa in January. Also, Rex is constantly flitting around Lili, moth to her flame, and won't give Seti a decent run-up to immolating himself. Until now, immolation has seemed the only failsafe way of getting her attention. The drab and timid moths get no breaks, of course; sizzling is their only choice. Meanwhile, the dumb, cocky, bright-winged ones give foot massages . . . oh, screw the metaphor. Rex is probably an *ace* with metaphor.

The one bit of headway he has made is with Mort. Though it's a stratagem better suited to Egypt than to America, Seti has spent a good deal of energy plying Mr. B — father-plying is for Lili a "major turnoff," he knows, so he's done his plying out of her sight. But befriending Mr. B was a goal he could pursue without becoming tongue-tied, without falling silent or falling down, and it at least *felt* like progress.

The upshot is that despite the age difference, Mort likely won't object. Seti has considered asking formal permission — "Sir, regarding your revered daughter: may I make bold to pitch my woo?" — but he figures that would be a deal-breaker with Lili. Mort said something the other day that might even count as encouragement. Shaking his head at the sight of Rex traversing the lobby with pants so low on his hips that a bright ruff collar of boxer short showed above them, Mr. B groused, "Couldn't she find a boy who owns a *belt*?" Then he seemed to glance at Seti's unimpeachably high-riding trousers, at the leather gird holding them in place, and there was nothing to disapprove. On Seti, only things that ought to be visible are visible.

But time is running out, and every time he's tried to ask Lili out he's been balked by something: her loveliness knotted his tongue, like this morning, or Rex was smirking nearby, or Seti was self-conscious about a blooming pimple or about the fact that much of his American vernacular, filched from screwball comedies of the 1930s and '40s, was out of date. One day last spring he finally worked up the moxie and gumption to touch on the subject, but when he asked how, in this country, a man who'd found the woman of his dreams should go about "making his suit," she'd thought he was asking for tailoring advice. "Your clothes are fine," she comforted. "They're kind of retro, really. They have a vintage-shop vibe. And suits are so, you know, eighties. Your girlfriend doesn't want you to wear suits, and even if she did you wouldn't need to home-sew them. Hit a discount barn. Ninety-nine bucks." For the next month, Lili had asked after his nonexistent "squeeze." At first he thought she'd figured it out, was teasing him about the vise grip she had on his heart, that ever-tightening pressure around his ribs. *My anaconda of love.* But the slang dictionary set him straight, and after that Seti kept his idiot tongue.

Thanks to Doug the Stoner and his friends, and later Myrtle, Seti's English had improved . . . but his nerve did not, so at last he had no choice but to force his own hand. He set out to engineer a situation in which *not* asking her out would cause greater humiliation than asking her out, and he has succeeded. Next Saturday, the minister of labor will be visiting New Orleans, and Seti has been invited to an afternoon reception at the consulate. He finessed a second ticket, made a point of saying to the chargé d'affaires that he would be squiring a beautiful young American. Word of this had, as he hoped and dreaded, reached the minister. Just yesterday a note arrived on creamy embossed stationery, a note in which the minister expressed his eagerness to remake the acquaintance of young Mahfouz and to meet the charming escort "whose loveliness has been whispered ahead of her."

So he's boxed himself in. There is no choice now.

The reception will be sumptuous. There will be dignitaries in full dress and waiters in sky-blue rustic-style *galabiyya* serving delicacies of home, bright wheels of blood orange and *mekhalel* pickles and bread and *mesh,* aged white cheese seeded with chili pepper. Fruit and fava beans and fish. Even Lili cannot fail to be impressed. Photographs will be taken, Lili radiant between twin bigwigs, honchos, nabobs: two important men wearing glasses that, bent to their wills, perch obediently on their noses. How could she not notice that Seti is marked for greatness, for future clout? How could she not begin to take an intimate interest in his successes to come?

From there the party — the *delegation,* Seti thinks he'll call it when he puts the proposal to Lili just a couple minutes from now (he has set the "Back in five minutes" sign on the counter and is headed to the central stairwell) — will proceed in a caravan of black sedans to the museum, to a preview of the *Riches of Pharaohs' Tombs* exhibit that's been touring Latin America and is now making its way north to New York.

After that, once Lili has had a chance to absorb some of the grandeur of Seti's ancestry — and he has reason to think there's plenty of absorbing left to do; when he asked last fall what she knew about Egypt, her response was, "That's the place with the really thick mascara, right? I loved Liz Taylor as Chemopatra. And that Bangles song? When Susanna Hoffs looks sideways in the video and you can see the whole white of her eye, that is *killer,*" and then she began a herky-jerky dance that involved holding her palms parallel to the floor and moving them horizontally forward and back — after the exhibit, he will crown the occasion with an elegant dinner.

He has made a reservation at a new fusion restaurant, a place called Kaiser Tut. In July, last time he was in town, Doug saw a review in the *Times-Picayune,* and he insisted on taking Seti down to try it. They sat in Jackson Square all day, steadily depleting Doug's supply of wallets — "It's almost not fair to sell here," Doug said. "The Quarter is a theme park of the weird, and if you offer the tourists something that's cheap and safe and eccentric, that can make them feel like they too are odd and artsy, you can fucking *print* money out here. If I stayed here all the time, I could buy a boat, man. But what would I do with a boat? I don't like boats. I have no need of boats. And it's depressing; these people don't really *want* my wallets. They're souvenirs of a day in Gomorrah. They'll take them home to Wisconsin or Nebraska and set them on the mantel and say, 'How strange New Orleans is, and I was there. Hey, I'm strange, too. I'm living on the edge. Look, I have a wallet made out of duct tape. And a voodoo spell, and a T-shirt with tits drawn in on the front.' It sucks, man, but on the other hand" — he reached into his fanny pack and pulled out a wad of cash — "it pays the bills. Let's go eat, bud. On me. Lucky for you I go for eats instead of boats."

Kaiser Tut features a café area with backgammon and actual hookah pipes and tarry black *kahwascitto* like that of home, though for the sake of fusion — the Kaiser half of the equation — they play oompah records and have waitresses in Bavarian skirts carrying giant steins of beer and make, in addition to serviceable Egyptian and Bavarian dishes, baffling things like spaetzle with tahine sauce and saffron-infused sauerkraut and weisswurst wrapped in papyrus. The restaurant is tony, with white tablecloths and napkins fanned up into scallops and candlelight and elaborately faked hieroglyphs on the walls. There *is* an unfortunate mural of Wilhelm and Tut standing shoulder to shoulder, Tut wearing the piked helmet and Wilhelm the golden headdress, grinning like sailors on a binge, but Seti has asked to be seated as far away from it as possible.

To top it all off, to make sure Lili is so overwhelmed that she might begin to envision a life as Madame Hydrologist, he has arranged a limo — okay, more precisely it's an off-duty medical transport van that will be driven by a friend of Doug's, Micah, a jazz oboist trying to hook up with a band that will embrace his brand of "mournful scat." Micah is willing to drive the limo/conversion van that is his day job, even to wear a livery cap (would a Greek fisherman's lid do?) and open doors and all, so long as Seti agrees to feign a broken leg and zero English if the cops stop them. And Seti will have to keep his date occupied until twelve, which is the earliest Micah can get loose from his audition: "That's the thing about jazz oboe. Only at a certain hour of night and level of drunk does it seem like a good idea. You've got to run them right past gloom and regret and on up to the edge of despair, you know? You want a 4 A.M., Kafka at Ice Station Zebra kind of vibe. So finding the right band takes patience. Patience and serious booze."

The windfall of the keys could not have come at a better time. Because of it, his nerve resurgent, Seti has come to be striding up the stairs with Lili's book clamped under one arm. Or what the hell, under one wing — there is nothing like impending victory to induce one to forgive metaphor for having foxed one last time. He lets his fancy flow. *Here comes your moth, my darling.*

He feels dashing, giddy. He feels like Errol Flynn himself, perhaps. Seti would never pry into the contents of his beloved's book; it is precisely that principle that he is upholding by getting it back to her. He has not opened it, would not. But he can't help noticing the cover. The title is no lie: Flynn sported a mustache that was perhaps even thinner than a pencil — a barbecue-skewer-thin, a car-radio-antenna-thin mustache, not unlike the one Anwar Sadat wore on the poster above Seti's boyhood bed. Seti would gladly consent to grow such a thing, if his darling Lili desires it. The back cover is even more helpful. It reports that Flynn played, among other things, a swashbuckler, Robin Hood, some famous American cavalry general. A buccaneer for homemade justice; that was Seti. He tries not to think about what "cocksman" might entail, and he does his best to ignore a couple other phrases his eye has chanced upon. What, for instance, is the White Slave Traffic Act, and how might a movie star fall afoul of it? Or "jailbait teenybopper" — is that even English? He sets these questions aside and listens to the steady percussion of his footsteps on the risers, the sound of inevitability. He is a cavalryman on the march. Now is his moment.

At the third-floor landing he hears above him a bell — not a measured tolling but an alarm. His friend Myrtle, his fellow warrior librarian . . . she is in trouble. What would Errol Flynn do? Seti grasps the book in his left hand and takes the steps two at a time.

12.

Bouncer school turned out to be a single two-hour session at the alternative-music club just off campus. The class consisted of ten burly college boys and Myrtle. Each of her fellow students seemed to be cultivating some raffishness, some signature idiosyncrasy: a do-rag studded with rhinestones, a Walt Whitman beard. ("You got to *volumize*," she overheard Big Beard explain to an admirer — a guy trying to eke by with a wispy Amish number — as they milled about waiting for training to start. "I won't shit you. It takes some effort. Afro-Sheen is good for glisten, and I bind it with rubber bands if I'm going to eat sloppy foods, like, you know, sloppy joes.") One guy, the shortest and unburliest of the bunch, was wearing a battered stovepipe hat, as if he feared he'd wash out of training unless he could occupy a space at least six feet tall. *To check IDs and boot drunks you must be at least this high.*

Myrtle sat alone at the bar and wondered how they'd treat her: the only woman, and elderly, and unequipped with a bull ring under her nose or a cardboard Burger King crown or a pair of yellow lobsterman's boots. Who were these children, and why were they vying so desperately for attention?

This was the generation whose couplings Myrtle would be busting up, and they were a cipher to her. Neither in daily life nor at the law firm had she had much interaction with them. She had no siblings, and Milt's sister's kids, though the right age, lived near Seattle; her dealings with Sasha and Colby consisted of sending twenty-dollar bills on birthdays and Christmas, and never getting thanked.

Myrtle didn't want to be condescended to . . . or adopted, God forbid, as a mascot: the little old bouncer from Pasadena. Butting into her classmates' conversations would only feed their stereotype of the garrulous blue-hair. So she contented herself with eavesdropping in every direction at once. Most of the boys seemed to be trying to move up to security from bar-back or dishwasher, but a couple — Bull Ring and an Adonis wearing jeans so ruthlessly and artfully acid-washed that they appeared more absent than present — had worked at music clubs before, as errand boys or bouncer's aides. She overheard their stories about being sent out to assemble backstage spreads, the contents of which were apparently written into bands' contracts in minute detail: Cocoa Puffs and slivovitz, surgical masks and a mesh bag of tangelos (which weren't touched, just demanded to make sure the band had enough clout to get their whims fulfilled), *X-Men* comics and a gross of condoms in rainbow colors. With unconcealed awe, Bull Ring told of a famous metal band whose instrument cases and packing crates were lined with closeup photographs — several *hundred* — of what he called "groupie quim."

"Sometimes there's a guy in the entourage whose whole job

is to scout babes in the audience," added Adonis. "He's called a trim coordinator." He pronounced the last two words the way boys of her generation had said "astronaut," or "president."

She saw a few guys sneaking glances her way, aware she was listening, and finally, when Bull Ring reached the predictable punch line of his story — during a break, the metal band's drummer had emerged from the tiny dressing room and given him twenty bucks to *fetch some film* — Stovepipe came over to introduce himself. His name was Kyle, and he doffed his elevator headgear and begged her pardon. No pardon was necessary, she said, and tried hard to embark on a course of small talk that steered safely clear not only of groupie genitals but also (he had resettled the hat on his head) of Abraham Lincoln and undertakers and circus barkers.

One by one, the rest drifted over to say hello. They were polite, nervous, even sweet. A guy in a blue dog collar did everything but kiss her hand. Bull Ring caught her staring at his disfigurement and said, "It doesn't hurt, if that's what you're wondering. I figure if I'm going to let every woman I meet lead me around by the nose, I may as well give 'em a place to hitch up. Want a tug?" She had an interesting discussion of hair processes with a young black man with a shaved head and one of those crimped, terraced pharaoh beards; it looked like an inverted oil derrick depending from his chin. Their oddities extended no deeper than a single item of wardrobe or facial hair, though. They turned out to be like suburban yard signs for a security system that wasn't hooked up — empty menace. Beneath the tattoo ink and the metal studs and the sheened or crimped beards was unlined skin, even innocence. They were like teen girls who'd broken into the makeup case to play at being vampy.

Myrtle found it agreeable to be surrounded by muscular youth. It had been thirty years since she'd been in close quarters with so many young men. She felt a flush, a kind of electrical flick and flitter. These boys were like she'd been, more or less . . . only it had been far easier to attract attention in the mid-1960s in rural Texas. Back then, a little mascara was enough to do the trick, for boys an extra half-inch of sideburn. For a girl, being easy made you damn near a town legend; now virginity might get you closer to fame, or at least to infamy. Nowadays, even if you made it all the way up to rock or rap star, the pressure to stand out didn't subside. You had to get your nose sewn onto the side of your face and demand two contortionists and a wheelbarrow full of petroleum jelly in order to separate yourself from the other prima donnas with homely haircuts and more money than sense. These kids were running through the catalog of idiosyncrasies at an alarming rate. What would be left when they were fifty but a brick split-level and canned beer and old TV in an undershirt?

What amazed Myrtle most was how much *work* was required, these days, to carve out a niche of uniqueness: rubber bands when you ate, haunting flea markets in search of a good livestock brand, finding an old-school haberdasher to reblock your hat. You had to brave the buzzing needles and autoclaves; you had to shop for neckwear at pet stores. Subtlety was out of the question. You needed to stake a claim to individuality, and bugger the mild or interior forms of it — who could spot those? What you needed was something *conspicuous.* Yet underneath the hairdos and the hardware, these were law-and-order types like the boys in Ozona thirty years before: conventional-minded, courtly, not terribly imaginative. They wanted to be bouncers because it was cool, sure, but also to keep the peace. It was a chance to belong to the protesters and the National Guard at the same time.

Now they were clustered around Myrtle's stool like a coterie — her fresh-faced attendants. For a moment she wondered why, and then she realized. *She,* Myrtle Rusk, had trumped them all, had laid claim to the ne plus ultra of eccentricities: She's an *old lady,* dude. If you couldn't beat her . . .

Their instructor burst through the outside door in full sail and mid-sentence: ". . . to teach you some techniques," he began, "that will enable you to move drunks like they're wind-up toys. Look and learn. Look and learn." He was a buzz-cut muscleman, handsome and African-American, with a set of nunchaku draped around his massive neck; the word SECURITY strained and rippled across his chest. The timbered door was still shivering from the blow he dealt it. He hadn't entered the room so much as he'd concussed it, and there was a blur of heat rising off him as off summer asphalt. A pair of mirrored sunglasses perched on his forehead, and there seemed to be an implicit threat that he might at any minute flip down the visor and return to a cool in which you would not be included. You didn't want that.

First he went around to inspect the flashlights they'd been required to bring. Myrtle's classmates' models ranged from a lowly four-cell all the way up to twelve. It was like being in a junior-high boy's locker room, an experience she'd missed out on. The guy with the four-cell, Big Beard, having clandestinely measured the competition, wore a blush, and she knew he'd be looking into enlargement. As the instructor made his way down the line, she saw Big Beard turn to Adonis and whisper, "Hair care ain't cheap, friend, as I guess you know. Had to *economize;* when you volumize one place, you got to turn it down someplace else." There was only one twelve, Kyle the Top Hat Boy doing his compensating on yet another front, and the instructor stopped to marvel at it. It was a thick, black, brutal thing; it looked like an artillery shell. "Nice deck, dude," the instructor said. "Internal bleeding is our specialty!" The one Mort had given Myrtle was a perfectly respectable eight, and this too won her some respect. "You be totin' large," whispered the Burger King. "I like a woman what totes large." This, whatever it might mean, seemed genuinely respectful, and Myrtle thanked him for the compliment.

Their instructor, whose name was Brass (no one asked, thank the Lord), said he didn't have time in such a short session to deal properly with the history of bouncing and concert security, which grew out of the mercenary tradition of ancient someplace or another; suffice to say it was a rich and noble history. He would touch on bouncing philosophy later, but anyone who wanted the longer perspective (it wasn't clear to Myrtle whether this was a joke; Brass didn't seem like a man to joke) could sign up for the ten-week masters course. For now, he was going straight to the action. "A short class ought to be," he said, "like a Kung Fu flick. Can the talk, and break some legs.

"If you have to hit a guy," he said, "if it gets that far out of hand, delicacy goes out the window. You can't mess with a nine-round TKO. You've got to end things with one blow. I want to see urine in his piss."

"Blood in his piss," corrected a big blond guy, a late arrival, at thirty-five or so the second oldest of the trainee enforcers. Good posture, hair parted in the middle, 1970s style, and a bushy gray-blond mustache. He looked like an adult-films version of the Brawny man. He too wore a SECURITY shirt, but with a caret and the letters IN inserted in red at the beginning. The existentialist porn-star bouncer.

"As I *said*."

"You said 'urine in his piss.' I'm sorry to have to be the one to break it to you, but —"

"Sorry, okay, blood in his piss." Brass resumed the lesson.

"Or blood in his urine," interrupted the blond.

"Are you done with the ringing the changes, cuz? Okay, to achieve this blessed state of blood in piss, or sangre in urino, or whatever, you'll need to plant a short, sharp blow to the kidney."

The blond guy raised his hand. "Is that sort of kidney-shaped?" he said with a smirk.

"Please be quiet, sir," said Kyle. "We need to learn."

"Make me, you little punk." The blond took a step toward him. Kyle glanced around for his deck, spotted it across the room, towering uselessly over ketchup bottles and Tabasco at the waitresses' station. The blond took another step, whacked the top hat away.

"All right, clown, you're done," said Brass.

"Am I?" The blond raised his fists. Brass crouched and lunged, popping him once in the thigh, hard, with a flashlight, and the blond crumpled, yelping in pain. Brass put him in a half nelson and ushered him to the street. He returned to applause. When the ovation was over, he said, "That was a demonstration." The blond reappeared at the door, and a couple of the bigger guys moved toward him, decks raised. "No, no," Brass went on. "As I say, that was a demonstration. I'd like you to meet my chiropractor, Biff Baines."

"Ouch, hombre, I think I need an adjustment right now," said Baines in a booming dinner-theater tone. He was walking like a rodeo cowboy. He stopped to rub his leg for a few seconds. Then he handed out bright blue cards to everyone: SPINE BY BIFF. He shook hands all around and left.

Brass waited for the hubbub to die down, for the cards to be pocketed. Then he confirmed that the way to inflict maximum damage was to take a swing at the kidney. But maximum damage was to be reserved for dire circumstances. "The kidney punch is a last-resort maneuver. Urine in your piss" — no one dared correct him — "is serious business, and you want to stay out of people's renal tracts to whatever extent possible. Folks tend to be kind of possessive about their renal tracts. You're liable to get sued, and the bar too.

"These are deadly weapons, is the point, and you need to show restraint. Do what's necessary, nothing more. It's never personal, NEVER. And don't hesitate to call the cops if something looks like it might escalate. Intervene only when necessary, Kyle, and always keep your deck handy. And rethink that lid, brother. It's like an invitation."

Brass explained that being a bouncer was not about violence; it was about the constant, overt threat of violence. "Everybody's idea of a bouncer is a guy with a neck so big it makes his earlobes lie sideways, and I won't kid you, conspicuousness is your job. You're a reminder that actions have consequences. I want you to look vicious and pitiless. I want you boys — and girl — to *clank* when you walk. Armed to the teeth, and looking like if the arsenal down low failed you'd be willing to *bite*. That's the point of the working out and" — he trailed a hand across his pecs like a game-show girl touting a Radarange — "the tight T-shirts and so on. It's about intimidation. But in thirteen years of bouncing, I have never once had to take a swing at anyone. Except poor Biff . . . who, by the way, will give half off to any of you for the first session. The man can crack a back like nobody."

Brass explained the value of calm and professional threats and put them through drills in which Myrtle found the boys' politeness especially charming. They called her "ma'am" — as in "Don't make me whip your ass in front of your friends, ma'am" or "Just leave quiet and I won't make you bleed, ma'am." Her favorite was from Kyle, who said, "Not even a twitch, motherfucker ma'am."

Eventually Brass circled back to physical training. He taught his pupils how to position themselves behind an "offender," holding the flashlight at its middle, then to insert it quickly between his thighs — 99.5 percent of your troublemakers were men — turn it sideways, and bring it flat against the front of the legs; his balls would then be just above the back of one's hand, and in peril, which tended to promote docility. "The bouncer should pull gently back while grabbing the back of the collar with the other hand and quick-walk him out on tiptoe."

Myrtle wasn't condescended to. She had to give Brass credit for that. He had the class demonstrate this technique on one another, and the intimacy of sticking her flashlight beneath several guys' testicles, of having a harem of young men shyly insinuate their clubs between her legs and duck-walk her out of the bar, gave her an atavistic thrill. When I was their age, Myrtle thought, I could have KILLED any of these guys in the sack. "Your deck should never leave your side," Brass warned again and again. "It is your best friend." Myrtle could remember her father saying the same thing about her virginity, way back when. That advice was as useful — and as likely to be heeded — as this. Myrtle was not, of course, going to don a second-skin security T-shirt and devise her own signature weirdity and carry her eight-cell around the library so as to be able to sneak up on a man violating the no-sex policy, stick a flashlight between his thrusting thighs, and duck-walk him, nude and with a glistening remnant of erection, down the stairs and into the main campus quadrangle.

She briefly fantasized about spicing up her marriage by

sneaking up behind Milt as he shaved; his wide stance would make it easy to show off both her deck-twirling abilities (she was warming to the lingo) and her new forceful manner. The Dominatrix Diogenes, carrying her lantern from house to house — or at least room to room — in the search for an honestly horny man. Cockwalking Milt back to the bedroom, back to the altar, back to the childbearing years: *that* would enliven the relationship.

But she couldn't tell him; she couldn't. Her main fear was that he would say, tiredly, "We're too old for such shenanigans," his response two years ago when, in a last attempt to salvage their sex life, she had sausaged herself into a twenty-year-old negligee and brought out a pair of handcuffs. His eyes barely left the PBS special on some recently solved math conundrum. "We're getting too long in the tooth, old girl. Now shoo." He had patted her rump and given a half-smile and leaned around to see the screen, on which a rumpled tall man could be seen writing silently at a blackboard. Myrtle would have settled for even a fleeting flare of panic in Milt's eyes, something to say that, after all these years, she'd surprised him, had revealed new depths of character or of depravity. Nothing. Nothing but the vimless rump-pat, a couple old-fashioned words, a reminder that Myrtle was no longer allowed unpredictability. *You've made your sarcophagus, my dear. Now lie in it.*

Not a word about the teddy, which smelled powerfully of dresser sachet and which *fit*, albeit snugly, after two decades; not a thought about the sacrifices she'd made. She had borrowed a wig and dark glasses and taken a long lunch to drive across the river to a boutique called Leather Pleasures, where the woman behind the counter wore a banana-colored catsuit with a long zipper down its front. The zipper's grip was a cock ring, and the woman fiddled with it habitually. "Ah!" Chiquita shouted, in response to Myrtle's shy query. "That would be over *here,* in *Restraints.*" She gave her cock-ring zipper a hearty plunk.

Did Milt not realize the psychic cost to Myrtle of such an excursion? Did he take no note of the love required to make her brave the whips and bridles and scratch-and-sniff panties ("Lingonberry"? "New Car"?) of Leather Pleasures? Did he have any idea how humiliating it was to have Chiquita say, "I'm guessing you want a kind of cuff that won't scar your antique headboard. And no spikes or straps. Am I right?"

What Myrtle had wanted was something to arrest, at least for a second, their slide into civilization, a word that more and more seemed to have the whiff of the grave about it. But she'd waited too long, too late. As she changed out of the nightie (nice to be able to breathe again) and dug the sales slip out of the trash, she realized she'd been like the woman who, in bed at night, spends long minutes summoning the nerve to say something important, something utterly *necessary,* then realizes that her lover has fallen asleep . . . and as she lies there can't be sure she doesn't feel *relieved.* Maybe she'd even noticed the deepened breath, the skin gone to dough; maybe she'd *wanted* him asleep, had never intended to say the thing except in the futile whisper she tries now. Maybe she'd been waiting for the hush that would mean the night was safe, at last, for self-pity. Had Myrtle somehow *enjoyed* the agonies of Leather Pleasures? Maybe the point all along had been autoerotic, not S&M but M by itself. Or maybe a *little* S, but not aimed at her phlegmatic husband. Myrtle found herself looking forward to Chiquita's questions when she returned for a refund. She found herself planning a minor vengeance, and she had to admit that the thought had an erotic charge. No need, anymore, for the wig and the glasses and the abasement. She would go as herself this time, and the straitness of her lace, her moral probity, her ferocious — why shy away from it now, character being destiny? — her *dignity* would make Chiquita, after Myrtle left, yank the zipper up an inch, pop in a stick of gum to combat an incipient sourness of mouth. Myrtle would say nothing derisive, would not so much as indulge herself the shadow of a sneer. Dignity alone would be her weapon. Chiquita might not even notice she'd done so, but she *would* give that quick upward tug, *would* unwrap that gum, and Myrtle would have left her little wake in the world.

It was time, past time, to acknowledge that this was and would be herself. What she would leave in the world was not a child but a chill, a tiny eddy of cool like the ones ghosts were said to stir. And that was something. That would have to pass for something.

So self-humiliation had been the point, and she'd been marking the passage into asexual old age with a last, pro forma gesture of defiance. She'd known Milt had long since drifted off to sleep, drifted off to celibacy. All along she'd understood how he'd respond. Why else hadn't she crumpled the sales slip and buried it in the kitchen garbage under stove grease and chicken fat? Why had she laid it gently atop the cloud of crumpled Kleenex under her bedside table, where, later, it might easily be reclaimed and redeemed?

But these things were best unthought of. There was, at long last, a boy's hot breath on her neck again; there was a fist between her thighs. Bull Ring kept whispering *Sorry sorry sorry sorry sorry* as he shoved her in a savage tango across the sunny bar floor and out to the street, and no sound could have been, in that or any moment, sweeter to her.

13.

By the time they finished their rondelle, everyone having practiced on everyone else, the benefits of the exercise had nearly disappeared. There was too much friendliness and good will, too much collaboration. People were very nearly hustling *themselves* out.

Brass called for a break. As the culmination of training, he said, to approximate real-world bouncing conditions, he liked to bring in a few barflies. "I want you to have a chance," he said, "to deal with different brands of unruly, and with different body types. I've asked them to go all out. Sit tight. I'll be back in a couple minutes."

It seemed that Myrtle's boys had been coddling her for only seconds — the held chair, the glass of water, the neck rub — when Brass flung the door open again, held it, and here they came in their street-motley, the group Myrtle had seen clustered on the sidewalk along the seedy row of pubs and ink parlors and plasma centers and head shops at the edge of campus: a rogues' gallery, the hophead all-stars. At the front, carrying a sample plate packed with seared fish and wasabi, was Marley-san, whose grilling cart could be seen through the window, chained to a meter out front; behind him was Sybil, playing a carnival air on the accordion no one ever saw her without; then Levi, loudly confirming over and over again, to Sybil's accompaniment of — good grief, was that Carl Douglas's "Kung Fu Fighting"? — that he'd negotiated an extra round for "loss of trade," loss of trade meaning, here, that he'd closed the velvet paintings and the brine shrimp into the back of his camper top for a few minutes; and crazy Lorenzo, with his fur shako, Beefeater of the street, drum major of the gutter.

Myrtle expected to hear her fellow bouncers badmouth them. But it didn't work out that way. She should have seen it coming, she supposed. These people were celebrities, campus legends, known to all, famous for not selling out (though to whom, for Lord's sake, could they sell out, given that their skills tended to be insanity and/or alcoholism?). They dared walk to the beat of a mute accordionist. They breakfasted on day-old Danish and scalded coffee from the Christian charity café called Hot Cross Buns, then spent the rest of the morning soaking up sun on the sidewalk in front of the Church of Elvis Bar & Grill (a splinter tavernacle devoted to the addled and bloated King of the 1970s, and the skinny-Elvisians of the mainline denomination — fair-weather friends — be damned).

They'd been here, so Myrtle heard, since time immemorial. They endured, and they outweirded her. Her reign was over. She couldn't help feeling a pang of jealousy as Big Beard's fingers ceased their rough magic at the back of her neck and he strode away to welcome the new Regents of Oddity. Marley-san's sample plate was devoured in seconds, green horseradish and all, and Lorenzo was mobbed, treated as a hero precursor by the boys who'd adopted eccentricities of headgear — they immediately surrounded him to ask hatting questions. Myrtle had to admit that his matted and crusted shako was impressive. But did these young men not realize that choosing as their hero precursor a foul-smelling lunatic who thinks he controls traffic with a pennywhistle might not forebode a happy future? Sybil, meanwhile, segued into a high-tempo version of "Roll Out the Barrel." She seemed to be getting impatient.

Then there came a second wave. Wino Ike presented Brass with a sheet of paper ripped from a spiral notebook — a contract, most likely, and scribbling it against a car hood outside was the source of the delay. This was a rare chance to practice his old profession in service of his new one. Legally guaranteed drinks, forthwith, to the due designee, now and hereafter. But his arrival was a drag on her buoyant mood. She'd known Ike, slightly, a dozen years before, back when his name was Tom Corcoran, when he'd had a family and been a partner at one of the big local firms . . . before his wife and daughter were killed in a car wreck that was his fault, before he began his slide into sodden Eisenhowerhood. He seemed to her a figure more tragic than comic. Behind him was Sketchbook Byron, head down, in full mutter. And then, at the back, a sixth, a boy who looked stricken, confused. The boy from the library. *Seti.* Myrtle would have thought him more likely to sell plasma, or Mary Kay, than to volunteer to get thrown out of a bar, and he did look like a draftee: he stepped hesitantly, and his eyes darted about, as if he expected at any moment to be assailed by goblins or flying monkeys.

"We'll take our libations up front," said Wino Ike. "Beers on the barrelhead. We're not Olivier, you know. If we're going to act impaired, you have to let us get into character."

Brass seemed annoyed at this, but he assented. "Ten-minute break," he said. "We'll fill out our paperwork." He disappeared into the back office, and the bar's owner came out to pull the beers. Meanwhile Myrtle caught Seti's eye. He looked relieved to see her, a rose among thugs.

14.

Seti gaped at the row of taps along the back wall (all those logos, like a scale model of commercial sprawl), the shiny hammered-copper bar, the tabletop crowded with metal clubs lined up from smallest to largest, a torturer's socket set. And who were these odd-looking young men who would, if he'd understood aright, beat and harry him from the tavern after he pretended to misbehave so grotesquely as to merit being thrown out? And what was Ms. Rusk doing here?

"What are *you* doing here?" Myrtle asked, looming up before him.

She noticed, again, what a beautiful boy he was — objectively speaking, she was speaking objectively — that combination of Muslim asceticism and Victorian reserve, overlaid by a thick-lidded leonine grace. He seemed like someone capable of going with the flow, like someone capable of making any adjustment. Coming to America, being a bouncer's prop . . . he would take her late career change in stride.

"I don't know. I was on the road to the bakery and stopped to talk with the friends of my friend Doug, and a forceful man came out — the black man in the black shirt — and they all stood up, and they said I had to be invited along with. Mr. Corcoran patted his stomach and said they needed a mezzo-morph, and the black man of muscle sighed but asked if I would help out at his school of bounce for a few minutes, and I had never before helped out at a school of bounce, and such an invitation might not come again. I am avid for new experience. And they made me come. So here I am."

I am avid for new experience. The poor kid. Just then Myrtle saw a blissed-out Wino Ike — Mr. Corcoran, rather — down the bar, holding up six mugs at once like a *Biergarten* girl. They looked like a bouquet, or like a superhero's magic fists. She could do the math; bringing in a teetotaler meant an extra three brews for him.

Seti pointed at the tabletop arsenal. "What will be done with those clubs?" he asked. "What exactly is a school of bounce?"

Kyle came by to tell Myrtle it was her turn on the paperwork. "One minute," she said to Seti. "Just a minute. It will be all right." It took all she had to resist chucking his chin, patting his head.

15.

Everybody else seemed satisfied, even bored, with the instructions, but Seti was at loose ends. He'd been told to stir up the kind of trouble that would get him kicked out of a bar, and that beggared the imagination. He remembered with horror (mostly horror — okay, at least *some* horror) his other foray into a saloon, that day he and Doug and the little red rickshaw forded the flood. In a saloon you could take off your clothes and drink child starlets or fruit daiquiris from whirling aquaria and gamble and swear and frug yourself against others at will — what was disallowed? How to get oneself banished from a place where nothing but virtue was forbidden?

He was half-glad to be there, too. All Seti had in Louisiana — until he finished his seventh lap around Lili's heart and blew the trumpet flourish that would bring down the walls at last — was his righteousness, and it was nice to take it out for a test now and again. He understood that his pleasure in American vice depended on not having quite succumbed to it, on having safeguarded a kernel of Egyptianness. He was a mole, a spy, an alien, not be to assimilated.

This was the one thing he might have vaguely in common with the Islamist fanatics who were gaining prominence and supporters back home. One of the group that coldly executed sixty tourists in Luxor had for a time been Seti's playmate, a rich boy who'd loved toy race cars and had the disconcerting habit of walking up to a person, barking "Vroom! Vroom!" and then turning on his heels. This vrooming boy and the others had been sent to the West to train, to sharpen their contempt and deepen their rage, and part of that training, it was rumored, was immersion in the underworld of strip joints and barrooms and brothels. Trial by fire.

Some terrorists washed out, ended up as exiles from both home and heaven, hollow-eyed drunks who carried at all times a dozen singles specially creased for G-strings. The others, like the vrooming boy, emerged as holy flames, fanatics annealed by the sensuous heat of America. Seti heard U.S. commentators ridicule the hypocrisy of these Muslims who indulged in all sorts of fleshly wickedness, but hypocrisy was rarely so simple as it looked. To voice a principle and then consciously flout it, for personal gain — that would make one an oaf, maybe a sociopath, but not a true hypocrite. A hypocrite was faced with the far dicier challenge of doing contradictory things while believing them compatible with, even necessary to, one another. To be a holy man and get lap dances too, indeed to arrange it so that being cosseted by a bottle blonde's surgically enhanced breasts, those warm loaves of *eesh baladi* warming each cheek as she straddled you in your chair — to arrange it so that enduring such breast-cosseting *guaranteed* you a chamber of heaven filled with pliant virgins, with their bud-vase bosoms (not unlike Lili's) . . . Enough.

The point was that the terrorists might be monsters, but they weren't cynics. They *believed*. It took a sick genius to be able simultaneously to delectate and revile, to displace self-loathing — Seti's faithful companion — onto someone or something else. *The blame for my being set about and brushed and haunted by milky bosoms lies on . . . America.*

Seti imagined the vrooming boy, pie-eyed on liquor, teeth gritted in anger or in ecstasy or in anger-ecstasy, in the fluorescent cave of one of those race-car arcade machines in some dive bar, careening around the oval and bumping or cutting off other drivers, causing their cars to explode and tumble in flames into the overprivileged American crowd. Shifting gears, yanking back the bolt of a gun — they required the same motion.

Seti, though, was blessedly incapable of such feats of hypocrisy or violence, and he had to settle for the chance to lay his virtue an easy task and to find it sufficient thereunto. How to get bounced from a bar? He didn't know, but he'd make an effort. He would be sure to take the last spot in line, and he would observe the masters at work.

He had come to enjoy spending time with Doug's friends, this krewe of the cracked — the Chimes Street legends, plus assorted silk-screeners, barmaids, dogwalkers, smalltime dope dealers, croupiers, makers of jewelry from beads and bottle glass and Monopoly tokens — people for whom a job was simply a means to an end, cash for cigs and weed and whiskey and concert ducats. They felt no pressure to take a profession, to (as more than one of them scoffed) Contribute to Society. Their lives lay elsewhere: in being beholden to no one, in the pursuit of good times.

They were a reminder that, no matter what he did, he could never be an American; he was not born to it, not bred to it. For Seti, pleasure was a hard quarry . . . and there was much to do (much to do, much to do, much to do) back home. Meeting Doug's friends lengthened the shameful list in his notebook, but in a pleasing way — with jobs that exerted no hold on him. Pamphleteer; blood donor; tattooist. Car-wash attendant; night clerk at the Kwik-Snak or the Alamo Motel. Temptations easily withstood. Nothing to keep him from his duty.

They were kind to him, too. He was a spaz and a geek, they said, and they seemed to take pleasure in his affable unhipness. (*Spaz* was not to be found in any dictionary; *geek* seemed to imply that he bit the heads off live animals. Seti had done no such thing, but it seemed intended as a compliment.) They made him feel welcome though he would not smoke nor drink, though he wore earplugs to their poisonously loud concerts, with amped-up electric axes and hashish clouds and mosh pits and, on one occasion, a madman eating a live bird on stage. On that night Seti had cupped his hands and shouted into Doug's ear, "Ozzy also is a geek! He is my companion geek!" He raised a thumb, a gesture Doug hesitantly returned.

In recent months Seti had begun to *hang with them* — even the alien geek may command a slang or two — when Doug was out of town. Seti accompanied a group to Denny's sometimes on Saturday mornings. "Oddfellows Local 2.99," Wino Ike called them, and they looked like maimed veterans: the veiny-nosed ex-president, the Nippon Rasta, the sketch artist hiding behind bottle-glass specs and a greasy scrim of bangs, and Seti the Lovelorn. (Sybil was busy at the Church of Elvis, where she made a few bucks by playing accompaniment for Saturday services. Her specialty was a stately, lugubrious "Suspicious Minds" while the collection plate was passed. The accordion was a reminder of hardship, a way to undercut the Caesar's Palace glitz. The Shtetl of Vegas.)

Mr. Corcoran ate a huge, decadent American breakfast: hot-cakes drenched in syrup, eggs, toast points tinctured with bright yellow butter spray, limp gray bacon. For ninety-nine cents each, plus a two-dollar tip, everybody else got a bottomless mug of coffee and free salt crackers and the use of a leatherette booth, and for an hour every woman they saw, each of the dozen bustling waitresses — heavyset Sweet Mary, Filipino Lou, Gold-Tooth Sondra, and the rest — greeted them by name and called them "Sweetie" or "Darling" and sometimes might nudge the back of someone's head with a shoulder or an armpit as she reached to re-fill a faraway mug or draw a blind. (Seti had to try hard not to recognize in these nudges an echo of the vrooming boy and his ji-had madmen. It was *different*. A shoulder, an armpit.)

Seti came to enjoy these kaffeeklatsches. Ike ran off at the mouth as usual — never letting his slurring or his chewing get in the way of his impeccable grammar — about everything from what various cultures use to keep salt shakers from gumming up to the proper temperature for rinsing whipped-butter scoops and the boffo lawsuit that might result from a certain restaurant chain's negligence in failing to observe same, and Marley-san in-terjected a random remark about spliffs or flying-fish roe, and Sketch Byron had begun a series of short-order still-lifes *(Pie Safe*

#9, *Whirling Rack with Order Slips on It #5)*, and Seti just sat there drinking dishwater coffee and waiting for the next chance to be called "Honey."

16.

Myrtle tried to go last, but four of the young men insisted — underneath their paper crowns and body ink these were the Dixie chancel choirs of yesteryear — that she go ahead of them, ladies first. Finally it occurred to her that she should make sure she was opposite Seti, and by accident she was, and she tried to make sure that circumstance didn't change as they moved through the line. She remembered making similar counts in the idiotic ballroom-dancing class her parents forced on her when she was twelve — she had made use of whatever devious means were necessary (usually it had taken only minor vigilance and math skill) not to end up dancing close to Lem Swayne, who smelled of the Vienna-sausage factory, or Boo Lovejoy, who liked to press against her the avid twig of his erection. God, she'd hated that class, at the Wood-men of the World Hall, among folding slat-chairs on which were stenciled the names of the honorably dead. What kind of parents envisioned for their daughter, in 1950s Texas, a future of crino-lines and watercress sandwiches and the Virginia reel? What kind of town thought the most fitting tribute to its sons killed in action was a cheap stencil on a cheap wooden seat, an item to be used mainly for gum parking or, on those occasions when Mr. Estep got wound up, as a clumsy, clattering tango partner? Occasionally there was a free dance, when the boys speed-walked across the floor to vie for their favorites — this was a part of the class, too, to develop their skills in small talk and politesse by making them cajole their partners a little. On one of these occasions, she re-called Lem Swayne — that revolting smell of soft pug sausage — saying, "Myrtle, you're a-sittin' on my grandpa. You *got* to dance with me this time."

The ultimate pickup line: *You're a-sittin' on my grandpa.*

Wino Ike was first to perform. He executed a spectacular facefirst fall from his stool, then ordered another drink from the floor. He lay on the checkerboard tiles with his hands pinned under his belly, heaving himself lumpily forward like a walrus and barking, "Bushmills, Bushmills, Bushmills!" There was an altercation afterward in which the bulky Ike cursed and struggled and finally, loudly, farted on the hands of the bouncer Walt Whitman, who was nearly moved to fury but was able in the nick of time to call on his vast reserves of poet's tolerance. *I believe the toot of a sot is no less than the journeywork of the stars . . .*

"Nice restraint," said Brass. "This is a good reminder to all of you about real-world conditions. You've got to be prepared for secretions. The ammo is always live. Make sure you wash up before the diploma ceremony, dude. Next!"

It went on in this vein for a while. The barflies had the rough grace of stuntmen. Marley-san did a tremendous imitation of a movie monster, including a lurching walk, thrashings of the head, and roaring, but he kept giggling at himself, and in the end the Pothead Godzilla went mellowly; Lorenzo pawed at the ground and snarled, then tried to butt Pharaoh Beard in the thigh with his hat, but he missed and thudded harmlessly into the side of the bar. "Olé, you fucking nutball," said the bouncer matador, scooping him up. Sybil, it seemed, had some acrobatic training. She executed a nimble ninja move and tapped Kyle on the back of the head with her accordion, all the while playing "Lady of Spain." Sketchbook Byron was the hardest case, and he caused the first casualty. He hurled his reeking coat and shoes at the trainee, then curled into a ball on the floor, whimpering, his sketchbook cradled against his belly. Burger King circled for a full minute, looking for a handhold he could live with. Finally he bowed to both Byron and Brass, twirled his deck one last time, and left. "A man knows when he's licked," said Brass to the survivors. "There's no shame in washing out."

Seti's attempt at stirring up trouble was meager. He took a mincing step into the circle, buried his eyes in the floor. "Madam," he nearly whispered, "I am fuddled with drink, and no woman is safe from my rude advances." She made no move toward him. He took another tentative step. "I am a mosher, madam. I am a cod." *A mosher? A cod?*

There were a few seconds of silence during which Seti ransacked his files for a suitable way to give offense, and then something came to him. "My name is Mort Bozeman," he said finally, and started reeling sideways while reading an imaginary book. "I have a Special Assignment for you."

Myrtle yanked his collar and threaded her deck between his warm, surprisingly tensile thighs and conducted him across the tile floor, her left arm looped around his rib cage, her nose planted between the tops of his shoulder blades. She wrestled him through the door. He smelled of almonds; her fingers interlaced his ribs perfectly.

"Ms. Rusk!" said Seti when she let go and unthreaded the stick. He looked flushed.

"Coffee at one," she said, "and I'll explain. At the student union. Now go!"

"But the class is not over. I have not been dismissed."

"Go! This is no place for you." *Get thee gone from this unholy spot.* Myrtle felt like a reluctant witch — the needle nose, the gnarled hand — banishing from her wood the sweet little morsel she's determined not to eat. As she turned to go inside, her thick black broomstick still held some of his heat.

"Nice job, Myrtle," judged Brass, "good stick-work. But you were carrying the deck a little high. You don't want to cop a feel, ha ha." He paused, seeming to realize that this old chestnut might not work quite as well with a forbidding old wench as with the homophobes he was used to. "Excellent work, though, graceful. Do you have some dance background? Hey, where's the kid run off to?"

"You told me to scare him off," said Myrtle, "and I scared him off." She smiled and snapped her deck against her open palm. The applause was deafening.

17.

Coffee was awkward. They sat on wrought-iron chairs outside the campus bookstore, each trying to banish the sensual specifics of their encounter at the Ecole de Bounce: for her, the mesh of ribs his and fingers hers, the way her chin had notched against a knob of vertebra, her nose in the complicated pleat at the back of his shirt. It was like . . . no, it was like nothing at all. He was a child, and she was not. Simile was perilous, likewise memory. She mangled and remangled a coffee stirrer, asked cheery, idiotic questions about his homeland. Did sand get into your clothes and shoes all the time, like at the beach? Were there really snake charmers, and did they wear those pointy silk slippers that curl up at the tip like world-record fingernails?

Seti assiduously forgot, and forgot, and again forgot the feel of the back of her slender hand against his buttock, his perineum. *That* hand, the one that now expertly scissored the tops of three Sweet 'N Low packets, the one now ineffectually stirring her coffee with a crumpled plastic Z.

Myrtle told Seti what she couldn't admit to her husband: the nature of her new job. He told her what he could never confess to his parents — about his list. And then they were confidantes, and the conversation grew easy. They lingered for forty-five minutes, exchanging rhapsodies about Egypt and about the Law, before they could force themselves to leave.

As they stood, Seti reached across the table to unroll Myrtle's diploma, with its gold sticker (who would have imagined that even bouncer school had a valedictorian?), and congratulated her again. He scrolled it back around the massive black paperweight that anchored it against the wind.

"I'm sorry," she repeated as she stuffed flashlight and imitation sheepskin into her handbag. "I really am. I hope I didn't hurt you."

"You are the gentlest of ruffians," said Seti.

18.

In the fifteen weeks since Myrtle snugged her club to Seti's testicles and carried him away, they've spent dozens of hours together, gabbing, usually over coffee and pastry at Shaheen's Lebanese Bakery, just west of campus. In summer the library is quiet, so there's time for long breaks, which (as Doug and Wino Ike have impressed upon Seti) are not a mark of laziness and cheating and disrespect for his host nation and institution but rather a grand tradition, the legacy of the country's proud labor history. It would be an insult to the memory of Samuel Gompers and Joe Hill and the Wobblies and Cesar the grape guy . . . to fail to stroll over for a pistachio puff now and again would be to allow the fat-cat capitalists, yet again, to grind the working stiff underfoot with their wingtip jackboots. Look for the union label, they told him, and don't begrudge yourself the second cup.

It's remarkable how freely he can speak to Myrtle. She is a motherly figure, but altogether unlike *his* mother, motherly in a way that allows too for muliebrity. Which is to say that she is an American *woman,* that fantastical creature, independent of body and of spirit . . . but one safely past sexual allure and its unbearable complications. Though Myrtle is pretty still, in her way, with an unlined face and slim figure, she has a severe and antierotic way that sets him at ease. She has boundaries, and they are garlanded with razor wire. Put it this way: Rex would never dare to twirl the anklet that Myrtle would never wear. She is not that kind of girl. She was never that kind of girl.

It's ironic: the one American woman he's comfortable talking to is one who wears a kind of *burqa,* a full-body veil of impregnable professionalism, stingy speech, dour dignity. Those crisp-cuffed neutral pantsuits, the minimal makeup. With knife and fork, Myrtle carves her *ashta* into eighths, eats it without smirching either hands or face with cream or pistachio.

There's something vaguely illicit, too, about their relations, though those relations are (on this point he must insist) entirely unexceptionable, blameless in every respect. Still, he finds the intimacy intoxicating. But those words are too strong, beg to be handled with the kid gloves of quotation marks. Better to say that he finds the "intimacy" "intoxicating." Best of all is to say nothing, and so he keeps it — keeps her — to himself. This is not stealth but discretion.

He catches glimpses of the person beneath. To him Myrtle lets down — by an iota, perhaps as much as a scintilla — her guard and veil, and he sees hints of the strong-willed, fun-loving, but virtuous girl (like Lili, he thinks) she must have been decades ago.

For a while he thought the off-duty Myrtle would be different, unrecognizable. She would wear looser clothes, a looser face, would be carefree and talkative. But two Fridays ago he was making one of his long sunset walks down the levee — comparing, as usual, the Nile's south-to-north beeline to the Mississippi's wayward, looping energy, or indecisiveness, or deviousness; thinking about the black land of home, the *kemi,* like this Delta mud except that the nutrient-rich *sebakh* was the debris of ancient and glorious cities, whereas here the silt was foully nouveau riche, the effluent of livestock lagoons and the runoff from golf courses and lawns upstream; and there was the astonishing difference of scale — the molehill *sadd,* feeder ditches dug with a crude wood mattock or by hand, versus the mountainous and uniformly sloped and massively engineered levees, the highest promontories in south Louisiana, with their cement culverts in whose seams grew opportunistic trash trees (no nebneb or tamarisk, just spindly mimosa and elderberry), and farther down, at the edge of the riverbed, scabby-looking larger trees scarred and ringed round by illegally dumped appliances and car parts, and beyond the *batture* was the sluggish and slatternly river herself, a sulfurous stew filled with chemical barges and faux paddlewheelers for gambling and flotsam (bloated corpses of fish, beer cans, rusty barrels, sheet metal, the joyless confetti of Styrofoam coolers); and the only animals to be seen were those leashed to dogwalkers (sleek, cheerful weimaraners rather than grumpy donkeys with a pannier at each flank or camels that showed their tongues only in wrath, not panting docility); and along the river road below whirred bicyclists in bright teardrop helmets, the women in sports bras and the men in obscene compression shorts, their genitals clumped into padded fists, all this pointless scurrying in contrast to the dusty fellahin he might see along the Nile in rural Egypt, conserving their energies for more work, curled under a mud wall with rags over their faces to hinder the unhinderable flies — and as Seti strolled and compared, he spotted a middle-aged man fussing with the legs of a telescope tripod, and beside him . . . Myrtle.

The man was trying to lock the legs into place, compensating for the levee's steep slope. Nearby, on a blanket, sat Myrtle, wearing work clothes and a grimace and, in short, the full black shawl and cowl of her self-possession. As he approached, Seti didn't hear or see a word pass between her and, it must be, her husband. Milt (that was his name, Seti thought he recalled) tried to right first this tipsy foot and then that one, but he wasn't in a hurry; the dark would come when it came. Milt stopped to drink from the can he'd propped against a small cooler on the slope. Seti presumed it was beer, but he couldn't be sure, because the can was wrapped in a sheath of cloth or plastic, a disguise.

Myrtle paid no heed to the bustle around her. She was sitting upright, back to the river, feet tucked beneath her and to one side — an askew kneel. Her shoes were on; though the light was beginning to fade, Seti could see the clunky black soles. She was eating something from a jar. Her head never seemed to swivel, but by the time he got within forty feet, Seti knew she had seen him, knew too that he must not stop to share with her the latest additions to his list: ocean-floor cartographer, glassblower, beadle (she'd recommended Dickens), ufologist (this had in some way to do both with bladder infections and spaceships); nor to tell her the hypothesis he'd learned in class this afternoon — it struck him as yet another confirmation of Egypt's early advancement, moral and technological, and thus as worth believing — that the Great Pyramid had been designed not as a wastrel's necropolis but as *a colossal pump for water.*

No, to stop and be introduced to Milt would be somehow to

violate the rules. He couldn't have said why this was so, but it was, and so he sailed by with only a subtle nod, which she returned with a similar tilt of chin and a little backhanded flourish with her fork, on which was speared a lovely Ping-Pong-ball-sized stuffed olive from Mr. Shaheen's.

19.

There's silt in every psyche. Which is to say . . . which is to say that we are none of us bathtubs, or rather beakers, or rather we are none of us the distilled water that might fill a beaker. It is our nature to flow and mingle. We're rivers. Or, sure, mostly we're not *rivers,* more like roadside ditches, sludgy brooklets, hog lagoons, storm runoff bleeding through drains blocked by sticks and bread bags and empty fifths and electrocuted sparrows. Oh, forget it. To each his own trickle or torrent. The point is that there's silt in every psyche. That's Myrtle's point.

So the person who cries surprise at the dirt carried in his or her dark currents is a fool and a liar. Oedipus can pluck eyes till the cows come home, but he can't expect us to believe he didn't have an *inkling.* It's too late for blindness. There's no unseeing now what needs to have stayed unseen. He'd like us to think that the thing he can't banish from memory is the physicality of incest, the image of his heaving hips, of Mummy's lockbox; but what really festers is the fact that in some way he *knew,* knew all along. Destiny is just another name for the weaknesses we can't deny ourselves. We are rivers; we follow our courses.

So it's best to know our snags and shoals. Myrtle is a championess of auger-eyed self-knowledge (and both those auger eyes in their right places on your face, Oedipus — enough with the drama, really, cut it out). She believes in psychic hygiene, just as her aunt Lettie used to. All it took was warm vinegar water and a squeeze or two.

Myrtle's figures of speech are badly tangled: beakers and silts

101

and eyes, homecoming cows and lockboxes. But that's the point, too, this unavoidable stew and scramble. She will not be deterred. We are made of waters and metaphors promiscuously mixed. She will follow her thought to its logical conclusion, until it empties into the sea.

So here goes: As bowel, so brain. The high colonic in excelsis, all the way to the top of your skull, the uppermost edge of your banks. We are rivers in need of enemas.

With all that in mind, it wouldn't be accurate — it would be inaccurate — to say that Myrtle was *surprised* by the insight that came unbidden when she saw Seti walking toward her along the crushed-oyster track at the top of the levee. She was . . . better to say she was *taken unawares*. Until she saw him outside his usual context, it hadn't occurred to her that for three months she'd failed to mention to Milt the existence of her young ward — for that's what Seti was, what he had become: her naïf, her protegé and protectorate, an innocent in a strange land.

She'd said not a word, made not a peep. And she knew immediately and decisively that she didn't intend to tell Milt now, either. If need be, she would pretend not to see Seti, and tomorrow she'd make an excuse for what must look like shadiness: *While leveling his tripod, my husband — Mr. Rusk, that is — will not abide interruption. We all have our quirks.*

She had good reasons. To introduce Seti to Milt would be to mingle incompatible worlds, acid and base, matter and antimatter: one world in which she was a streetwise sex cop, a woman of respect, a licensed and highly decorated (valedictorian!) asskicker, and on the side a mentor, a friend; another in which she was a sterile drudge playing out the string. Milt was no fool. To introduce Seti would be to divulge everything, including the details of her employment. What she feared most was that Milt would laugh at her, at the caricature she'd become: on the one hand what she'd seen in Miss Berryhill, the battle-ax, bitter old scourge of lovers, Enema of the People; on the other a simpleton, a textbook case, the fruitless woman who's compensated by divvying her maternity in two, into parts tender and harsh: half surrogate mother, half tough mother.

Though Milt was not unkind, had never been, this might strike him as a fitting end. She'd always suspected that her failure to get pregnant could be blamed on her frolics in youth, if not for medical reasons then as nature's revenge on her for having twitted and flouted and skirted it for so long, for having made resort to pills, pastes, pessaries, prophos — ah, those foil wrappers she learned to tear open one-handed, without having to look; she was always clever of finger, could handle buttons, snaps, hasps, rubbers, soundlessly, effortlessly.

Over the years, without her ever revealing the history, Milt had clued in. He could scarcely have failed to, given the gauntlet of leers and whispers when she made the mistake, eight years ago, of venturing home to Texas for her mother's funeral. By the time they lowered the casket, it seemed there were more people there — paunchy middle-aged propane men and druggists, tackshop owners and drywallers — to mourn the passing of her hot pants than to mark her mother's end. She saw a real tear or two from several of those quondam boy toys — Walt Skeen, Darryl Probert, some tubby blubberer she didn't recognize — men whose only thoughts about her mother in life had been to worry whether she'd been peering through the screen door, taking down their license numbers, when they came in the small hours to drop off her ruined daughter.

That girl, she could imagine them thinking, wistfully, *she was somep'n. A wild thing. Took a hog to the prom. A Berkshire, I recollect. He was a fine black thing, but gone to ham by now. So are we all.*

Myrtle had appreciated the show of emotion, and she knew that Walt and Darryl — ordinary Texans squinting into blaring sunlight and wearing flammable suits with ties their wives had had to knot — believed they were crying for the departed. No, the fault lay with her. *Her* eyes had been dry. During the eulogy she'd caught herself counting obelisks farther up the hill: the rich and their obelisks. Guilty, guilty, guilty. Then as now, everything eventually came to grief. Or went to ham.

It hadn't escaped her, either, that guilt was the chief thing she and Seti had in common. Theirs was an unusual intimacy, one that consisted not so much of sharing confidences as of artfully sidestepping them. She knew about his crush on Lili; anyone could see the way he looked at the girl. He must know that Myrtle shut down when the subject was children, must know she held herself responsible for her unblessed state. Beneath every item of gossip or explanation of idiom or story of home was, for each and both of them, that inmost private corm: *I am a hypocrite; I am failing those I love.* But it was never acknowledged. What exquisite relief it was to share the burden without having to speak its name, without having to violate its sacral hush. What a relief to hold the guilt in tandem while holding it aloof, keeping it for one's own.

It was too late to tell Milt about her new life, and so she was pleased that Seti's tact matched her own.

Milt took another nip at his beer and moved to the lens, began spinning the oculus. He grimaced westward as if to chase the last sliver of sun over the horizon, hummed "Stardust Memories." Myrtle nibbled at the clove of garlic at the center of her olive and resettled her feet underneath her.

She has to admit that she's warmed to the task lately. Deputy of Nookie has become a role she plays, a mask that serves her; she was Miss Berryhill's apt pupil. Like the Iron Maiden, too, she's been smart enough to base her role on a version of herself, a part, and to let people think it the whole. The key is to believe in the task, at least temporarily, to forget it's a role, and to an extent she's succeeded. No one could shush so savagely as Ivy Berryhill without believing in the justice of her cause, and the same is true of Myrtle, who prowls with perfect conviction, who thwacks the deck stingingly against her palm.

And Miss Berryhill's racetrack mechanic, with the bandannas flowing from his rear pockets as he tinkered with his engine? Those bandannas like a magician's scarves, bright and inexhaustible; a girl might unfurl for a thousand yards, wrapping the car like a maypole, without pulling that last one loose. That handsome, dusky man — that other, better life, held in reserve and kept to oneself. Myrtle has none.

Enough of that. Yes, perfect conviction . . . yes, the justice of the cause. These lusts need to be shushed, and harshly. College is all about gratifying students' vanities. Everybody is smart and young and pretty and promising, or close enough to those things for grade inflation to make up the difference. It's all about reassuring you that you're keen of mind, comely of face, deserving of praise. Are you loved? You are, and you are, and you are. And then you're sent out into the indifferent world to age and cave in and turn into the saggy hypocrite-to-be, and then no one loves you. Then you are unloved. Love seems a myth, a chimera, an insupportable foolishness that must be stamped out. You possess the wisdom of age, and it's about time you started sharing it with your juniors. You are right for the job.

She's even begun to give Mort Bozeman some credit for having ferreted out this aspect of her before she knew it herself. He has continued to evade the question of how he learned about her departure from the law firm: "Should it surprise you," he asks, "that you have built a reputation as a woman of great moral sinew? That this reputation extends far and wide, hin and yon, fore and aft?"

Which brings to mind a long-buried phrase, used by an angry boyfriend to give her the gate: "I hope you get the clap fore and aft, Myrtle. Keep on whoring around with Kendall Janes and you will for sure."

Moral sinew and the clap, fore and aft. She'd courted the latter, maybe, but it was the former that she eventually caught — a case of it that is, more and more, looking to be terminal.

But bring it on. *Ring out old shapes of foul disease* . . . And ring in the new. One has no choice but to adapt, right?

Necessity is the motherfucker of self-invention.

20.

Mort did what he could to speed her conversion. One day early in her tenure, after a visit from a department chair who demanded to know why *Misty of Chincoteague* was in restricted shelving and thus unavailable to her granddaughter, he called Myrtle in so he could blow off steam. Sure, he said, mistakes occur, but these people need to see that you can't make an omelet without breaking the wills of all the little perverts, without keeping one step ahead of them. Steaming withers and whatnot, fragrant manes, pasterns, fetlocks, those rubbery black lips and flaring nostrils . . . she saw his thrust, right? He wasn't going to stand aside while LSU bred a whole generation of Catherine the Greats, or Catherines the Great, whichever was correct — now there was a pretty pickle, grammatically speaking.

"Yes," Myrtle had agreed, listlessly. "A pretty pickle."

He explained that part of Myrtle's appeal for him had been a background in law and order rather than academe. He assumed she wouldn't be squeamish about so-called censorship. *So-called.* Let him be clear: these books were in the collection and available for checkout. Mort was not infringing upon anyone's right to see them. He was merely instituting a ritual, giving people extra opportunity to consider their motives.

All this had the look of intimidation to Myrtle, and of course there was Mort's borderline insanity to consider — what student would relish an interview with Savonarola the Clown? — but in principle she was all for a priestly caste whose job it was to mediate between the people and the books. To help, guide, aid; and to thwart, if need be. Intimidation had been her stock in trade for all those years at Gedge & McGillis. Mort had, by some mysterious method, figured her right.

She thought naggingly of Donatello's bronze *David,* a reproduction of which had stood in her favorite plaza on campus when she was an undergraduate. She'd sat on the pedestal, leaned against his feet, and read through many a sunny afternoon (over time the metal stud at the corner of her jeans pocket had rubbed a bright spot in the patina, and she noticed it every time she hurried by, the comet above his ankle, *hers*). David, with his cocked *contrapposto* hips, that languid look, wearing only a country cap covered with grass and leaves, as if he's just now climbed out of the hay — and those S&M boots: Wouldn't Mort, these days, the cynical, tenure-denied Mort, not Young Mort of the Masturbated Jesus, have stashed it in a hinter-room under the watch of a matron or a nun? He would have.

But this had troubled Myrtle only slightly, and for a second. Nowadays all museums had guards to keep kids from humping the ephebi. If you let them alone, they would hump the ephebi blind, and on film too, most likely. The pictures would go up on their Web sites. Myrtle wouldn't mind caging *all* the books, if that would give the kids a proper respect for them again. Mort's Take-Back-the-Stacks campaign was a hopeful gesture, in its way — he *wanted* books to be dangerous again, rather than props and relics. He had to see the pointlessness of the exercise, had to see how corny and prudish it looked. He knew that keeping kids from reading about colostomy bags or about bruin-screwing or about Mafouka, the man-woman of Montparnasse, would make no difference. He was just trying to hold the world together. It made him feel good to think that books change lives, as they used to. But they didn't. Not now.

The most shocking thing (Myrtle reflected as she sucked the garlic marrow from yet another olive and took a quick look at Milt, still trifling with the telescope's eyepiece and waiting for the last light to fade) was that Mort's paranoia had turned out to be, it seems, *right*.

Under every rock she's overturned have been teeming beetles coupling like there's no tomorrow . . . or rather uncoupling as soon as she arrives bearing the light of day. In her first three months she hasn't caught anyone in flagrante, hasn't had occasion to peal her bell, but she's flushed a half-dozen pairs slightly ruddy and disarranged, has heard plenty of giggles and whispers and retreating footsteps, has found all sorts of graffiti and contraband.

At first she felt Mort must have arranged this menagerie of sickos to impress her with the gravity of the problem. Already on her first afternoon she found two inflatable sex dolls — man upside down, woman right side up — pressed together, crude Orphan Annie mouths to surprisingly lifelike genitals, among the bound master's theses (they'd been pinched into the right angle between the shelves for 1968 and 1969). Myrtle had unwedged and separated the mannequins, used a hankie to yank open the air stems at their navels. Then she stood atop them to banish the bad air. She was embarrassed at first by the giggling crowd that gathered — drawn, she guessed, by the protracted sigh and hiss. As the number of onlookers grew to six, then eight, she'd been tempted to stomp or squeeze or fold, bend, and mutilate the dolls to hurry the process along, but she realized what the laws both of dignity and deterrence demanded. She stood patiently on the pink chest of one and then the other, let them sigh their long sighs, hiss their long hisses — the lady doll's pillow-breasts wore gray footprints, size 7B, and the man's stalwart penis was the last part to subside — and by the time she scooped up the limp corpses (which smelled like the beach rafts of youth) for disposal, the kids had dispersed to their desks and carrels, and Myrtle had begun to grow into her role.

A week later she found an eight-page homemade erotic comic whose cover featured a grotesque fat man in a brown cassock, the crotch of which had been cut out. His hands were above his head, as if he were riding a roller coaster or directing a symphony, and one fist held a leg of mutton, the other a squat brown blood sausage that was uncannily echoed below, where a serving wench knelt. The magazine, still warm to the touch, had been hastily and imperfectly concealed in a concordance to the short fiction of Henry James. It was called *Friar Fuck*.

Myrtle had been tempted to conduct a stakeout — the deviser of such a thing should not be allowed to roam the streets freely, much less the aisles, *her* aisles — but she contented herself with picking it up with a tissue and delivering it, in the decent wrapper of a campus-mail envelope, to Mort.

Shortly thereafter, looking through the narrow vertical window of a faculty study room, she witnessed a scene whose principals were a sixty-year-old man, a twenty-something female student in a blindfold, and a row of tiny hoteliers' pots of jam. The girl was wearing a maid's apron over a tight white T-shirt, and the apron-strings looped from the back of her neck around the sides of her bulbous breasts, calling attention to what could scarcely need, or even bear, emphasis — the most prominent nipples Myrtle had ever seen, like the upper knuckles of twin pinkies. Myrtle saw this girl dip a finger into a ramekin, lick the finger contemplatively, close her eyes and say a few inaudible words, then move on to the next jar. When the man — distinguished-looking, on the verge of elderly, with a loden-green sport coat — leaned back and his hand moved toward the crotch of his worsteds, she pounced.

Professor Schlöndorff of the Food Science Department and his assistant waxed indignant, claimed she'd disrupted an important experiment in the field of "wild berry *Konfitüre*," and eventually raised enough of a stink that Mort made Myrtle go to the professor's office to apologize for the "misunderstanding." When Myrtle finished mumbling and turned to leave, the girl escorted her to the door and gave her a little pipkin of boysenberry, a parting taunt or gift. "You look like a woman in hard need of good preserves," she said, winking. "You might want to try them sometime." With that she leaned forward and tugged the fringe of her collar until Myrtle could see a row of gluey purple fingerprints at the top of her left breast. The girl grinned. The nipple pointed Myrtle the way out.

Not long after that there began a plague of totems. Late one afternoon Myrtle had rushed to investigate a squeaking shelf on the second floor and found only a hastily abandoned box of tissues. The one caught in the sleeve at the box's top, waiting to be plucked, was twisted into a parody of a Victorian's pocket handkerchief, an origami orchid. It looked both genteel and obscene.

In the days that followed — and always on the floor of an aisle, always after she had pursued her prey the way a jungle hunter does, by following rustlings of the native foliage, in this case tin

109

shelves — she discovered all sorts of items: an old-style sewing pincushion, liberally pierced, in the shape of an apple; a Barbie wearing Band-Aids for bra and panties; a white chess rook against which shiny two golf balls leaned.

None of this rattled Myrtle. There was an abstraction to it, a condoling whiff of bookishness — far better to harvest symbols than to have to roust the young spooners and sparkers and noodlers. The dolls and pincushions didn't have dewy furzes and eager tongues, didn't scowl or hiss or mutter "Rent-a-Nun" under their breath. She felt she was dealing, this time, with an adult, someone who understood subtlety. She knew how to play this game. So when the fruits began to appear — a banana, the next day a peach — she'd made a point of gobbling them down where she stood and dropping the peel, the wizened pit: messages. She would not be condescended to again.

She suspected Mort himself. Was he trying to get her started, laying her a path into the woods? It seemed an extension of her training, and innocent, like the deceptions of parents at Christmas, when Mom sets out cookies and eggnog and Dad polishes them off, and the kids are none the wiser. He left her fruits, and she ate them.

After the peach, a week went by before she discovered, on the bare floor of a microforms aisle in the basement, a yellow crookneck squash with its tip lightly imbedded in a tomato. The droplet of red juice on the floor marked an escalation, the first sign of serious trouble — and sure enough, Myrtle rushed upstairs to discover that Mort was in class, had been for two hours.

So there really was a Fiend Greengrocer, and on top of the new explicitness he was dabbling in a cryptic kind of miscegenation: fruits were getting it on with vegetables. What did it mean?

The next morning her foe grew bolder yet. When Myrtle emerged from her cubicle behind the circ desk, five minutes after opening, she could see his offering for her already, among the reserve books . . . *behind the counter.* This was a violation of everything she held dear, and a vindication, as if she needed another, of her hatred of open stacks. No one observed the boundaries anymore; there were no boundaries anymore. Not of age, not of species, not of *anything*. It had become a free-for-all.

One day at Gedge & McGillis she'd returned from the comfort station and spied a cheeky associate trying to slip behind her desk. She'd routed him out with a huswife's broom and a fishwife's curses, and no one had dared renew the invasion. But here, now, the malefactor had made it easily into the sanctum and left his vile calling card: half a canteloupe, scooped out and glistening, with a gray wig of Spanish moss arranged along its rind.

It had turned personal now, and Myrtle began to wonder: Had Mort conjured up this monster by appointing her to look for him? Until there's a watcher, is there anything to watch?

Worse, had she encouraged him? She'd meant the banana peel and peach pit as evidence of her ferocity. Had he interpreted them as *foreplay?*

For two weeks there was nothing, at least nothing in that line. In the aisles she found only the usual junk: slips of papers with call numbers, candy wrappers, brown and withering apple cores. She began to doubt herself. Could she have been overstating the problem? True, the pincushion might have dropped from some grandmother's sewing bag, and the doll had been modestly if unconventionally attired. People get colds; noses must be blown. Even the squash and tomato might be explained innocently, if one thought it through. Someone stopping into the library on the way home from the grocery . . . sure, sure, to double-check a casserole recipe on microfilm. This domestic perfectionist had cut the recipe out of the *Des Moines Register* in 1988, if memory served, and now it had gone missing, and she needed to check: a dash or a pinch, and of coriander or cumin? And she'd leaned over to pull out the reel, and maybe she shouldn't have tried to save trees by declining the double-bagging . . .

During those weeks of respite, Myrtle devoted herself to the run-of-the-mill offenses: toenail painting and make-out sessions in the lounges, porn boys hanging ten, and in a study room a game (interrupted early, thank goodness) of what appeared to be Strip Pin-the-Tail-on-the-Donkey.

But none of this, indeed nothing in all her life, had prepared her for the horror to come, the last of the fruits. This was the end of August, the semester's opening week. Myrtle was directing the expunging of graffiti from the help counter on the third floor when she heard a grunt, then the song of a shaken shelf. She tore through the oversized folios of sacred music and rounded the corner to see only a flash of green — a duffel? — and the stairwell door clanging shut.

On the floor of the aisle was a grapefruit, badly misshapen and leaking juice. It looked like a lumpy yellow balloon left to pucker and deflate. Myrtle unthinkingly picked it up. What she saw next — a flash of pink innard — wobbled her legs and her resolve. There was no mistaking it. This was not the innocent aftermath of juicing, wasn't the result of a dutiful child following Mom's prescription for avoiding scurvy or warding off a cold. The fruit had some kind of *glory-hole* cut into its underside. She was holding in her hands a *raped citrus*.

She dropped it — she might even, in a momentary descent from dignity, have let loose something not unlike a shriek — and sprinted toward the bathroom, thinking only of soaking her palms for the next ten minutes.

But after a few steps she shook off this paltry impulse, which was beneath her. She turned into the central stairwell and scurried down, puffing for breath, her flashlight so heavy that it seemed to yank her elbow out of socket with every step. She rushed through the lobby and out the front door.

Which way to go? Classes were in mid-change, so a few thousand students milled in the main quad in front of her. Surely he'd slipped away by now. On a hunch Myrtle chose the covered walkway to her right, the one that led toward the English department. *If you're looking for an apple,* her father had used to say in his rare sage-advice moments, *don't look in an oak tree.*

Her guess paid off. She hadn't gone twenty feet before she saw a faded military duffel being held by a boy, his back to Myrtle, who was chatting with a pretty brunette. Myrtle switched her flashlight to her left hand, secured it as invisibly as she could against her forearm, and walked past the pair. She slowed and glanced back over the poor girl's shoulder . . . when the boy's eye caught hers, she found the confirmation she needed. He recoiled, almost invisibly; he casually cradled the bag to his chest, kept the conversation going with great show of casualness.

He looked like a typical graduate student — that is to say, like a pervert in training: stubble, sandals, short hair moussed into spikes, glasses with square lenses half the size of his eyes. He wasn't Charles Boyer or Cary Grant, but he was handsome enough to find a mate within his kingdom, she thought, perhaps even within his phylum. Myrtle was tempted — *Can the talk, and break some legs* — to jam her flashlight between his thighs right now, grab his collar, and drop him to the gravel, where he might pick up an abrasion like the one Mort suffered, on almost this spot, the day she met him.

But this was a public place, a potentially hostile crowd. She'd already seen a few students pointing as she passed, whispering her nickname, the one she's aware has lately stuck and spread: Madame Flashlight. If she took this punk down with her deck, she'd be the lead story in the school paper tomorrow, the *Baton Rouge Advocate* the following day. By next week she'd be fodder for talk shows, and the library would be padlocked forever. Discretion, discretion. Myrtle turned away and kept walking. Around the corner, she circled back to observe. Sure enough, he broke off the colloquy in less than a minute — not his type, Myrtle thought grimly, that girl is not his type — and Myrtle followed him upstairs to (just as she'd suspected) the English mail room, then stepped into the departmental office and called the campus police. She patrolled the hallway, cutting off his escape routes, until the officers arrived.

The kid willingly surrendered the bag to them. It held a treasure trove of evidence: plantains, kiwis, a honeydew, several limes, and a possibly unrelated cheese sandwich. Myrtle stopped peering around the door frame and entered the fray. "See?" she asked the cops. "I told you. He's a menace."

"Who is this old lady? I saw her outside a few minutes ago,

staring at me. This is harassment," the kid said. His cheeks reddened, though no one seemed to notice but Myrtle.

"What's with all the fruit?" asked the lead cop. He had a butt the size of a beanbag chair, looked like a man fresh produce might offend, but his tone was disappointingly blasé.

"What? Can't a guy eat healthy around here?" Maybe the kid would claim he had simply misunderstood the food pyramid. When it said six to eight servings a day, he'd naturally thought it meant . . .

"Free country," allowed the officer. He glanced at Myrtle and shrugged: *I tried, but he's a tough nut to crack*. His partner was still holding the bag, but he'd ceased to investigate it. He seemed to believe that his shoes might commit suicide at any moment.

"Explain the cheese, then," Myrtle challenged. Tangle the fiend in his lies.

"Okay, you got me, you food nazi. I've got a rock of baby Swiss at home, too. With intent to distribute. Cuff me."

"Ma'am," said the lead officer, "would you let us handle this?"

Myrtle took the other officer aside and explained that there was irrefutable proof available, but he seemed disinclined to conduct the decisive sniff test, and he was no more enthusiastic about doing a rape kit on the grapefruit. Are you kidding, lady? *A rape kit?* What are you trying to prove?

The kid started squawking about illegal search and seizure, so they returned his duffel. The policemen seemed more embarrassed than anything else, harried. Cretins. Probably they wanted to rush down to the public-safety building and try out the box of oranges Aunt Bitsy sent from Boca Raton.

But Myrtle had learned her lesson from her encounter with Nipple Girl and the Fruit Spreads; she knew when she was beaten. In a lax world, the strict suffer. She contented herself with a fiery warning that the kid had better not show his face in the library again. She gripped her flashlight with white knuckles and shook it.

"No sweat," said the kid. "You freaking fruitcake." The dullard cops seemed not to notice the taunting reference to his crimes.

It hadn't ended the way she'd imagined, but still she marched to Mort's office with her heart riding high. Every priest and every cop has a First Collar, and it's special. She hasn't seen the punk since.

On those days when Myrtle's will was iron and her face was stone, all went smoothly. She was an avenging angel, stalking the aisles to throw big light on big wrongs. Chasing tail, someone else's or one's own; either was futile. But on other days, at other moments, memory sneaked up on her and made her sigh and waver, made her see even that she was a little in love with them: her quarry, her children. She'd hear the jangle of hasty bucklings, the scurry of feet, and she'd feel like yelling out, "Get your pleasure while ye may, before it pall or cloy."

She feels six ways a hypocrite, but so much of adulthood has turned out to be about making peace with betrayals — the world's of you, then (fair turnabout) yours of everything you used to hold dear — wildness, joy, spontaneity, time-wasting. Nowadays you brush your teeth while you sit on the toilet before bed: multitasking, they call it. And the flashlight/nightstick is a perfect symbol of the new you. Dual purpose. First there was the clock radio; now this; next they'll devise a warhead with an evergreen sachet, to give nuclear winter a nice pine scent, at least.

"Myrt, the scope's ready," Milt called then, finally, and she screwed shut the jar of olives and got to her feet. It was full dark now, but still she imagined she could see Seti walking the levee, a blade cutting through the blackness a few hundred yards off, going away.

21.

But Seti, as he sprints up the stairs to help Myrtle, misjudges a riser and takes a spill. *Errol Flynn: Cocksman with a Pencil-Thin Mustache* flies out of his hand, bounces off the iron newel post, and ends up splayed facedown on the fourth-floor landing. It's a flimsy paperback, and he's afraid its spine is broken. He can't fool Mort by putting back a misshapen husk of the book he took . . . borrowed, borrowed. He snatches it up and tries to knead it back into shape, to smooth Mr. Flynn's dashing mustache, and as he does a slip of paper falls to the floor.

It's a birth-control-pill information pamphlet, and tucked inside it a card, dated yesterday, for an appointment — patient's name "Lily Flynn" — with a gynecologist at a storefront pregnancy clinic across town, something outside the university health plan, outside even the realm of possibility.

Betrayed by a fellow Second World striver, this Dr. Alicon Chandrasekhar; worse, worst, betrayed by Lili. He tries to exonerate her: she has a friend named Lily Flynn, or she is seeing the doctor out of excessive prudence, years early, about how to take precautions when Seti's courtship finally, inevitably, concludes in matrimony. She is — what would Jesus do? — trying to convert the heathen Indians one at a time, starting with Chandrasekhar; this is research for the allegorical play she's writing about a pince-nez and a diaphragm.

If their evening in New Orleans were already scheduled — just that, one date held in prospect — Seti might be able to torture the facts into the desired shape. But "Lily Flynn" is too paltry a disguise. Why else did she want this book back? Why else had Rex bounded up the stairs after her?

Lili has used him. He is the love-starved pet who will do her bidding. *His heart breaks* — an odd American idiom. Back home that organ is not so brittle and fragile; it is the seat not of lust but of reason. But he has let his *qualb* shrink, wither, until it is merely a heart, a small frail thing that breaks.

He knows what he must do. His love for her is a broke-leg

camel, and in desert crossings — he sees now that his years in America, in this wettest of places, turn out after all to be just a desert crossing, a long dry season, and all else was a mirage — the broke-leg camel gets the mercy of the knife. He must never see Lili again. He couldn't bear it. By the time Mort gets back, Seti will have threaded the jailer's key into the lock and left the forbidden cabinet ajar. Once Mort has a chance to take in the scene of the crime, Seti will carry the purloined book in, place it on the desk, lower his head in shame. He's seen enough cop shows on TV to know the drill: He will *spread 'em*. Mort will palm the top of Seti's head as he shoves the *perp* into the backseat and takes him *downtown*. There Seti will *wave at his Miranda* and be *booked into Writer's Island*.

If he is to be banished from the library, even deported, so be it. The sooner he gets home, the better. Really. His parents need him, and his country does. But he can't bring himself to inform on Lili. The rough justice he requires is for himself, punishment for being a simp. He is a fool and a donkey, and he curses himself. He'll tuck the appointment card into an envelope, and he'll send it to her. He cannot turn his back on her entirely. Maybe that creep Rex has forced her, is even now pressing himself upon her. His pleas and blandishments, his slangings. *Rock and reel. Get busy.*

Maybe she needs Seti more than ever right now. He may have to see her once more.

But no. No. Remember: *the mercy of the knife.*

And then the bell sings out again, close by, and Seti feels doubly guilty, doubly selfish. While he pities himself and plots a ceremonial surrender, his friend Myrtle is in distress. He grabs up book and appointment card and sets off running again.

22.

Myrtle can't fathom the couple's response, or nonresponse, to her alarm, her bold, clear *gotcha*. Hey! It tolls for *thee*, and *thee*. You're busted.

As one second ticks by, two, she tries to keep her mind on the fun of reporting this to Mort. She will do so in dispassionate legal Latin, without trace of a smirk: "Subjects were engaged in an act of in situ cunnilingus, ex machina habeas corpus delicti. Veni vidi vici."

But two seconds become three, and on goes the pleasuring, heedlessly, and each clapper-clang vibrates down Myrtle's arm and into her chest, her jaw, her temples, until it all seems a cartoon, as if her head has deformed to a bell shape and is gonging her across the room. And if tintinnabulation will do no good, her only choice is to bring out her club, to *smack* the world back into shape . . . but the eight-cell has never seemed so dead in her fist. It is a weight pinning her to the floor, or she might float away.

The bouncer must immediately seize control of the situation. But how? They are deaf, and she's struck dumb.

Since her campaign began, she's seen Lili with this boy a number of times, of course. A couple months ago, early on, she happened upon them in the old third-floor smoking lounge. They were sitting on a stained and split-cushioned vinyl couch, dental surplus, and Rex was rubbing Lili's neck. Two fingers of each hand had crept inside her Peter Pan collar, the top button of which was undone. Myrtle didn't even have to waggle her flashlight to make them jump apart as though they'd been scalded, and Lili pinched the fabric shut over her throat and looked away. Shortly thereafter, in the same place, Myrtle ambushed them in a kiss. Yet there was something about their posture — they were seated side by side, knees together, spines straight, torqued toward one another at the rib cage, and Rex's hands were on Lili's shoulders and Lili's gripped lightly at his kidneys — it was the kind of four-feet-on-the-floor buss that passed muster in the filmstrips of her youth, that wouldn't have violated the Stone Age parietals rules of her college dorm, so when Lili spun away in horror and thrust her hands between her knees and looked up pleadingly, Myrtle had given the stern nod that meant she would, this once, leave it off her report.

Around then they seemed to clue in to Myrtle's schedule, to the thorough but predictable way she covered her beat. The few times she's seen them since, they've been sitting, prim and unmussed, six inches apart, like purebred youngsters of yore on the porch in summer, not daring to make the swing creak lest Dad come running.

But now — six, seven — Lili's atop a public platform, in her father's last bastion of chastity, and Rex's head is at the root of her, and his wrigglings and her cries make it seem, for a moment, as if he's trying to unbirth himself . . . and both of them are nude, or rather *naked,* which isn't strictly required for the act that keeps going on and on, unabated, while Myrtle continues to flog the bell — eight, nine, ten — until the flesh of her face feels like it's melting off her cheekbones.

What happened to the Peter Pan collar, the bloomers, the knee socks? What happened to that pleading look? Where has shame slunk off to, and what can Myrtle do to bring it back?

She is no longer hunter but prey. Just as Mort drafted her into service, Lili has now conscripted her too — as witness, as town crier. But to what? What announcement is this, what demonstration? The peals of the bell begin to sound to her like a call to worship, and Myrtle has to stop.

Lili seems unconcerned by either the noise or its cessation. Her eyes don't flutter open until Rex slowly lifts his head and turns to glare at the arresting — the arrested — officer. And then the glare melts into a sly grin, and his soul patch wears, oh my word . . . and if Myrtle knew how to faint she would do it now. There he is, Donatello's *David* come to life, his hands retaking their places on Lili's rump, his eyes swinging up to meet hers. His back muscles are ropy, articulated; on one shoulder blade is a tattoo of an anvil landing on the head of a coyote. And on high, above all petty concerns, Lili, her slender arms spread for balance, each hand clutching the top face of the stacks, each leg occupying a stool of its own, and a blissed-out smile spreading across her face. Behind her midsection one shelf of books is tipped back, more toward the middle, less toward the sides, in such a way as to record the impression of her derriere. There is something filthy about this, more disturbing even than the unimaginable foreground. The page edges tipped up by her bracing against them; books with their faces lifted in awe, their red or green or gold-filigreed underskirts showing. A row of hosannas. "Almost there," Lili says, tapping her lover's forehead, "finish me," and Rex . . . Rex returns to the task at tongue, and Lili locks eyes with Myrtle before the younger woman's slowly close and the writhing below recommences, and with it a low complaint from the footstools, soon echoed by Lili's moans.

The brazenness, the scandal. Myrtle makes one last effort, begins ringing in a frenzy that sounds horrifyingly like the church-bell fusillade that used to announce a marriage. They are so smooth and supple, like albino seals. They are beautiful. They may be right.

Myrtle is repulsed, is trying hard to keep up her repulsion, but she can't turn away, and Rex and Lili seem to know she's transfixed there, seem to be continuing as much for her benefit as for theirs. When will someone come and break the spell, tip the balance? When will someone come and gasp indignation and thus return the wobbling world to its axis? Myrtle finds she doesn't have the strength, the nerve, the history. She drops her deck on the carpet, damps the bell. It's all she can do to keep her feet.

23.

Seti is only ten rows away when there comes a new flurry of bell-ringing, an agitato, a charivari. There seem to be no other rescuers at hand. He's seen no one except the sorority girls in their sound-proof study room, using smuggled hair dryers to quick-dry their party cups. Everybody else is either downstairs in the reference room, shut into carrels, or gone home already to flee the crush of football fans. This is his chance at redemption: Myrtle is in peril, and he can come to her aid. His friend, nearly his *only* friend on this godforsaken continent. Afterward he'll tell her everything he hasn't dared confess before. She must know it all now: his love for Lili, the way he's been cruelly used.

And then he's four rows away, three rows, two, one, and he

shifts his freebooting friend Mr. Flynn to his left hand and, with the right, grabs the last shelf to fulcrum himself around.

His momentum flings him to a stop within three feet of Rex, who starts, and then Lili sways on her stools and sways back and falls . . . right into Seti's arms, and there she is, more gorgeous than he could ever have imagined, and more naked, and so *warm*, and she says, "Seti, oh, I'm sorry, I'm sorry," and she flings her arms around his neck and squeezes, and meanwhile Rex is quietly removing his backpack from where it's wedged into the stacks, and at the other end of the aisle stands Ms. Myrtle, looking forlorn and immobile, her bell and flashlight at her feet. Seti realizes that the biography has slipped his grasp again, and he sees it ten feet away, between Rex and gray-faced Myrtle, a mess like a roadkill bird with one matted wing flopping back and forth, hanging by that last stubborn ligament. The empty shelf Lili had been clutching with her left hand is vibrating an eerie music like that in science-fiction films. Rex is lifting from his bookbag a . . . towel?

"Your book," Seti begins. He is drowning in a pit of sand. Here is his besought destiny, his fondest wish, transmogrified into torture. He has the urge to cover her posterior from the prying eyes of Rex and Myrtle, but they have seen all already, and their eyes aren't prying. They seem lost in themselves, Rex calmly attending to the chores of dressing, Myrtle in a coma of introspection. Only now does it register that Lili is wearing his pince-nez; it has devolved into nothing more than a sexual aid, a toy, a costume, like fishnet cabaret-stockings or a hangman's hood.

Her bare skin, though, makes his fingers burn, and then — as the embrace imperceptibly tightens, another turn of the screw, and another — his palms smolder, and then his forearms kindle, and his cheek and neck, and it feels as though someone has snipped off the top of his head. As long as his nose is pressed into the hollow behind her ear, as long as he's enwrapped in her aroma, nothing else will be real. The tears begin to flow. "I have brought the book you wanted," he manages, finally.

"It doesn't matter now," says Lili, "it's too late, hush, hush," and then again, "I'm so sorry, Seti. I never thought you'd leave the desk, never thought . . ." She pulls her head back, reaches out to lift Seti's chin, and with it his eyes, the eyes she must not see and enchant again.

And Seti does what he vowed he would never, once he had Lili in his arms. He lets go. He disentangles himself, reclaims his forehead, his neck and cheek, arms, hands, fingers; the only part he can't retake, yet, is his eyes, which grant him one last wet, fleeting glimpse of her, and of his spectacles. He turns and goes, ignoring Myrtle's calls as she emerges at last from her fugue state and starts toward him. He breaks into a sprint.

24.

Come back, Seti! What has Myrtle done? She blew it, blew it twice — first by being paralyzed, next by being so self-involved. How could she not have leapt up to keep the temptress from laying hands on him?

Rex is pulling on his pants, and he hands Lili a bath towel as Myrtle tries to squeeze by. She has lost interest in them. The spell is over, the magic fled, and they have ceased to concern her. But Lili bars her way. "Ms. Rusk," she says, wrapping the towel modestly around herself, "tell my father whatever you want. Rex and I love each other. We're getting married." Myrtle takes this in. "Today," adds Lili. "This afternoon." Myrtle doesn't move, and there's a moment in which she has to suppress the lunatic urge to give Lili a hug and whisper congratulations. She has been their Matron of Dishonor.

"You go see to Seti now," says Lili, and — holding the towel in place with one hand twisted behind her — she reaches with the other to touch Myrtle's cheek, a gesture of, is it *sympathy?* It's as though she's the adult, Myrtle the child. "I never meant to hurt him. I didn't think he'd see." She pauses. "Return his glasses, too, please. Something borrowed, you know. I'm so sorry."

Lili presses the pince-nez into Myrtle's hand, and Myrtle sets off. Her cheek burns, but somehow she knows the heat belongs to Seti, was simply passed on by Lili. Seti is beset by a fever, and she must find him.

But he's not in the stairwell, not at the desk, not in any of the smoking lounges, not in reference, not hiding among the metal boxes and roach tablets of compact shelving; he is not in the microfiche room, not holed up in a music booth to listen to the song of the muezzins or the nightingales. He is nowhere to be found. She takes up his post. Just for a while she'll cover for him, see if he returns.

But it's nearly eleven-thirty, and she doesn't want to chance seeing Mort, who will return at closing to check on things and, he imagines, to take Lili home. She can't face him. After five more minutes she has no choice but to give up. She wraps the pince-nez in tissue, tucks it into an envelope, scrawls a note: "Seti, you must call me. It will be OK. Call today, if you can. I am here for you. Myrtle. 346-8355." She feels awful for him, and to be honest it's a relief for a few minutes to have someone else to feel awful for. That's what friends are for, it seems, to put your own troubles in momentary shade.

As Myrtle signs the note, she sees Rex poke his head out of the stairwell, and after a brief murmuring he and Lili, fully clothed, sweep arm in arm into the lobby. It occurs to Myrtle that he was checking, on Lili's orders no doubt, to make sure Seti was away from the desk, that their departure wouldn't reopen his wounds. Lili veers over for a moment to set Myrtle's bell and lamp on the counter next to the envelope holding Seti's glasses, but she doesn't look at Myrtle. She keeps her eyes low, is demureness itself now. She steps back to Rex, who offers his crooked elbow the way an old-fashioned groom would, and she slips her arm in, and they nod sweetly when the connection is secure, the way Myrtle was taught to back in ballroom dancing. Rex is carrying Lili's book-bag. Again Myrtle is put in mind of the hilarious hygiene films of her youth:

Darla, may I carry your books for you? They are quite heavy, no doubt, and might impair your lovely posture.

Golly, Bill, that would be keen. My, what a thoughtful boy you are.

But the hilarity is long gone. When they've passed through the turnstile and security gates and the automatic door has clapped shut behind them, Myrtle looks at the bell, at the eight-cell that was once her pride, but she can't bring herself to touch them. They are ruins, markers of a false destiny. No, she must go home, to her bath beads and candles, her cracked and faded stars, her prosaic husband.

She is all but fifty. Now is the time for downshift, downturn, downslope. She saved plenty of money at G&M, and she can retire, at least take a year off and pick up a hobby, something befitting her age: bridge, mah-jongg, gingerbread. She'll make rubbings of old gravestones, organize her shoes, collect dented canned goods for a soup kitchen. She can look forward to Elderhostel trips, senior discounts; she can volunteer in the neighborhood branch library, which still has the varnished-wood date stamps she remembers from girlhood. She'll spend dozens of hours and hundreds of dollars decorating the yard for Christmas: "Milt, are the wise men crooked? Myrrh looks like he's falling-down drunk; I'll have to stake him down. Do you think it's sacrilegious to have Rudolph peeking into the manger like that? I want people to be able to see Jesus from the street, but I don't want it to look like he was born in a cathouse."

She'll grow old alongside Milt, her easygoing drudge, who is reliable if not much else. Give up, give in, take a load off. She has taken her last hormone pill; hot flashes will be the only heat left her.

Poor Seti, too good for this new world, too loyal, too loving, too sensitive. Poor Seti, to have to endure sexual longing for a lifetime yet — that treadmill, that pointless boulder to shove up that pointless hill. That's what makes her sorriest of all. She is quit with it. She heads home to wash off the taints of the day, plus whatever acid Lili left on her still burning cheek.

Poor Seti.

25.

Seti stands in the second-floor men's room, his head under the spout of the hand dryer, which offers the double balm of its world-blotting din and its artificial simoom, the hot wind of home. He wants to feel scoured. No one has come in, fortunately. He is not eager to seek refuge in the Kama Sutra of a stall, where he would be confronted by limericks and line drawings that would shatter the composure he's been working hard to regain.

I am Seti, warrior-librarian; I am of Egypt.

If invaders shoot the nose off the Sphinx, it doesn't collapse or complain. It endures, noseless. It soldiers on. It has a home, and it knows enough to stay put.

This is not my home.

Tonight he will burn his notebook — or no, that would be to grant it too much power, to give it the honorific of a pyre. He will stuff it into the trash beneath the scales and fins of the *feseekh,* putrid mullet, that he will buy to feed his legion of cats, a special treat for having preserved him through time of peril.

But first he will resume his work, do his duty, take his lumps and deserts. He will not yield again to the ammoniac pinch in his nostrils, behind his eyes. He will not be seduced again, either. Even if in the next twenty-five minutes a blonde with velveteen quilt pills in her hair and sleep at the corners of her eyes hands him a book for checkout and plops alongside it a spiral notebook on the cover of which are depicted three beauties in bikinis and bathing caps astride four musclemen, the whole beaming pyramid — fleshly simulacrum of the shrine to Cheops — towed in crystalline water behind a motorboat, he will scarcely notice; he will not be sucked in again. Seti is impervious, is steely, is steel. The girl's shy smile will be lost on him, and he can barely be said to — or rather *could* barely to be said to, in the future, if such a thing were to happen, which it has not and surely will not — he could barely be said to have entertained for so much as an instant the feel of the shuddering yellow skis beneath him, their drumroll on the blue water as it slips and slaps underfoot, the pale, polished feet clenched and balanced on the taut wire of his deltoids. What view might loom above: a tawdry mystery that does not — would not, could not, will not — arouse in him even a fugitive fillip of curiosity. Such would be no fit job for him. He is Seti; he is of Egypt.

He fails to punch the dryer button the sixth time, and then, after a quick self-evaluation in the mirror, decides on one last bout of wind; he seems to have spilled water and soap on his thigh when he washed his face a few minutes ago.

As he dries his trousers, his thoughts turn to Myrtle, poor Myrtle. He must find and console her, must complete the mission in which, back on the fourth floor, he was so humiliatingly balked and interrupted. He must finish what he started. She has been his mentor, companion, bosom friend, has been one of only two people who've shown curiosity about his homeland, about the plan laid out for him. She is the one who's reminded him, again and again, of the superiority of that destiny over the stupid glitz of America. He has been deplorably selfish these last few minutes. Is his composure more precious than Myrtle's sanity, than her happiness?

She was stricken up there, terrified. For the first time she looked to him feeble and frail, looked *old*. Her shoulders stooped, face fallen, arsenal on the floor at her feet. Disarmed, disfaced, dissouled.

The hand dryer clicks off, and he swings open the door to look for her, to do what he can to give her succor before Mort arrives. Twenty-two minutes.

Poor Myrtle.

26.

Myrtle's goal: a bath. She will permit herself to think no further. If she's going to embark upon a life as a prune, fine, but she insists on being a prune that's rimed over with suds and that smells of almond oil. For the next half-hour Milt will almost certainly be out, having his neck scraped at the barber, or sitting at Java Man sipping a capsicum-infused Mexican brew — Café Olé! In truth, this embarrassing decoction is a step up: how she cringed to hear him ask, before, for a "Mighty Mochasippi, extra-muddy, please." He wore the foam mustache obliviously: the beige vices of beige men.

If she can get behind closed doors, steam the mirrors, fill her nostrils and cloud her mind, maybe the world will begin to seem endurable again. But at 11:40, when she turns onto their block, she sees Milt's Omni in the driveway, exactly where it was when she left this morning. He hasn't bestirred himself to go anywhere, and she doesn't hear him out back, mowing.

She's not feeling up to conversation — maybe she can sneak past him to her sanctuary, to her tub tea and unguents and candles, and by the time Milt realizes she's home the door will be drawn, and the blinds, and the bath, and that's one place he wouldn't dare disturb her.

Maybe her training will pay off at last; it's about time her stealth proved useful.

She doesn't hear the TV in the parlor, so — clutching her keys to choke the jangle out of them — she slips through the front door. There's the murmur of talk radio from the bedroom. Milt's probably reading magazines and listening to a right-winger rant about the embattled president, who can't keep his pants on; the other day Myrtle heard the phrase "Lollipop in Chief."

Narrow is the path of dressedness, and perils on every side. To the tub . . . to the tub.

Once she's navigated the kitchen and entered the hallway, she can see that the bedroom door is half-shut. She'll be able to sidle past and into the bath without being seen. She clamps her purse in one fist like a dead pheasant, and pads in her spy's shoes alongside the carpet runner, treading close to the wall so as not to excite any squeaks from the floor. She's within two steps of sanctuary before she wonders why Milt is talking back to the radio in that docent's drone he gets when the subject is sunspots or singularities. Shoptalk.

But of course. But of course. Where else could this day have been leading? *Even Milt.*

He keeps talking, and his girlfriend — Myrtle imagines she's an elementary-school teacher, plain but youngish, shy, slender, someone who looks better out of her clothes than in them, who wears peasant skirts and adjusts her glasses with a chapped-looking knuckle — whoever she is, she's mute, either overcome by his show of erudition or, more likably, bored to the brink of a coma and plotting escape. But how young? How plain? Myrtle steps into the doorway.

The blinds are down, and through the gloom she can make out two mismatched figures, lying side by side on their backs, wearing only briefs, and the short one's Milt, and the long one's, good God, *Mort,* and each rests a hand on the other's belly, and Mort is holding a big black deck — the smiting-hand-of-God klieglight twelve-cell of his dreams — and training it on this random stretch of ceiling and then that, and Milt is spewing every bit of stellar trivia he can, and there's a cozy intimacy to it, a lazy Saturday morning. This is not the first time, not by far. *Your reputation precedes you.*

Myrtle doesn't edge or hurtle forward, doesn't shrink away. She doesn't lapse backward against a wall and slide dolorously down like the grieving women of films. She tears nor hair nor new asshole. She simply stands there, a voyeur yet again, and takes in the astonishing scene: the covers flung to the bottom of the bed, the clothes stacked on the companion toile chairs along the wall, Mort's wingtips on the floor at military attention, the black socks rolled together and tucked under the tongue of one. There's something almost innocent about it, by comparison to what she witnessed in the library — this is a scene from a slumber party of forty years ago. The briefs, the flashlight, the rapt chatter. Myrtle's bell hand tingles, but she doesn't flinch.

Mort and Milt, Milt and Mort, like a hokey '50s comedy duo. And this seems something from a Borscht Belt routine gone awry. She half expects the joke to end with a merry blast from a bicycle horn or a plummeting rubber duck on a string. *Take my wife, please.* But Henny Youngman never took to his bed with a goliath Ganymede, did he? The marital bed, *Myrtle's* marital bed, with its inlaid headboard and serpentine posts, her hairnet displayed on the one behind Mort like a head on a pike. No, Edgar Bergen never put his ventriloquist's dummy through paces like these . . . and Shecky Greene never looked away suddenly from the ceiling and yanked his hand from the bulge of Mort Bozeman's rigid *Pinsel* and said, "Oh my God, it's her. It's *her.*"

Mort reaches for cover and in doing so drops the deck, which clatters onto the hardwood. That would fail him out of bouncer school, Myrtle can't help gloating; Brass doesn't tolerate panic.

"Please don't speak," she orders, her voice more weary than angry. "Don't say anything."

"Yes, Myrtle," says Milt, her obedient boy. He hangs his head, and in doing so seems the first person today who understands what it means to be caught out, snared, busted. She feels an inappropriate flare of gratitude.

Mort, meanwhile, mounts a sputtering defense. "Just a little stargazing. Astronomy lessons, you know. About time I got a hobby."

"Don't embarrass yourself, Mort. *Quiet* now. I need to think." But she doesn't need to think — what good would thinking do now? Her mind is empty, sucked clean. For the moment she can only marvel at the way they have scooted back to the headboard and sat up and are clasping one another protectively, like movie hostages. Against her better judgment she's touched. And maybe it's the dim light, or some hint in their embrace of a familiar work of art, but how young they look: unwrinkled, unmarred, and muscular. She noticed a couple of months ago that the old free weights in the garage had been dusted and oiled, but how could she have failed to see Milt's new biceps, pectorals . . . and could that be the nascent swell of an *ab,* a chimerical beast she's seen up to now only on rap videos and infomercials (unless you count the illusion, that time, in Mort's office, an illusion that turns out not to be illusory)?

Firm, hale, youthful. Even Milt's erection, that absurd boyish tent pole smothered in cotton, hasn't shrunk away. It's as though there's an erotic premium in being found out.

Meanwhile Myrtle has dwindled and receded, is on the verge of disappearing altogether. In the moment of pure instinct, Milt rallied not to her but to Mort. His first loyalty, first tenderness. He couldn't even bring himself to utter the black beast's name: *It's her. It's her.* She is here only in the abstract, as the specter that Mort and Milt have made her, the myth the world has whittled her to. The transition is complete. Sister Immaculata, the Holy Torch of Justice; My Frigid Wife. Shrew, husk, hag. She is dead already.

How can this day have taken her by surprise? Myrtle, of all people. Sure, sex is everywhere, was everywhere, has been, had been. *Will be.* She recalls the solace she took, back when she and life were easy, from reading Plato on stubborn Eros: the winged soul overwhelmed by the unruly left-hand horse of lust. Back then she had nothing but contempt for the ruly, the square. While they tugged at their ties and smoothed their skirts over their precious knees, the rest of the world was busy getting it on. Ask the old Greeks. *They* knew.

The guy she was sleeping with that semester, a budding philosophe like her, had from then on let her know he was craving it by shouting out — whenever the flesh arose and asserted its claim, wherever they happened to be — "Whoa, Nellie!" That phrase had never failed to make them laugh, and they'd giggled off to a cloakroom, a backseat, a hedgerow.

The horse wore no bridle, then. They gave it its head, and the poor winged soul crashed to earth at least once a day, on weekends sometimes three times, four. It was a game, like dunking the principal at a carnival booth. The soul needed muddying now and again; that was how you knew you still had one.

She retrieves the fallen flashlight, and Mort lifts the pillow as though to ward off a blow. They think she's going to hurt them. But Myrtle has no such intention. She has no intention at all, it seems. Intention is yet another thing she's left behind, a spent stage, a bit of tin fuselage tumbling behind.

All this conspicuous bashfulness — Milt cowering, Mort weaseling. Myrtle can't help making the comparison to Lili and Rex, and as always, youth wins.

She flips the flashlight, and it lands on the bed in front of Mort. "Always keep your deck handy," she says. "First lesson of bouncer school."

This seems to jolt him back to reality. "Don't do anything rash," says Mort, taking up his lost scepter — staging a late rally. He hops to his clothes, drapes his pants over his lap, runs his thumb across the rubber gasket that turns the flashlight on. "Let's talk this over. A lot is at stake, for all of us. You know how easily such things can become public spectacles. Think of how it would look, and not just for us but for the library. I'm thinking about the future of the li —"

"Shh!" hisses Myrtle, holding a finger to her lip, the finger not quite straight but held with the disdainful crook that was Miss Berryhill's stock-in-trade.

As she begins to back away, Milt, a day late as always, at last leaps up to explain — to explain! — but his fifty-three-year-old back doesn't work that way anymore (the dangers of geriatric weight training, she could tell him; you've got to hang all that new muscle on *something*), and then he's doubled over in pain, and Mort hurries to comfort him, and that's the worst of it, somehow, Mort's solicitousness, and she rolls her head backward so as not to have to watch, and looks at the ceiling, now more than two decades out of date, and this is not her life anymore, not her time, the universe has continued to fly apart, and the sky blurs over, she can't see it as well now.

The stars have shifted blue, and she's gone already, far away. We end in dispersal.

And then, from the madnesses of the day, a clarity is distilled. It's not until she's speeding past the campus lakes, down the oak-lined row of churches and frat houses, that she realizes where she's going. She feels herself in the grip of one of those decisive intuitions she has no chance or choice to trust, since by the time the question arises the trust has already been vested, the leap leapt. She's not sure what she'll do when she gets there, and in truth she's not particularly curious. She's beyond curiosity now, beyond motive and struggle. What have they ever gotten her?

And dignity, that ragged old flag . . .

27.

Any minute now, Mr. Bozeman will arrive and bring him to justice, and Seti will be cut loose to resume, at last, his own manifest destiny. The confession is prepared, the scene set: the key in the open door of the security cabinet, the contraband book on Mr. Bozeman's blotter. It's 11:57 on the lobby clock, three minutes to closing.

A graduate student stands before the desk. This is the last time Seti will induce a woman to smile by twirling his book stamp like a revolver in a western. The silver clamp attached to his ID card has ruined its last shirt collar. He will never again punch, for one beat longer than recommended, the five-minute-warning buzzer that ruptures eardrums and spikes heart rates on every floor, B through 4.

Or, well, *possibly* not. Probably not. The fates are toying with Seti — they seem to have laid some impediment in the path of his judge and jury. Mr. Bozeman is never late to pick up Lili, never. Not until today. He hasn't come and gone during Seti's unforgivable absence from his post. The book satchel is still in his desk chair, his nasal spray still propped atop it. One bullet dodged, then — or no, that's no way to think, since there would be no point or honor in dodging the bullet fate has designated for one, and fate is a crack shot with unlimited ammo, and . . .

But it is nevertheless true, as they say here, that justice delayed is justice denied, so if the law fails to show in the next two minutes and twenty-five seconds, Seti will have no choice — he can't very well fail to secure the Cabinet of Perversities overnight, can he? That would be a sin more grievous yet. And staying late isn't an option. What would Doug the Stoner, or Eugene V. Debs, say if he waited around like some timorous wage slave, if he lurked outside the library *on his own time* so that he might inform on himself to his tardy master? So if Mr. Bozeman doesn't come, Seti will have to wait until next week to hurl himself on the point of the knife, on the mercy of the court. He'll have to remove the key and carry home, for safekeeping, the Errol Flynn book, which might contain some clue to what happened to Lili, what drove her to Rex.

Two minutes to go. Through the glass wall of the reference room, Seti can see the last couple dozen holdouts — Asians South and East, Africans, a smattering of Latin Americans and nervous junior professors — stowing their notes, gathering their things. To his right a handful of people are turning in reserve books, and he can hear a few stragglers scuffling down the stairs.

One minute forty-five. He reaches into the drawer and takes the stubby electronic key that will lock the ingress. As he glances to the front, the glass doors whir, and Myrtle marches in, makes a sharply squared right turn, and strides to within ten feet of the circulation desk.

Without looking up, without any hint of hurry, she undoes the cameo clasp at her throat, tugs up her blouse to untuck it, and begins to unbutton, bottom to top. After twenty seconds she shivers the blouse off her shoulders, and it billows to her feet. She undoes the silver safety pin that secures her skirt, then unwraps the dowdy navy-on-charcoal checkerboard. She rubs her heels together to pinch off her shoes and leans over to unroll her stockings. She is wearing only a black lace bra — surprising for its color, its style, and the full bosom it leashes — and matching undertrousers.

Seti's first impulses are to feel sorry for her, to blame himself: if he'd done the right thing a while ago, if he'd disentangled himself from Lili and stopped his sniveling and rushed to help his friend, this wouldn't be happening to her, this public shame. Now Myrtle, who has seemed to him sanity itself, has cracked, and she's performed — in the library, right here in the main lobby, before God and the exchange students — some sort of slow-motion striptease, only there's no tease in it, she's in absolute earnest, and what can he do but gape? Her skin is pale and freckled against the pitiless lingerie, and she stands in a sickly light that makes her look blue and lumpy.

There is at Myrtle's feet a tidy pile of frumpery, and it reminds Seti — he wants to resist the unflattering comparison, but why should memory obey him when nothing else does? — of the morning when he first met Doug the Stoner. That barroom, their refuge from the flood: the rubble-heap of clothes on the floor by the entrance, the smoke-stained brassieres stapled overhead, the lithe and immaculate girls who had shed them. Seti recalls the sight of two beauties facing off across a daiquiri the size of a bathroom waste can, their lips pursed over straws, competing to see who could drain more of it. They were pulling comical faces, and they began laughing, snorting red slush, and then they leapt up and hugged, held one another's naked shoulders until they laughed themselves empty of laughter, and when they pulled apart there was juice all over them, and they laughed again.

It is hard to imagine that Myrtle was ever such a girl. As she steps out of her stockings and straightens up, he hears one of her knees crack like seasoned wood.

Water, water everywhere, Doug had said that day, and Seti hadn't quite understood, or had tried not quite to understand. But he'd noticed Doug's wistful tone, seen the sad way he shut his eyes as he fulcrumed the bottle up to his nose and downed the last of the beer. A fit of self-pity, Doug told him later, to be thrown off in a day or a week, *when I get it wet again. It's just that with a face like mine, you don't score much with babes like that. But any port in a storm, eh? There's no reason to dwell on it.*

Seti sees now, though, that there is a kind of drought that can't be ended even by flood, in which one has no choice but to dwell. Age encroaches: skin loses its oils and grows splotchy, riven, like an abandoned watercourse. Seti, of all people, knows what it is to live in a dry country. *Poor Myrtle, poor Myrtle.*

And then, only then, does she raise her head to look at him, and his eyes catch on hers. Her head is high, her eyes are dry, her feet are turned out like a general's, her hands grip her hips, and there is on her face a lofty, almost disdainful expression — like the one he's just seen in a book on the history of the pinup (what was the harm in a quick good-bye glance at the fabled cabinet, since he would soon be confessing to having raided it?). Back in the 1950s, nude models felt free to show a barely hooded scorn for the men whose eyes would rove their images, whose fingers would handle them. That is the look Myrtle has as she stands nearly bare before Seti's desk, before the Bier of the Book.

It is — what do they say? — it is *dignity*. Dignity is the quality that holds him where he is, is what paralyzes the others, the lonely migrant students and the library staffers and the fearful junior faculty and the sorority sisters, who are piled up like a ten-car crash at the base of the stairwell, holding their columns of cups like jousting poles. Seti sees eyes lifted, mouths opened. But nobody whispers, nobody moves. Three people stand motionless at the exit turnstile, afraid to leave. Behind them is a knot of early-bird football fans gawking through the windows.

Seti examines the spread of Myrtle's fingers, her thumbs hooked over her pelvis. The Statue of Liberty ought to have her hands on hips — that is American, the implacable demand, *Look at me, acknowledge me* . . . the naked need. It makes Seti feel in some odd way patriotic. In his country she would be covered from foot to forehead, and that would be meet and proper and right. Yet Myrtle seems to him a kind of beacon as she stands without the lie of clothes in this bad light in this public place. She is fascinating. She is, suddenly, somehow, *beautiful.* She has been his peer, his adviser, his friend, but until now he's thought of her as an affable gray eminence, his coffee companion, the nice old frau with the sex bell. But here she is; here she is. No fluorescent tube can stanch the glow of her skin, of her eyes.

A few tears have begun to leak down her cheeks, but any fool can tell they're tears not of capitulation but of rage. They must tickle her cheeks, her chin line, but she doesn't stir. She is a statue; she is a rock. And the world remains in stunned suspense — a dozen expressionless faces peer through the reference-room glass, the sorority sisters are still stacked before the risers, and now at least fifteen football fans look on through the doors. There is no sign of Mr. Bozeman. It is after twelve, and Mr. Bozeman has ceased to exist.

The lights buzz on and on and on. Everyone is waiting for something. But what? What will she do? The only way to carry this off is to stand here for all eternity, is to *become* a statue. Anything else would be a diminution, a disappointment, would free the world from its spell. The people now standing by in awe would run off to translate this miracle into an anecdote, a lie to be told and retold over the years to gales of laughter. Her austere beauty wouldn't survive to the first telling, and over the years she'd come to be described, for the story's sake, for the sake of banishing the true memory, as a crone, biddy, relic, bat, corpse, some crazy eighty-year-old prune who was, get this, bareassed at the university library. Her dignity would be overthrown, debunked, forgotten.

For now, though, there Myrtle is, in all her glory, standing in the broad plain of light, weeping. Her eyes have never left his.

He half believes she can do it, can stand here for all time. He *hopes* she can.

And then she nods, slightly but unmistakably, and it is as though Seti is a cataract of water suddenly loosed through a sluice. The gates have opened. He understands that all those assembled here are waiting not for her, but for him.

He knows what to do. He tips Lady Liberty's torch into the trash, his pince-nez along with it. He gathers his coat, steps around the counter. He goes to give refuge, and to take it.

This is his job.

Zugzwang

Chess. A position in which a player
must move but cannot do
so without disadvantage; the obligation
to make a move even when disadvantageous.

— *Oxford English Dictionary*

1.

Sam can't say he wasn't warned. Half an hour ago, when he disentangled himself from a picnic table at the Kiwanis booth, tossed
his gravy-slick plate into the trash, and made a beeline for the
french-fry stand, his friend Della said, "Easy, easy. Only an idiot
or a death row inmate would pack that in on top of smothered
pork and red beans. You know how important this night is to
Wilbur. Please don't mess it up."

The vendor handed down a mammoth paper cone of fries;
Sam doused them with vinegar, ketchup, Tabasco. He capped it
off with a gaudy circle of mustard that looked like police tape
marking off a disaster scene. "I hope," Della continued, "they
made those squares *jumbo.*"

Sam, having shut his eyes in a peanut-oil beatitude, paid her
no heed. She pressed on: "Queen's rook is no picnic, Sam. It's no
picnic, and you don't want to embarrass your boy in front of all
his friends. You upchucking in the middle of his big game is *for
sure* not going to make him stay. That's all I'm saying."

Sam was tired of sparring, was ready to start eating in earnest. He had no time for this. In twenty minutes, yes, okay, he'd make his way to the stadium and take part in this high-flown idiocy his son had dreamed up. Sam would assume his place alongside every ham or twit or publicity whore they could scare up in this burg. He would submit to being ordered around the stage by his own kid. He'd be dressed like a pudgy turret, doing a job usually handled by a thumb-sized hunk of plastic; a crowd would be witnessing the humiliation.

Before such an indignity, wasn't he entitled to a last meal of his choosing? After all, the chief joy of the parish fair these days was the availability of out-of-the-ordinary foodstuffs. A man didn't get enough cotton candy or funnel cake in daily life, Sam could tell you that much. Humdrum existence didn't yield bouquets of vinegared fries or fudge sundaes served in miniature Houston Astros batting helmets. At Piggly Wiggly they didn't sell delicious lemon corn scooped from enormous plastic garbage cans.

Still, he tried to mollify her. "This baby's cast iron," he insisted, patting his beltline. "No worries."

2.

But sure enough, just three moves in, Sam feels on the verge of exploding. The acid has crept steadily up his throat, down his innards: it wants out, one way or the other. He glances up at Wilbur, who's surveying the scene from the basket of a cherry picker borrowed from Cajun Power & Light. The boy is suspended over this end of the giant chessboard; across the way, grinning madly into the October sky, is his friend and opponent, Milena, a teen master who's come all the way from Prague to LeBeau, Louisiana, to stand in a loaner truck-bucket and shoo baffled townsfolk across a sheet of painted pressboard in the middle of a rodeo ring. Ah, America.

Thursday night of the parish fair, and Sam finds himself dressed all in black, including the watch cap Wilbur bought him for the occasion. He looks less like a castle than like a lumpy cat burglar, and his belly is on fire. In front of him are the darkened livestock halls, behind him the screech and whoop of the midway. The sky is a riot of glary colored lights and plinking music and carnival come-ons and children's howls. The terrified show animals, pampered all their lives to this peak of plumpness and glossiness, don't know what to make of the bedlam out here, or of their cramped pens among rivals they hadn't dreamed existed. They bleat and moan, snort and stink . . . and ever rises the gorge.

Surrounding the raised stage is the bullring — an expanse of raked cinders and clay and a few heroic dung piles left from yesterday's bronc-riding. Beyond the restraining wall a couple hundred people, mostly puzzled parents, are scattered through the bleachers, wondering (Sam has no doubt) what the holy hell is wrong with young people of the '90s. In Sam's day, kids tried to breed monstrous pigs or watermelons or flawless snap beans; they went to the fair to rope calves and drink rotgut behind the expo shed and maybe steal a kiss from a horse-faced carny while the Scrambler or the Himalayan Flyer groaned and flashed nearby. Kids hopped onto filthy carpet remnants and raced to the bottom of the big slide, hollowed paper targets from close range with BB guns, threw baseballs at pyramids of milk jugs (one on the bottom row weighted, to keep safe the sumo-sized stuffed animals they'd chained to shelves along the back of the booth — this was an introduction to the world's little treacheries). On the fair's final night, Friday, the town's two high schools waged gridiron battle in Judge Hughes Stadium, the centerpiece of the grounds.

In 1974, Sam scored a big touchdown in that game; a few hours later, Belinda Cooksey, a *cheerleader*, let him cop his first feel. Twenty-five years along, he can still see his hands disappearing under that luminous white sweater with the maroon megaphone across its front, can still feel the tiny knobs of nipple rising to his touch. The breasts of an angel in bloomers, or a bunch of nimrods in chess costumes — which would you rather bring to attention? Youth wasted on the young, again.

Now, thanks to Wilbur, LeBeau has gone stark loony over some foreign game where you push little dolls around, punch an alarm clock, then write in code and wait. Wilbur's sixteen, and he spends his evenings hunched over a board or a book, jabbering about the Sugar-Tit Gambit of London, 1883, or the Two Nights of Morphine in New Orleans, 1858. At the mall, instead of scoping out girls' naked midriffs or harassing preppies from Houma or boosting candy like a regular teenager, he sets up in the atrium and matches wits against eight opponents at once. Shoppers set down their parcels and rest their tootsies and watch a boy stroke his smooth chin and walk down a line of tables, chivvying little horses and churchmen across a checkerboard. The fools clap and hoot — Sam has seen it. It's not normal; it's not anything vaguely like normal.

3.

Wilbur has just started his junior year. Soon he'll be gone, and Sam — who's devoted these last five years, since Bea died, to ushering their boy safely to adulthood — will be left alone. Wilbur plans to go away, maybe up east, to college; Sam will stay here as always, will continue backfilling trenches and shredding tires and monitoring leachate at the parish dump, where he is a king of long reign. The caliph of crap. The rajah of rubbish. *Ain't much*, he used to reassure himself, *but it's mine.* Say what you will, not everyone's lucky enough to have an honest-to-God *domain.*

The boy, for his part, barely sets foot at the landfill anymore; he's lost interest. He used to ride alongside his father on the backhoe while Sam tidied hummocks of trash, used to help scavengers load wrecked washers and dented stoves onto their trucks. For a child, there is no greater playground, no richer trove, than a dump. How many times did Sam have to rout him out of a rancid pile of books or amputee dolls or, once, a box filled with dildos and vibrators of every size and description?

As recently as two years ago, father and son would put on their mucking boots and climb, at dusk, to the landfill's tallest peak. There, at the highest point in Cut-Off Parish, eighty feet above sea level, they'd stare over the massive steppes of refuse — the summits somehow beautiful, burnished, in the waning light, amid the wheeling and screeching gulls, and with just enough up-creep of steam to suggest the sluggish volcano below. Roughly forty feet beneath their boots, the detritus of Sam's youth was slow-roasting at 110 degrees. It was all still there, more or less, only hidden, faded, diminished in the small but steady way all memories are subject to: the pull-tabs from the Dixies he and his friends used to drink atop the levee, the clamshell burger boxes from the Dairy-O, the hulks of muscle cars they'd raced and ruined. Buckets from Kentucky Fried Chicken, now crumpled ossuaries for drumstick bones. Scroll-key Spam cans. And in snug anaerobic pockets, lightly yellowed copies of the *Times-Picayune,* some still coiled tight inside green rubber bands holding on after thirty years.

From the top of the tallest mound they could see it all — the brown skeins of bayou, the thickets of cane, the broccoli-crowns of live oak. They could watch cars creep through the distant downtown, headed home, could spot the blinking stacks of the chemical companies along the Mississippi. And, too, they could look over the cemetery, just a mile away, where Bea had found her rest. In south Louisiana the water table is too high for dug graves, so Bea is interred aboveground, inside a brick of polished cement.

Father and son would stand atop the mountain of trash, arm in arm now, and gaze out at the mausoleums and the scrolled iron gates and the thin towers the rich built to stake the first claim on God's attention, should He ever chance to look. At this time of day, the whitewashed concrete seemed to glow amid all the darkening green, and they'd silently count back seven crypts in the third row and Sam would squeeze Wilbur's shoulder and then they'd breathe in the sweetly foul aroma of the garbage mellowing beneath them and finally slog back down (sinking sometimes up to their knees) to the trailer, where they'd fetch the shotgun and, using the last of the light, knock off a few early rats for sport.

4.

There's no doubt what moment of these last few years Sam would freeze in time, if he could: The Night of the A-1.

In 1975 and '76, before he met Bea, Sam made a living by pretending to crack heads; he served what his future wife would sniffily call "a stint as a grappler." In those days pro wrestling was still low-rent, lowbrow, low-blow — it wasn't a path to action-figure stardom or beef-jerky commercials or the governor's mansion. Most of the guys were tough ex-jocks who drove trucks or humped crates around a warehouse by day, then donned bikini briefs and whaled the bejesus out of one another for kicks and an extra paycheck. As sidelights go, rasslin' had its appeal. It paid decent coin, first of all; it offered free access to weights, a bit of the old rough-and-tumble without the fluky perils of bar brawls (jagged bottles, pool cues, hopheads with blades). Wrestling had, too, a grubby glamor. It provided something Sam had been missing, truth be told, since the end of high-school football: a chance to flick towels and play the dozens in a locker room again, a chance to behave as a boy among boys. And, all right, maybe just a hint of vanity — wearing satin tights was still an option back then; he was young, slim-waisted, powerful. His biceps were grapefruits, or cannonballs; his pecs could be made to *boogie*.

The prettiest wrestlers got to be heroes, and they tanned themselves orange with quick-cream and days at poolside. They rated the private dressing rooms, the groupies, the fake ermine capes. Sam was a villain, but that had its compensations, too. The fellows were close. They were like a troupe of itinerant actors, only instead of breeches and buskins they wore bright red or black shit-kickers and satin coochies with stars across the crotch. This was a kind of amateur theater that no one could call homo. The villains and understudies would travel from gig to gig in vans, and while careening down the highways of deepest Alabama or Mi'ssippi they'd sit cheek to meaty cheek, draining forties and toking on a communal fatty and trading tips about wigs and masks (cotton stretched too much, and polyester was too frigging hot — a nice blend was *de rigueur*) and boot polishes and the use of Scotch tape or spirit gum to keep one's trunks from riding up. Kid Commie (real name Cyrus Hills; hometown Wheeling, West Virginia) would practice his accent, a thick-tongued cross between Tarzan and Dracula with strong undertones of Snuffy Smith. When he got tired, all but the Snuffy Smith vanished: "Behaaand the Arn Curtain," he'd say, "we kick some everluuvvin' ass, bawwys." Daniel Boom, his musket and coonskin cap safely stowed behind the rear seat, would try to shush everybody so he could read anthropology texts; he was a grad student at Ole Miss. Hours later he'd be stalking around the canvas, grabbing his crotch and basking in his fans' raucous and adoring song ("Daniel Boom was a man, was a BIG man"). The guys would demonstrate holds, tell stories, hash out changes in choreography. It was fun.

Sam was known as Bodo the Butcher, and they'd have him swagger into the ring wearing an artfully stained apron and a paper hat, all the while flinging sausage links and raw T-bones into the crowd, which clamored, sometimes nearly rioted, for the meat. You'd see two burly goofballs in the cheap seats, best friends, beating the crap out of one another to claim a gray and gristly lamb chop plucked from the gummy floor of a civic auditorium or C&W bar or armory gym.

Sam had a mean-looking Fu Manchu and a special niche; he was almost always pitted against the bleeders. These were lifers, not like the small-time moonlighters or the kids out for a brief adventure before settling into marriage and middle age. They were true professionals, men who'd spent years mastering the odd magic of exsanguinating themselves; they were not to be trifled with. They were closemouthed, grimly serious about their craft. Most carried doctors' satchels stuffed with solvents, scalpels, tools of torture; all of them could, by dint of mysterious "training methods," pretty much hemorrhage on command. Some of the blood was fake, to be sure — guys would conceal packets in their mouths and nostrils, tape them between fingers or under arms. But some bleeders were genuine artists, sorcerers who could work miracles with the limited palette of red, red, and red. They would go at themselves, before their bouts, with gutting knives, meat mallets, tattooing needles. Several took massive doses of niacin to dilate their vessels and came into the ring with faces ripely crimson. Most terrifying of all was Paul Plasma ("The Universal Donor"), who would lightly score his face with a serrated blade, get blood to pool near the surface, and stitch himself, barely, with thread or glue. Then, when Sam came on like Attila the Hun, showing his full repertoire of headbutts and helicopter spins and vicious souflexes, Paul Plasma would nick himself open as he fell, and all at once his face would be a gruesome tomatoey mask. Bodo the meatcutter would soon be wading in his element, roaring with delight, slobbering and licking his lips . . . and then he'd get bounced off the turnbuckles and the mat, pummeled and pinned and left there on the canvas, smeared scarlet, and the outraged Universal Donor would stand over him, looking like he'd just been flayed, and then would reach into Sam's limp right hand and produce, for the madly booing crowd, the razor blade presumably used to accomplish such butchery.

Sam had started wrestling out of boredom, as a way to stave off adulthood for a while. He'd been working at a tire shop, beating rims flat and waiting for his life, at long last, to begin. One night he went to see some rednecks rock and sock one another at the fairgrounds — the bouts were held in the same livestock hall he's gazing at tonight — and afterward he sought out the bossman. The guy was easy to recognize; he was the one wearing a tuxedo with baby-blue shirt ruffles, the one smoking a tiny black panatela . . . he was the one with tassels on his shoes. Sam stood outside the ring on the familiar dirt floor — to be precise, it was sawdust mingled with generations of hard-packed pig shit from every corner of the parish — tapped the sharp-dressed man on the shoulder, and asked whether they were looking for new blood.

Sam was wearing a T-shirt, and as he awaited an answer he wrapped his left hand around his right wrist, trying to flex his chest and arms inconspicuously. The impresario looked him over. "Good muscle tone," he judged, "but you got some acne, and your nose is too long for a hero. If you don't mind being a baddie. . . . Can you do accents? Rooshan, maybe Chink? We could use an upper-crust Brit, too — can you do a limey in a bowler hat? For God's sake, kid, quit flexing. You're in already. You're gonna blow a goddamn gasket."

In those days, being a wrestler meant doubling up in fleabag motels, eating at greasy spoons, but it was a way to travel without joining the military, driving a big rig, or taking up tent-preaching. But when he met Bea — lovely Bea, with her college degree and her ritzy ways (beer from bottles, museum prints on the walls, pajamas to bed) — she put a quick end to his days of being bled on in boondock towns. She brought him to heel, to home, and in late '76 he caught on as assistant manager of the landfill. (The "manager" in his title made it all right, though Bea made him bathe in rose water and wash his hands a dozen times a day.) He ascended to his current position three years later, when Lester Ballou moved on to the genteeler trash of suburban Jefferson Parish.

Shortly after Bea's death, Wilbur and Sam started watching wrestling together, and again and again the boy made his father tell the story of his days as a manslayer and hurler of meats. He answered every excited question: No, he didn't have to buy his own pound of flesh; day-old cuts were provided for him. Yes, they let him carry a real cleaver sometimes, but for insurance reasons it was blunted with a rubber sheath like on the end of a crutch. Yes, he got whupped by both Nature Boy Ric Flair and Bulldog Brower (the king of the bleeders, a one-man Peckinpah movie whose fans often rolled up their sleeves and kicked in a pint for their hero's nightly transfusions). Flair carried around a mesh sack of lemons to keep his hair blinding white; Brower was a prince who once let Sam test-drive his new riding mower. The weirdest place Sam ever wrestled? Inside a disused silo near Tupelo. The spectators were outside — a few dozen people watched from high scaffolding through portholes cut in the tin, and fifty others stood on the ground and pounded the walls as their buddies yelled down a blow-by-blow. It was like being inside a can, and Sam could still remember the yells that erupted whenever one of the wrestlers' backs slammed the tin and set it ashiver.

Wilbur insisted that his father show him tricks and holds, and a ritual developed. They'd start off in their twin recliners, silently watching the action onscreen, vertices of a happy triangle. During commercials, Wilbur would surf through whatever games were on (good internal clock on that boy, and a steady thumb — Sam had reason to be proud). But eventually one of them would mount a sneak attack, and soon they'd be writhing on the floor, whooping and hollering. These battles grew more pitched, more byzantinely plotted, and on the night when Sam would have liked to stop time, they were rattling the floorboards and bouncing off the chairs when Simons Cuthbert, rookie cop, burst in, his night-stick cocked and ready. A neighbor must have called. Sam was on the floor, pretzeled into a figure-four leg hold, pleading for mercy, and he saw Simons first. Wilbur loomed above his father, wearing only underwear and a stocking mask, roaring: "You can't whup me, old man; you can't whup me!"

"All right, Wilbur," said Simons in a low but frantic tone. "You're safe now. Go ahead and let him up. We're not going to let this scuzzbag hurt you. And you, Mr. Sam? How could you?"

Wilbur betrayed no surprise at this intrusion, kept his back to the door. Sam could see his eyes through the mask slits, and they gave away nothing. They were steely, impassive. It was as though he'd been awaiting this moment, this audience. Without releasing the pressure on his father's leg, he deliberately worked himself around to face the officer. Simons had been a senior when Wilbur was in seventh grade, and they had a nodding acquaintance; Sam had known the boy since Simons and his pop were regular customers, way back when, at the dump, where Cuthbert Sr. seemed to deposit a suspicious number of cracked mason jars and worn metal tubing — the waste products of moonshine whiskey.

Sam could see Simons blanch when he got a look at Wilbur's

chest, which was thickly lacquered with steak sauce. The officer's handcuffs jangled menacingly, and his grip on the club tightened.

Wilbur reared back and feigned a brutal stomp to his father's chest, and it was only then that Sam caught on. He groaned and let his head loll to the side, shuddered once, and went limp. And then Wilbur began his endgame. He proceeded step by step, with a certain dry savor, like a man splitting logs in crispest winter. He was a pro; he took his time. Sam's eyes were closed, but nonetheless he could see it all unfolding, could count off the cadence as Wilbur rubbed his hands together, held up a finger to let Simons know to hold off just a minute, all will be revealed in good time, sweet time, right time. The boy ground the heel of his hand against his gory chest, dramatically flicked blood onto his fallen enemy. Sure enough, Sam felt a light mist on his face. And then Wilbur leaned down and pried open his father's clenched fist and stared at his audience of one — perplexed now, nightstick lowered, car radio squawking in the driveway — and showed him the razor blade responsible for the bony, boyish chest looking like the wall of a slaughterhouse.

Simons Cuthbert squinted at the plastic safety razor (the best they'd been able to do with the materials at hand) and said, "What the hell, Wilbur? What's *wrong* with you people?" At that moment the father came alive and the son turned to welcome him back. Both convulsed with laughter. "Loons," muttered Simons, and he gave up, shoved his stick into its scabbard and headed off to hassle kids drinking beer in the graveyard or bust a few loiterers or save somebody's pet bunny that tried to eat a dish towel. Regular cop stuff.

Sam sat up, and Wilbur laid a hand on his father's sweaty neck, and they kept on laughing in loud sighs and sobs. That's the moment Sam would relive endlessly, were endlessly reliving allowed. That one right there. Night of the A-1.

5.

Meanwhile, the pieces arrayed on the fairgrounds board wait silently for something, anything, to happen. They're trying to stand still, to be quiet; this is the job of chessmen, but it turns out to be not so easy as it looks. Mayor Pendarvis, a white bishop, is scrubbing at an itch under his cockeyed miter and trying, no doubt, to figure out why he volunteered. It seemed like good public exposure, what with his reelection bid next month — the campaign trail doesn't offer many chances to dress up like a high muckety-muck of the church, and he's taken full advantage. He stationed himself at the stadium entrance a half hour before the opening move and handed out bumper stickers to arriving spectators. "Didn't know you was runnin' for pope, Bud," they kept saying, and the mayor had only smiled and said, "God bless you, sons and daughters, and by the way, cast your vote for Bud Pendarvis." But that was then; this is now. He hadn't counted on being allergic to this fucking *hat* (may the Lord forgive him), and he'd figured the game would last ten minutes or so. His scalp is aflame, and he can't — in front of the assembled voters — pull off the churchly lid and stomp it into a pulp and rake both hands over his head like a man assailed by vampire bats. If only that Communist chick would hurry . . . Ralph Broussard, a black knight, has tucked his broomstick horse under his arm and transformed it into a rifle; he's locked onto an imaginary raft of geese among the stars. Albertha Simmons, the white queen (or the "black white queen," as she's been referring to herself), has to pee something fierce, but if she did she'd have to go to a filthy Pot-o'-Gold, and while she was hunkered down in there amid the mind-blowing stench, her subjects would have to go unruled, and she'd be hearing, in her head, the mutterings of the racists in the bleachers: "I always knew them nigras had weak bladders. You don't see none of *our'n* runnin' off to make water." Too, the pawns (Ms. Warmoth's class from the progressive playschool) are grabassing a little. Each pawn is identified by a balloon (black or white, depending) mounted on a hair ribbon, and a couple of the boys are trying to prick one another's noggins with straight pins.

Wilbur and Milena seem not to notice the restive footsoldiers, and they pay no attention, either, to fires of belly and bladder and scalp. *A good general . . .* Sam muses bitterly.

"Pawn to king's bishop four," Wilbur calls, and the announcer shouts into his mike, "THE BLACK TEAM MOVES PONE TO KANG'S BISHOP FO'." There's a small buzz in the grandstand, but on the board nobody budges. Wilbur leans forward, lowers his voice. "That's you, little Brigit. Go forward two spaces. There you go. Got it. Thank you kindly." Brigit turns and stares up at him, her face clouded. Has she just been scolded? Sent to time-out? What did she do wrong? She's only five years old; what do they *want* from her? Wilbur grins beneficently. "This is a compliment," he assures her. "Now you're a *developed* pawn." Brigit beams at him, turns, and sets her hands on her hips. Her balloon headdress bobs proudly, there's a ripple of applause, and Sam thinks, My God, that little girl would rather be here, standing atop a tiny white square on a stage in the rodeo ring, than riding the carousel. He's got the whole town caught up in this. It's madness.

Sam's guts are in turmoil, his mind in disarray, but when he glares at Wilbur, he gets a genial wink in return. *Isn't this fun?*

6.

It wasn't long after the Night of the A-1 when things started going sideways. Time passed; garbage mounted. Every morning Sam went to unlock the gate and welcome the roaring procession of trucks, and the offal mountains grew gradually higher and less stable. It is, of course, the same with children.

In eighth grade, Wilbur limped home from the first afternoon of football two-a-days and announced he was quitting to form a jug band. Della and Sam were standing in the kitchen when the boy clomped in, still wearing his cleats and his grass-stained pants, which had slid down his hips so that the knee pads protected his mid-shins. "The hell you will," barked Sam. "Blowing over a pop bottle with the other mouth-breathers won't make you a man. What you need is to get set on your ass by the big kids. Get your helmet on and pull up your trousers, boy. We're going outside." For half an hour Sam threw bullets and ran one-man drills. The boy, exhausted, plugged on without a word. Snot strings swayed from the bars of his face mask. Finally, Della came to the rescue; she'd been inside, whipping up a pie that could melt an ogre's heart.

The next morning, when Sam went to wake Wilbur for the pre-breakfast session of football practice, his son was gone. There was a note on the pillow. "Sorry, Pop. I got the music in me." Della made Sam give up his rather vivid plans for punishment. "Let the boy be," she said, and Sam reluctantly did.

He was sure the musical group would go by the wayside in a few days, but Wilbur shocked him by practicing almost without cease, and by coercing his friends into constant work as well. The kids gathered at the dump ("Garbage don't want to hear that racket either," carped Sam, but he didn't chase them off) and played their loud mix of downhome and hip-hop in the recycling shed: Wilbur on a secondhand squeezebox he'd bought with proceeds from scavenging, his friends Bruce and Emile on banjo and drums, respectively, and a gold-toothed black kid named Rebar making old LPs squeal on a battery-powered turntable. They called themselves "Straight Outta Compson" (your guess there is as good as Sam's), and they'd saw away for hours at a stretch, playing to an audience of milk jugs and soda cans. Eventually they achieved a minor celebrity in New Orleans clubland (thanks to a song Wilbur composed called "Yo' Mama Eats Fig Cobbler") before breaking up because Bruce wanted to play bluegrass and Emile got a nasty case of the clap.

From there Wilbur moved on to what he called "guerrilla filmmaking," which career ended when he tried to shoot footage of his father in the bathtub and Sam heard the whir and took out after the budding auteur and beat his camera near to death with a toilet plunger. Wilbur said he quit because any natural-born talent would have foreseen this and placed a second camera in the living room, to capture the slapstick of the soapy naked man pogoing up and down with that orange rubber bell on the end of a stick. Whatever the horseshit explanation, Sam was grateful that the video siege was finally over. For three long weeks, every mundane activity — mopping the kitchen floor by penguin-walking a filthy towel over it; stepping out back for a late-night whiz (the hallmark of freedom, this one, the homeowner's right to water his shrubs in moonlight); potting a few crows and seagulls with the old shotgun — had been fraught with danger. Della made Sam sweep up the camera remains and give Wilbur two hundred dollars, and, grumblingly, he did.

It was then that Wilbur discovered chess, and suddenly he was playing all the time — on the Internet, at the mall, in parks and antiquarian shops in New Orleans. His enthusiasm was strangely and immediately infectious. Word spread that the high-school football team, traveling to a road game in Baton Rouge, had fifteen boards running in the bus, and Wilbur — who'd taken the job of statistician just, it seemed, to shame his father — was roving the aisle, dispensing tips. The idlers who'd been playing listlessly out front of Cherry's Feed and Seed for years were suddenly surrounded by kibitzing kids who babbled about "irreal positions" and "indirect batteries"; the parish library was mobbed by patrons who wanted to see their collection of whittled chess sets.

And then he started venturing to tournaments and racking up ratings points, and what the hell was a father to do with a prodigy? Wilbur began amassing a reputation, and one morning this past summer a woman from New York showed up at the fill. She was a flat-faced matron in square-toed shoes, blunt in every way. She asked Sam if he didn't want his son to "escape all this" — she gestured disdainfully to the mesa of rubbish where Sam had made his career, the one that overlooked his wife's final rest, and asked whether she could whisk his only child to some sort of fancy academy where he'd be tutored by grandmasters. She kept her wary eyes on the ground, as if suspicious that a speck of Dixieland mud might leap up and soil her. She looked, Wilbur thought, like someone who'd be better off if she'd stepped in dogshit a few million times in her life.

"We can train him among others with his gift," she finished. "All expenses paid. He's a very unusual young man, you know."

"A few years ago," said Sam, by way of explanation, "Wilbur and I used to wrestle in front of the TV, and he'd have steak sauce all around his pie-hole and smeared on his chest. What's happened to him?"

Flat-Face looked terrified; she seemed to think that the unorthodox use of condiments in the home was reason for the board-game authorities to step in and steal a boy from his old man. "Look," she said. "This is a fabulous opportunity. Do you want to keep young Will down on the farm, down in the dumps? He has a special talent, and you're in, ahem, no position to foster that talent. Think about it."

Flat-Face is wrong. It's not that Sam wants to squelch Wilbur's personality, kill off his so-called gift . . . and he never meant to sentence the boy to a life in LeBeau, cheek by jowl with his father, plowing garbage with a bulldozer all his life. What he *did* want seems simpleminded now, on the verge of appalling. Sam thought Wilbur might go a little further in football than he had, might land a scholarship to LSU, where he'd study to become, well, a scientist of trash, a garbage archaeologist who'd solve the world's waste problems via landfill analysis: he'd take core samples, catalog them, calculate rates of decomposition, perform chemical tests. On their jaunts to the garbage pinnacle, years ago, Sam had often peppered Wilbur with questions about dumpology: What's the largest sanitary landfill in the world, Bubba? *Fresh Kills, on Staten Island. When it has to close in 2005, it will be over five hundred feet tall. It's fifty times as huge as the Great Pyramid.* You got it, Bubba. What's the difference between "trash" and "garbage"? *Trash is dry; garbage includes the gross stuff.* What killed off the great ancient civilizations? *Improper waste disposal, Daddy. They drowned in their glop.* Amen, my son. Smart boy.

What Sam had foolishly imagined was that the son would be like the father. The apple wouldn't fall far from the tree. Furthermore, the son . . . the son would be *with* his father. Bea would want Sam to hold the family together for as long as possible; absolutely she would.

"He's staying put," Sam told the shovel-faced woman. "For as long as I can make him."

The woman scowled and snorted and then, giving up, minced her way across the puddles and the oyster shells to her rental car. "Checkmate, baby," whispered Sam.

7.

A gulf has opened between them, as wide as the one separating chess greats like Alekhine or Capablanca from Paul Plasma or Bodo the Butcher. Sam's youth is long gone, and his wife, and now even Wilbur seems on a perilous verge; another loss looms. Already the world has begun tilting. These days the old call-and-response has been supplanted by a listless call-and-mumble, with roles reversed. At dinner Wilbur poses arcane questions, then answers them himself. *Do you know the derivation of "checkmate," Pop? It's from the Persian "shah mat," or "king dead."* Didn't know that. *Some great players were madmen who could slobber and rant and at the same time carry out three-pronged attacks on multiple boards. One world champion won his crown while having to play in a straitjacket. He committed himself to a move by sticking out his tongue and licking the piece in question. Then he'd call out the coordinates, and an assistant in rubber gloves would carry out his instructions. How 'bout that?* Mmph. Not surprised. *I lied, Pop, I made that last part up. Did you know that the queen wasn't even female until a few hundred years ago, and couldn't move but one square, diagonally? Before that the piece was an aide-de-camp, an unarmed yes-man. When the king was threatened, his counselor might scurry around and raise a fuss, but he couldn't help.* Hmm.

And now, as the game has evolved, every pawn wants to grow up to be a queen. They yearn to reach the back rank and put on the crown. Early feminism. The king is a figurehead: old, weak, slow. The real power belongs to his queen, who can go anywhere. Chess was ahead of the curve. Pretty cool, huh, Pop?

8.

And now this . . . this ridiculous exhibition. Della has been an eager conspirator all along. She handled every detail: booked the rodeo ring, borrowed the cherry pickers, arranged for the construction of the board, hired the announcer, obtained a visa for the Czech girl. Della has served as casting director, caterer, seamstress, impresario, innkeeper (Milena is staying with her). She mobilized the community. And it was Della's hectoring — her blackmail, not to put too fine a point on it — that made Sam at last accede to being a lowly and dyspeptic rook.

Ever since she began seeing Sam, three years ago, Della has been Wilbur's friend, advocate, protector. Her constant, chipper praise grates on Sam, actually, and now and again she's forced him into unseemly bluntness. The nastiest discussion was about chess school, and it was only resolved when Sam rolled out the heavy artillery: "Sure he's smart and funny, but can the boy kick ass? Can he work his will on the world? Not unless the world is an eighteen-inch square he can't. His training isn't done yet; I still have things to teach him. Besides, I'm his father. Della, *I* am his *father.*"

Not to speak ill of the dead (Sam always adored Bea, still does), but it was Wilbur's mother who got him started down this path to disappointment, she with her big-bug ways, her grand ambitions. "Nobody's smarter than you are," she would tell the boy. "Your horizons — do you know what a horizon is? — are unlimited." Talk like that is poison. Not everyone can be a hero; you never know when something trivial, something you can't control, a scattering of zits or an aquiline nose, will stand in your way.

Better by far, Sam thinks, to hold down your hopes to what you can be sure of. What's wrong with the bright bit of horizon you can see from the top of the trash heap, a horizon that embraces your father's hometown and a legendary river and cane fields and factories and the sunlit grave of your mother?

And did Bea's big ideas help when she got sick? No — all that "no limits" hogwash, and then she ran up, too hard and too early, against the one final barrier. But she passed her lunatic confidence along to Wilbur, and Della (well-meaning Della) encourages it. Sam is the lonesome voice of reason.

9.

Milena is one of Wilbur's Internet friends and adversaries. She's come to the United States, it turns out, to study at Flat-Face's academy in Manhattan, but she stopped off here to get a feel for small-town America . . . and to meet Wilbur. The two of them have been spending afternoons in New Orleans, eating muffalettas and gumbo and checking out the haunts of their favorite eccentrics: an infamous hot-dog vendor (Sam gathers) named Ignatius Reilly and "the great Paul Morphy," who around 1860 retired from chess at the height of his powers and spent his last years trying to thwart evil barbers who were, he believed, united in a plot to slit his throat. Sam could only sigh when Wilbur — breathless, happy Wilbur — reported these escapades. Of course, sure; a person has to be nuts to live in the Big Sleazy, and the crazies who roam those fetid streets deserve one another. The whores and the hucksters and the paranoids — doesn't Wilbur recall what Sam told him about the absolutely *repulsive* refuse generated by New Orleans? *Garbage in, garbage out.* Was this where chess would lead?

On Monday night his sense of alienation from Wilbur reached a new nadir (though no doubt, things being what they are, a momentary one). Sam was watching football, and Wilbur was in his room, alone; Della and Milena had gone out for Sonic burgers and line-dancing. Sam yelled to Wilbur to come catch the replay of a spectacular touchdown. No response. During a break, Sam cranked himself out of the recliner and padded down the hall. As he stood outside the bedroom he could hear the soft tones of some sort of pointyhead classical music, and he threw open the door to find his son lying atop the bedspread in his briefs. A comical schoolboy boner pointed toward Wilbur's left hip, and for an instant Sam felt a father's pride, but then the rest of the picture came into focus. His son's hands were serenely behind his head, elbows out, and he was wearing a black silk blindfold.

"What in Cheezits' name are you doing?" Sam asked.

Wilbur, imperturbable as ever, did not shiver guiltily, did not rip off the blindfold and leap to his feet and begin stammering excuses. Unhurriedly he yawned, crossed his feet at the ankles, cracked his toes. And then — to the father who's done everything he can to raise his only boy right, and alone, too, these last years — he said, "Fairy problem, Pop." What? *What?* Sam started to crumple, to sink to his knees.

Wilbur must have heard the strangled cry. He didn't move from his pillow, but he said, "Fret not, Pop. Not to worry. Chess term. Just a chess term."

That's his usual reassurance, when he leaves Sam gasping for air: "You couldn't possibly understand, Pop. *Chess term.*" But how is a father not to fret about a son who uses the word *fret* while lying in the semi-dark behind a soft black blindfold, pondering, to the accompaniment of lightly plucked strings, a fairy problem — whatever the hell that is? A father frets. Believe it: a father frets like mad.

10.

Which leaves Sam here, again, thirty minutes into this endless game, still marooned in the back row — his stomach pains unabated, nerves worn, patience shot. His only move has been to castle, which meant sidling around whoever's underneath the ridiculous kingly outfit — could it be Bruce the fiddler? He can see everyone flagging a bit. The pawns' balloon heads have begun to pucker and sag, the knights' plumes are wilting, the queens' corsets and buttresses must be dragging them down. Even the bishops look sour. This had better end soon. This will be a hard lesson for Wilbur, and you'd rather your child didn't have to learn through public disgrace . . . but Wilbur had to find out that this was a fad, a passing fancy. Real people don't go for egghead pastimes like chess. He has some growing up to do.

"Rook to king's bishop four," announces Milena from her yellow roost. The call gets relayed to the booth, and the muddy PA announcement washes through the stands. A few halfhearted cheers rise up.

Above Sam's head, Wilbur calls out, "Is that a check?" His voice has an angry edge.

"It is," answers Milena.

"Do you take it back?"

"I do not, American swine." There is a sudden flash from her right hand, and a fusillade of Roman candle flares whizzes over Wilbur's head. "Take them!" she yells. "Take them *now!*"

"CHAAAARGE!" shouts Wilbur, and Sam finds himself engulfed in chaos. The knights gallop across the board and start fake-pummeling one another with their broomstick steeds; the pawns are rolling about in an ecstasy of violence, loudly bursting one another's heads. The bishops are going at it tooth and claw, every man for himself. Mayor Pendarvis has already vanquished the black bishops with a brick concealed under his surplice. Now he comforts the other white padre, who seems overwhelmed by this breakdown of *agape* and Christian charity. The man is sobbing theatrically, seems not to know what to make of the unconscious priest he's sitting on. Has God really demanded of them, as he did of the Crusaders, say, that they *wreck some ass?* Or is this mayhem Satan's work? The mayor gives a quick and decisive answer. As he cradles his grieving colleague's head, he pretends to bash this Lamb of God several times with the brick, then stands and lifts his arms in exultation. The crowd is in a frenzy now, roaring and booing and hurling ice.

And then the queens are in the middle of the board, ass over teakettle, their capacious skirts gaping, petticoats flapping in the breeze. They battle for a while as the fans hoot and whistle, until all the frippery has been ripped away and stomped on, and the two svelte women — Albertha Simmons the black white queen and Jennifer Astley the white black queen — are facing off clad only in bikini bottoms, sports bras (Albertha's ivory, Jennifer's ebony), and, improbably, their tiaras, which are askew but intact amid hair pulled wild in the fracas. Albertha chases Jennifer off the board, and only then does Sam realize that he is among the last three figures standing.

The two kings are lodged quietly in their corners, looking unperturbed. Everyone else is massed alongside the stage now — inert, quiet, their faces blank, their battles apparently forgotten. When Sam looks up, the kings are still poker-faced, immobile . . . but each is advancing a single space. The black king, at Sam's left shoulder, takes a stately step forward, and the hem of his cape whispers over Sam's shoe. In the bleachers, the fans begin stomping in unison, and on each eighth beat, the kings advance again.

And now they are met in the center, and they stop again. The stomping goes on and on, increasing in intensity until the sound seems unendurable. And then the ermine-collared capes fly off as though from a centrifuge; one lands at Sam's feet. The crowns are flung down, and they spin and sparkle as they carom across the board and over the side, into the muck below. Bruce the fiddler and Emile the drummer are revealed. Each wears wrestling tights and boots of his kingdom's color, and suddenly, to the crowd's ecstasy, they grab one another's shoulders and begin rocking mightily. They clobber one another in turn, and suddenly the board is a welter of blood. It's flowing in impossibly copious amounts — gallons, buckets, pools.

Sam looks up now to see that Wilbur has clambered into Milena's bucket, and the boy beckons his father with a hand. Sam's feet are sore from standing, and the fried food has settled around his midsection like the gold-laden belt that drowned a legendary thief. He must hold his ground; he must not jump overboard.

"Come on, Pop," calls Wilbur, and he beckons again.

And then, against his will, his grain, his every fiber, Sam finds himself descending the stage steps. His belly has ceased to knot, and his head is clear. He feels a bizarre tingle of reconnection, of recollection, of helpless love. *This has all been for him.* For the first time in forever, he understands his boy perfectly. Wilbur has given him a glimpse of the game he loves.

Sam knows, without thinking, what is expected of him. The cherry picker starts on the first try, and he pounds it into gear, begins the slow procession past the grandstand and toward the bulls' chute. The kings are still pummeling one another — the stage is awash in blood — but the fans' attention has strayed. They are standing as one now, cheering and waving as Wilbur and Milena pass. Their numbers seem to have grown; the grandstand is packed, the crowd maybe five hundred strong. The mood is of jubilation.

And there's Della, flailing with a handkerchief from behind the rail like a woman waving from a departing ocean liner, and Sam admits to himself what he already knows, has known for several minutes now: the boy is through traipsing and rifling through garbage. Come Monday, Wilbur will accompany Milena to New York.

Sam shouts up through the din. "The blood, son. The blood. It was A-1?"

Wilbur nods. Sam can see Milena's mouth: "A-1? What is this A-1?"

Sam keeps his hands on the controls, his misty eyes on the path ahead. He does not have to read Wilbur's lips, does not have to see him grin and press his mouth to Milena's ear and whisper it.

Chess term, dear. Not to fret. Just a chess term.

Kidnapped (A Romance)

Mother, he was the kidnapper who might have been; he was my chance at deliverance. You could have saved me so much grief, so much time, so much good love thrown after bad. Why didn't you let go that first time? Why didn't you leave me when abandonment was still only reckless, before it turned cruel?

He was the kidnapper who might have been, Mother. Sometimes I wish he had taken me home.

Brooklyn, 1951

Under a dark stand of hemlocks near the low wall he waited. Prospect Park was quiet. Behind him stretched the meadows, the rococo bandshells, the well-lit lovers' walks. In front of him was the wall — smooth, stone, sternum-high. The smells of soot and roasted peanuts hung heavy in the August air.

He leaned casually against a tree, his left palm flat against its trunk. He had held this pose for nearly an hour, waiting for the crowd from Ebbets to disperse; he had watched the soft bark beneath his hand wane with the sun from a dappled cinnamon to flat black. During that hour he had twirled a screwdriver in his right hand, surprised at the honest iron heft of it — whatever its use, for good or ill, the screwdriver remained purely a tool, and it felt good to hold it. Tools functioned; they didn't judge. What did it matter, really, what material one plied with them? Leather, lumber, ladies — all the same, in one way of seeing. Material to be

161

worked. The raw stuff of craft. There was no need to think beyond that.

About now, in their cold-water walkup in Gowanus, Darla was gathering the boys around her in the narrow bed. The apartment was cramped, drafty, infernally loud; there were rats the size of hams. But Darla and his sons were well fed now. He had bought them tenderloins, cashews, French cheeses, a new hotplate, milk in bright, cold, dewy bottles. If not for his nightly predations, his wife and sons would be going to sleep with nothing in their bellies but cloudy water and bread mottled with mold. That had happened before; it would not happen again. The screwdriver would see to that.

Darla asked no questions about their sudden wealth; chewing made inquiry impossible. She only smiled at him, worked her jaws with a passionate gratitude. Mornings, she pressed her pretty snub nose to his shoulder blade as she slept, spread her newly fattened fingers along his flank so that they seemed like extensions of his ribs. He loved her dearly. He stole for the boys, for Darla. If that made him a criminal, so be it.

But larceny had its more personal pleasures too; that had to be admitted. He felt a raw, rude, thrilling power whenever he waggled his screwdriver in front of the stricken face of some naïf. The tool was sleek, shiny, unscarred; he had never had to use it on either a recalcitrant screw or a headstrong patsy. And he was good at assault, better at banditry than any of the dozen or so jobs he had held (or failed to hold) before. He set his own hours. The wages were good. The work excited him. For the first time he felt like a man deserving of the love of his wife and children. Breadwinner: winner of bread. Man of respect.

And after all, he was no lowlife crook — he had style. He found it astonishing, his ability to allay his victims' fears, but all it took was sweet breath, a smooth bow, a crisp grammatical phrase or two. He won them over with sheer etiquette. Victims, it turned out, were suckers for grace, for proper syntax. Often one of his marks peered up at him as she handed over her cash with something not far short of gratitude. He wouldn't hurt me, she reasoned, a mannerly boy like that — if there has to be crime, better him than some foreigner with a homemade blade and greasy hair.

He wielded his screwdriver as shyly as a country suitor, with something like real tenderness; sometimes as he pressed it up under a matronly breast he had the urge to say, "This is going to hurt me more than it hurts you." He had come to treasure the frightful intimacy of his crimes. On dark street corners his victims stood hip to hip with him, ransacking their purses almost eagerly, seeking to please. Their painted lips parted; their shanks bled heat. Often his breath and his victim's mingled like lovers' sighs. Women craved attention, it seemed to him; robbery was a subclass — shabby, not a little cruel, but nonetheless a subclass — of courtship.

He could only marvel at his fame. During the six months of his spree it had become a badge of distinction to be accosted by the dashing young robber — a sign of conspicuous wealth or beauty or both. Rumors had flourished, myths. Eventually, the *Eagle* had dubbed him the "Gentleman Brigand."

The Gentleman Brigand reveled in this sobriquet, pored over the paper for news of himself as he rode the commuter trains. Forenoons he whiled away on the IRT, the BMT — going nowhere in particular, just reading his *Eagle* as he traversed the city, exchanging pleasantries with his fellow businessmen. He nodded, winked, bowed, greeted; he never met a morning he couldn't call good. The Gentleman loved to hold that crackling rectangle in front of his face (folded, of course, into courteous fourths), loved the slant of the jentacular sun, the slightly acrid odor of the newsprint, the snappy headlines: "So It's Muggy? Don't Go Buggy If It's Ugh-y"; " 'Take That, Reds' — Truman"; "Joe, Ez in Encore Dispute." His favorite was this: "Gent Breeds Copycat Crooks — 'They're Not Sweet, They're Thugs,' Huffs Double Victim." Every sentence or so he was jolted from his reading by the jerk and rattle of the great city passing beneath him. Tenement windows exhaled the sweet sizzle of lard; laundry flapped its cheerful semaphore on the wires outside; in the streets, kids played stickball and tapped

163

hydrants for relief from the heat. Grocers stacked fruit into pyramids. The train clattered along on its blessed track. The Dodgers kept winning.

The paper made the Gentleman Brigand feel like a vital part of the life of Brooklyn. Everyone, he thought grandly, has a part to play. He looked himself over: his shoes shone like russet stars; a fresh carnation nestled fragrantly in his lapel; his fedora (he had swiped it from a haberdasher to tip during "performances") sat regally on the seat beside him, a touch of class. The Gentleman Brigand had a reputation to uphold. The exploits of lowlifes weren't chronicled by the *Eagle;* lowlifes had bad manicures, bad skin, bad intents; lowlifes packed heat, threw politesse to the wind.

His reverie was brought abruptly to a stop by the sight of a woman emerging from the gloom of the boulevard. Only twenty feet away. Alone. A bundle in her arms. Her heels clicked invitingly on the pavement, and the sidewalk mica sparkled beneath them. Under the hemlocks the Gentleman Brigand flexed his powerful legs, brushed the harmless splinters from his palm. Dark enough now. Time to move. To work.

The woman was lovely; she couldn't be more than twenty, he figured. But there was something hard about her . . . the stone corbel of her jaw or the point of her elbow as she shielded her eyes from the streetlamps or the wiry strength with which — one-handedly — she wielded her package. The Gentleman was astonished when the bundle, the carelessly swung parcel, turned out to be a little boy. The mother was trudging along, scanning the city sky like a tyro navigator — lost. Very nicely dressed, it appeared. Her head was bare, but a huge Dodgers cap gaped over the child's face, making him appear headless. Though it was seventy degrees, the boy was swaddled in a heavy mackinaw coat.

Still squinting into the sky, the woman stopped to regrip her child. The Gentleman Brigand looked up, too, into the glow — the city's permanent nimbus of excitement. In Gotham, things happened. It was his job to make sure of that.

The pretty young woman kept sweeping the sky for clues.

She'd be the perfect victim, thought the Gentleman. An out-of-towner, here most likely for the Bums' game this afternoon. Her clothes were expensive, but they looked awkward on her; she didn't wear them often. Feet bound by tight shoes . . . wearing a starchy dress, itchy nylons . . . hair newly bobbed in a bumpkin's parody of city style. A woman loaded with greenbacks, starved for affection, saddled with a child she didn't want. His kind of woman.

She'd like him.

As the Gentleman Brigand vaulted the wall — nimble as a prince, quick as the coming of night — the weapon clicked smartly against the concrete coping. The fedora didn't budge. He landed silently and stood before her, a panther in a well-dented hat. His screwdriver found a shaft of lamplight and took its chance to glint.

The boy was asleep on her left shoulder, so the Gentleman Brigand switched his weapon to his left hand. He slid it under the woman's right breast as subtly as a caress. She lifted her eyes to his. He smiled, lifted his hat. "Madam," he began, "I would mightily appreciate it if you'd give me all your money. And please don't make a peep. This is a dagger," he explained, wiggling the screwdriver against her rib cage in a friendly way.

He looked into her eyes and was shocked to see that she wasn't frightened. She didn't shrink from the pressure of the weapon. "That's a screwdriver," she said matter-of-factly, nudging its dull tip with the underside of her breast. "By the feel of it, I'd reckon one of those new Phillips heads." She said this as though she were teaching an infant the names of things. Her accent was thickly southern. She reeked of peaches. She was beautiful.

"This is a robbery," he repeated. Hadn't he made himself clear?

"Where's the Prospect Park BMT station?" she asked.

Silence. Damn it, did he look like a highwayman or an information kiosk? He would have been enraged but for her beauty. It was extraordinary. But her hip was a wall, chaste and cold; it gave nothing away. Her indifference thrilled him.

"Madam," he began again, "this is —"

"I heard you," she snapped. "I hear fine."

"Listen," he said testily, "I am holding a weapon. You are carrying a child. I will hurt you if need be. Either of you." He paused, thinking of his reputation. "Now please do as I say."

The woman's pale eyebrows arched, and a smile teased at the corners of her lips. She lifted her right hand mockingly to her forehead, and the Gentleman Brigand noticed how dark that hand was, how coarse, how sinewy: maybe she wasn't the easy mark he had thought. "My God, you big dark handsome brute!" she sneered. "I ought to throw a Buick at you." She swung the little boy to her other shoulder. The Gentleman dropped the screwdriver to his side, let it dangle there.

"Give it to me now," he ordered.

"I'm a stranger here," the woman continued. She paused. They stared at one another, hip to hip, the bandit and his victim. He thought of peaches blushing like spanked bums, saw in his mind's eye a line of pies cooling on a windowsill. This woman's feet, under her stifling shoes, would be broad and flat and brown, country feet. Her skin gleamed dully in the dark.

"So?" He could barely contain himself. Live by civility, die by it. A beat cop might happen upon them at any time.

"What kind of welcome is that? Do you want to prove every nasty thing I've heard about New York? You don't scare me, tough guy."

He raised the screwdriver to her throat. This was too much, pretty or not. Way too much. "Goddamn it!" he spat. "Hand it over, miss, or I'll gut you right here." He pulled back the screwdriver, embarrassed; it had left a mark like a tiny love bite.

The woman didn't flinch. A smile spread slowly across her face, and she said, "That's more like it. You should have said so in the first place. If you walk the walk, you have to talk the talk. *Now* I'll pay you. Here."

As she spoke this last word, she thrust the sleeping boy into the Gentleman Brigand's arms. He had to yank the screwdriver's blade quickly downward to avoid spearing the boy's bottom with it. The mother dug through her purse obliviously. What was she doing? She had handed him her child. He was holding her child while he robbed her, and she seemed to think nothing of it.

The boy, he noticed, was about the age of his own youngest son. The Gentleman brushed a few flecks of peanut shell from the coat the child was wrapped in. He removed the baseball cap. The boy had a fine head of yellow hair under it, a pug nose, pale eyelids the size of pennies. There was a smudge of chocolate on his cheek. The Gentleman looked at his charge's mother, who was rummaging through her purse intently, then licked his finger and wiped the stain away.

The child was blood-warm against his breast; the Gentleman could feel the boy's heartbeat. It suddenly occurred to him: this woman didn't deserve her son. She had given the boy away. He should turn tail now and run, take the boy home; over the wall was the safety of trees. A new life waited there. Darla would think that the towheaded youngster, like the warm clothes and marbled meats and impossible winter berries he had brought before, was precious manna — best not to ask where it came from. They could take care of him, love him as the boy's mother hadn't. This boy could be his — not his plunder, but his son — flesh of his flesh, fruit of the city. His.

But of course the Gentleman Brigand couldn't steal the child. The notion was crazy, and it passed as quickly as it had come, almost before he could register it. He squeezed his almost-son with something like regret, something like love, and the child's eyes flashed open.

The Gentleman Brigand stared down into the boy's clear, tiny eyes. There was no sound — but slowly the boy raised his chin, then just as slowly lowered it. It was unmistakable, couldn't have been anything but a nod; the child bobbed his head deliberately, almost solemnly, and then shut his eyes again and slept.

The Gentleman shuddered, shook the lunatic vision from his head. Crazy. A two-year-old boy in cahoots with his would-be kidnapper — it was absurd. Amazing, the things one thought to see. After this, he'd sleep well tonight. The fancy new electric fan he'd bought them would guarantee that.

The woman snapped her purse shut. "Here's your dough," she barked. She pressed a knot of bills, bound in a web of rubber bands, into her assailant's hand.

"Thank you very much," he said, peeling a five-dollar-bill off the roll and handing it back to her. "The BMT is straight up this street. Three blocks. Nice boy you got here." He hoisted the boy like a tankard, as if to show her which boy he meant. "Take good care of him. I hope he makes the bigs."

"I hope he doesn't," answered the woman affectlessly. "Baseball's nothing but trouble." She shook her head. "You ought to get a gun if you're going to be a real crook, mister," she added. "You're not real good at this. You ought to go to the picture show now and again, see how it's done. Read some Chandler. You want me to spell that?"

The Gentleman Brigand looked at his shoes. "Well," he said through bared teeth, handing the boy back to his mother, "it's been nice doing business with you, madam."

It was only then, my mother claimed later, that she realized what she had done. "Scared witless," she said, "scared speechless. Crazy with fear." But I knew better. I was there.

Mother, say what you will: it's true, I'm sure, that there was nothing like romance in it, that my version is spiteful and sexist and wrong, dead wrong. He was no swashbuckler, no stud, certainly no gentleman — just a garden-variety asshole, a stupid beast with ruined teeth and a shiv made of sharpened tin, a vicious creep who preyed on women. Just a criminal, nothing more, nothing less.

I know that. I know that, and still — sometimes, a little, if only to make you hurt like I have, like I do — sometimes I wish he had taken me. Sometimes I imagine his rough, strong stranger's hands under my armpits, his hot breath on my forehead; I feel the sureness of his grip, this man whose claim on me has no blood in it, no emotion, no history, no love; and I feel safe, Mother, safe at last.

Hooper Gets a Perm

1.

Hooper peers out of his cage, past the wrecked carpet slide and the wormy carousel, past the funnel-cake booth and the dry-docked swash boats. The park is dark and still but for the faint grumble of traffic beyond the live oaks at the gate. Another weird Friday night, in a lengthening string of them. But this marks — this must mark — a new low. Here he is, hunkered among piles of monkey scat in a cramped pen, a prisoner in Turvyland. He's scanning those oak leaves (well, where else to turn?) in search of nothing less than a savior. Don't sneer: when the tough find themselves trapped after hours in seedy amusement parks . . . well, like anyone else, the tough start flailing for straws.

Hooper can't be sure he's seeing the oaks' leaves, exactly — better to say he's staring into that billowy intensity of darkness that he figures for foliage. This two-bit carnival has a dozen security lamps, but only two are lit. The others have had their eyes put out by vandals. Even the working fixtures cast only a shy, sickly circle of blue; they whine in tune with the mosquitoes. Since childhood Hooper's favorite refuge in times of boredom has been reading, but the only available material tonight turns out to be crude homemade signs that must be the work of the park's owner, That Asshole Breaux. Cartoonish drawings on plyboard tout the traditional midway foodstuffs; placards above the restrooms read, mysteriously, "Pointers" and "Setters" (oh, now he gets it); and so on. Hooper can make out two nasty hand-lettered warnings in his corner of Turvyland, the pitifully dirty mini-menagerie: "Do not feed the albino otter funyuns THIS MEANS YOU" and, along the

169

slack barbed wire of the goat's pen, "Stay back unless you want to loose a finger. The MGMT." If he ever gets out of this mess, Hooper may use that last sign in freshman comp on Monday as an example of bad spelling and badder ambiguity: it's not clear whether one's finger will be taken by the animal or, per Cajun-Islamic justice, by the MGMT.

So here I am, thinks Hooper. Home again, home again, jiggety-jig. This isn't funny, doesn't sound even vaguely funny. He's behind bars in a chimp's box, parsing the scrawls of That Asshole Breaux. His manacled wrist hurts; the balls of his feet have gone rubbery; he has to pee. There are nasty mounds of turd all around his Italian loafers. And that's just the tip of the iceberg, the turd-berg. Tonight, his whole life is going to shit.

Hooper likes to think of himself as hyperarticulate. He is, after all, in his five-classes-per-semester-and-minimal-benefits way, an English professor. Now he summons up the word *scumber,* which he's pretty sure means "dung." He's not sure whether it applies to primates or only to dogs and foxes, but who's here to call him down? Who'd rob a schmuck handcuffed into a monkey pen in the swarming darkness of a Baton Rouge summer night . . . who'd deny him the pleasure of a recherché word to roll around his mouth while he waits for the cops to come and his life to start unraveling in earnest? Right, right. So Hooper, thank you very much, squats amid the scumber. Around him pullulates (uh-huh) the pestiferous (yes!) world.

Being in a cage sucks. Hooper supposes that's not a profound insight — hell, it's more or less the thought that brought him out here in the first place, in a halfwit attempt to save Taffy the Chimp — but it's a conviction he can hold, now, with new depth of feeling, with the credibility that comes from having been there, done that: Folks, let me tell you, being in a cage sucks! Some people, Hooper reflects, aren't cut out for social justice; they should do whatever it takes to choke back the urge. Next time he feels called to mount a spur-of-the-moment solo rescue, he'll resist. He'll go home and chase off (or at least numb) his foolish sympathies by smoking some bud and listening to Billie Holiday.

Hooper's parents are on the way into town from Fayet-
teville, Arkansas, and his house desperately needs defagging. Six
months ago, after years of doubt and then months of creeping re-
alization, he finally made the big lifestyle change, and he hasn't
found (oh, shut up!) the right way to break the news yet. Every
time Hooper talks to his dad, the old man makes a to-do of shoo-
ing the Mrs. and then whispers conspiratorially, "You been dip-
pin' the wick, son? Life ain't all litty-ture, you know." How do
you tell an old goat like that, a rough-and-tumble ex-sheriff, a
muskhound whose truckbed toolbox, all through your boyhood,
harbored porn mags called *EEEE-normous* and *Mountain Do!* —
you're his only son, he's your only father, and with your frail build
and crisp pleats and fragile sensibility and your goddamn book in
your goddamn hand all the goddamn time and your lack of interest in bow-hunting or cracking lawbreakers' skulls or college football you've already departed from him in virtually every way —
how do you tell this man (be it noted that he's the man, too, who's
retiring your graduate-school loans and buying you a new car and
still sending you, at thirty, a healthy allowance) . . . how do you
tell your dad, who thinks the only thing you have left in common
is a mutual appreciation for the feminine chassis, that you're
horny for boys now, sorry to disappoint but there it is?

Anyway, it's nine now, and they'll be in town by ten. Hooper's
mom has a key to his place, and he doesn't want them wandering
in to find the shrine to Antonio Banderas, the "Looking for the
Perfect Elf" votive candle, the inevitable musical-theater playbills.
And the bedroom — he can't even begin to think about the bedroom. Hooper's parents are old-fashioned; for God's sake, his
mother collects Hummels and antique finials. She has to have
known forever that he's gay, had to know it already twenty years
ago, when he ditched the motocross bike his father had just given
him and slunk into the house to help sift through earrings for
something to match her blue moiré dress — though she certainly
never bothered to tell Hooper (which might have saved him a lot
of time and trouble). If he made an announcement now, she'd be
supportive, in her baffled way; but Hooper can easily imagine what

will happen if, unwarned, she enters the bedroom. His mother has always had trouble when confronted with explicitness of any kind (hence the hiding place for Papa's porn), and Hooper's own assortment of finials and figurines will stop her heart in a hurry.

The upshot of all this is that Hooper's parents, finding his house deserted, will wonder what's happened to their boy and will investigate; they'll find plenty. When he comes home from jail, disheveled and exhausted, his fingertips black from booking, wrists raw from the chafe of the cuffs . . . well, it's not going to aid his argument that he's perfectly normal, the same son they've always known. He knows his father will boil the story down, as usual, to a lurid headline: HOMO IDJIT MAROONED ALL NIGHT IN CHIMP CAGE — NO GODDAMN SON OF MINE. Hooper's mother will get out the peroxide and bathe his wrists and weep soundlessly. Finally, she'll dredge up from unseen depths of feeling a few practical words: "Martin," she'll say, the tears watering her cheeks, "don't you keep mercurochrome in your medicine chest? You know you should."

The night has not begun well. Being in a cage sucks.

2.

Hooper has a sister, Lenore, who's eight years his senior and a minion of Lucifer. There's ample evidence of this; even as a child, Lenore bore enough Marks of the Beast to cover a whole squad of Antichrists. Besides her spite and meanness (and you wouldn't need more substantiation than that), there's always been her freakish ugliness. Lenore at sixteen: her hair was outlandishly big and butter-yellow, her nostrils flared so wide that you couldn't plug one with a thumb, and she was more or less unequipped with eyebrows, which was an obvious sign though nobody appeared able to read it but Hooper . . . this despite the fact (pay attention, people!) that she penciled them in as Mephisophelean curlicues, which she used to fence in her hellfire-orange (clue!) eyeshadow.

Thanks to Lenore, Hooper's enduring vision of Beelzebub is a cross between Dionne Warwick and Cyndi Lauper. Instead of a pitchfork, Lenore wielded a thin aluminum file, with which she sawed at herself nonstop. The rapid-fire rasp of metal on fingernail followed her everywhere, a skin-crawling accompaniment; this was the sound of sinners being peeled. Hooper cringed and pled for it to stop.

Still and all, the yokels of northwest Arkansas — as a kid, already, Hooper knew that though he found himself among them, he was not *of* them — had the bad taste to consider Lenore pretty. This bothered him until he realized that it was Satan's bounden duty to deceive mankind. It was beyond him what the Prince of Darkness would want with the homecoming tiara from Hindsville High, but the ways of the PoD are subtle . . . and Hooper reasoned that a reject from heaven might well yearn for crowns, even chintzy ones that seemed to be made of plastic cutlery.

But the proof was the monkey, the devil's animal familiar. When he was eight, Lenore got a pet capuchin monkey, a castoff from a small circus that was, Hooper thought he heard, "going to funk." (He was a sophomore in college when he suddenly realized, reading an e. e. cummings poem for class, that the word was *defunct;* and a weirdly intense feeling of letdown washed over him. He hoped — being nineteen and of a lyrical turn of mind, Hooper remembers, had sucked just as much as being locked in a dung-filled cage — that adulthood wouldn't turn out to be just a long, languid drift away from mystery, a chance for everything to resolve itself into the same old tedious crap. Would he wake up one day to find himself with a wife and kids? Would he be wearing hand-tooled boots, a manhole cover for a belt buckle? Afraid so. And not long after that he'd find tufts of fur bursting from his rapidly expanding ears, which would leave just the one sad step, or slide. We all make it: Hooper to funk.)

Lenore named her ringtail Dobie. For weeks Hooper heard her droning at it, working her witchy will. When he walked past her bedroom door he saw the monkey hanging upside down from a dowel his father had mounted in the corner, and Lenore would clam up and glare and her nostrils would gape and she'd point: There, my pretty, there is your target. The thing would — he swears it — turn its beastie head and bare its yellow teeth at him.

Lenore trained Dobie to attack whenever her brother made so bold as to leave his room. For a full year Hooper spent his home life encased in an astronaut helmet, fleeing from Lenore's pint-sized goon, who wanted to claw open his skull and eat his brains. Hooper got used to the sound of Dobie skittering after him with murder in mind, got used to the excited nickering as the monkey looked for a gap in the defenses, inured himself to the sight and sound of its tiny, strangely beautiful fingernails as they roved over his face shield. What Hooper couldn't stand was the creature's breath, a hybrid of brimstone and spoiled fruit. This stench was in his clothes, his thoughts, his dreams, was inside the helmet . . . was inside his head.

For a time Hooper thought conspicuous terror was the key to vanquishing his enemy; he'd be so pitiful that his mom would have to step in and save him. He tiptoed around the house in his space helmet, sweating, often with the screeching Dobie in pursuit. The situation finally came to a head when Mrs. Hooper got a call from school one day. Mrs. Warmoth couldn't understand: she'd decided, as a treat, to read the children a Curious George book, and little Martin had dived under his desk and started whimpering. Was there trouble at home? Did it involve — she didn't mean to meddle, but if you'd seen what she saw — could it be possible that Martin had been, well, menaced, maybe by a lanky man in a yellow hat or possibly other yellow clothing? These things could be taken care of nowadays by therapy — had anyone been making, you know, unnatural advances toward the boy?

Her sympathies engaged (nothing like public humiliation to do the trick), Hooper's mom plumped that evening for banishment of the offender: "Roger," she told her husband, "how do you expect Martin to grow up normal if he lives in a spacesuit and wears a monkey as a headdress? What kind of life is a boy going to lead who's scared to death of Curious George?" This sensible argument looked like it might carry the day . . . until Daddy's little girl burst into tears. Then Hooper's father reconsidered in a hurry: "He's a goddamn sissy in waiting," he said, ignoring his wife's frantic shushing gestures. "Maybe being chased by Dobie'll build him up some backbone. Now climb out from under the table and eat like a man, Martin. And get that geek flowerpot off your head. Fucking Buzz Aldrin. Just what the world needs: jarheads on Mars."

So, left to his own devices, Hooper plotted for months — idly — to get rid of his foe. He'd blow it up with M-80s; sell it to the first organ grinder he happened across; hire a swarthy hit man to whack it; stab it with a stalactite from the eaves of the house, then let the murder weapon melt untraceably away. He never did anything, mind you — and that, too, seemed a disappointment to his father. Imaginary vengeance was for pansies. A real boy would strangle his tormentor with bare hands and stomp the corpse into jelly. Hooper, unreal boy, dutifully strapped on his helmet whenever he was home. It wasn't so bad once you got used to it. The constant sweating kept him from turning pudgy, and he liked the feeling of being in an echo chamber. He pretended he was on Apollo 21, the mission to save all their sorry asses from hell, where Satan could be counted on to sic her man-eating gargoyles on the astronauts. Once subdued, they'd be flayed alive with giant emery boards. Hooper learned to play the TV loud so he could hear through plastic and over the frantic squeaks of his living wig. He snacked warily, his visor flipped up. He developed the only slightly paranoid notion that the world was fraught with perils that wanted to fly at your head. In short, Hooper made unmanly peace with his situation. To his shame, he learned to make do.

But then the monkey died. One day Dobie escaped and tried, with only fleeting success, to dangle by his tail from a high-voltage line. Hooper was immediately suspected. God, this was so simple: he'd been toying with a plan that involved lasers, a pig suit, and some arc-welding expertise, and it turned out all you had to do was leave the side door ajar and the stupid thing would go fry itself posthaste. Hooper couldn't be sure he hadn't somehow done it; at any rate Lenore was sure he did. "I'll kill everything you love most," she promised. "Pleasure is over for you, bucko." She pointed her file at him.

This is where the guilt began. Hooper was thrilled, of course. He could barely contain his pleasure. He watched his father scrape the charred remains off the roof of the Carons' van, and he felt like dancing. Had he really done it? Had he juiced Dobie? Had he started outside, come back in for a glass of Tang, seen the monkey scurry past, and then pushed the door shut behind it? As Dobie twitched and shrieked and smoked on the wire, had Hooper watched from the window with a ghastly smile? Had he, on his way out to "see what the commotion was about," calmly dropped his helmet — once and for all — into the trash? Memory is tricky. Hooper has vivid recollections of all these things, but neither more nor less vivid than his memory of gutting the monkey with a porch icicle and then being foiled by that damnably clever kid detective, Encyclopedia Brown. No . . . surely that helmet was too big to fit in the narrow kitchen can, and even Hooper — even at nine — would have covered his tracks more cleverly than that. But he'd wanted Dobie dead, and then Dobie was dead. Wasn't that enough? All afternoon Lenore sobbed on the porch swing, her eyebrows bleeding down her cheeks. She seemed a scintilla less evil than usual. She'd clawed at her coiffure in grief, rubbed away six inches of its height, and with lank hair and muted makeup she looked nearly human. When Hooper gave her a box of Kleenex, she didn't bother to threaten him. She took the tissue without looking up, honked loudly; it was a sound like a person might make. He'd planned to suck down a half-dozen Cokes and give Dobie a sarcastic twenty-one-belch sendoff, but he thought better of it. By the time his dad finished digging the hole, a pink Vesuvius of wadded tissue had mounted alongside Lenore, and it was almost kind of pathetic. Hooper's euphoria had disappeared. The scritch of the shovel in wet earth — how could this be? — seemed to him unutterably sad. Lenore made her father intone some fake Latin over the grave, and the four of them stood in the backyard and mumbled together. Hooper did not cry; he did not.

Later, he overheard his parents discussing him. "That," said his father, "is the most passive-aggressive child I've ever seen. He's got plenty of conniving, but no goddamn balls."

"Roger," scolded Hooper's mom. "He seemed all broken up this afternoon. You don't know that he had anything to do with it."

"Oh, no, not Mother's angel. You should have been there when I was chivvying old Dobie into the body bag. 'Do you think it hurt a whole lot, Daddy? Do you think it did?'"

Then, worriedly, Hooper's mom: "What did you say? I hope you were gentle."

"Hell yes I was gentle. I said, 'Naw, Junior. Gettin' sizzled to death feels kinda sweet, really.' The son of a bitch just stood there and smirked at me. And all that pissing and moaning over the corpse is just one more example of the kid not having convictions. For Christ's sake, either kill Dobie or mourn him. You can't do both."

What Hooper doesn't want to admit is that maybe it's the old passive aggression that got him in this reeking cage tonight. Maybe he not only wants his parents to know, but wants them to make the discovery in the most agonizing way possible. He can hear his father now: "Naw, Junior. Having an only son who's a faggot feels kinda sweet, really."

That wouldn't make Hooper smirk, but he can't say there wouldn't be a morsel of pleasure in it. Maybe his dad was wrong: maybe you can kill those you love and then grieve for your victims. Maybe you have to.

3.

Hooper knows why the caged bird sings: nothing else to do. It's quarter to ten. If he marched out of here and drove straight home, he might head them off. But his marching range, just now, is about eighteen inches. The trees have yielded no miracles, and won't.

So he pokes once more through the evening's ruins. He left the CD shop, his final stop, at five to seven — had every intention of limping home, playing out his role in the sham he calls his own. But when he heard the final segment of *All Things Considered,* everything seemed to click into place. It was a report about That Asshole Breaux, who'd been feeding Taffy and the others sawdust and stale cotton candy because park attendance had plummeted. The creep admitted, too — proudly — to calling cosmetics firms, asking if they had work for a chimp who'd outlived her usefulness: maybe they'd want to run a few thousand volts through her, ream her with lipsticks to see if they were carcinogenic, something along those lines? One company spotted a rare opportunity to make points with the animal rights lobby: Look! Here's a prick who's worse than us! They ratted Breaux out, and it became a national story.

Several things murkily entered into Hooper's coming here tonight. Taffy's situation was another black eye for Baton Rouge, which made news only for chemical spills, vampire cults, Nazi office seekers. He felt a twinge of injured civic pride; all those urbane Yankees in their Saabs and saltboxes would think the people of Red Stick were jackbooted Draculas who habitually fed their chimps spun sugar and chipped wood. Say it loud, say it proud: Hooper had a surge of good citizenship, idealism, patriotism. He did. Here was a chance to do something noble, more or less, and by God he needed it. Think globally, act locally: Hooper would take his cue from his brave colleagues with their brave bumper stickers. Okay, so there wasn't much he could accomplish, practically, to save this broken-down ape. But that wasn't the point. Quixote got credit for his wigged-out shit because he meant well; why shouldn't Hooper? Sure, his thoughts weren't strictly rational right now, but reason is the hobgoblin of puny minds, or however that goes.

And, all right, it didn't hurt that Taffy could play proxy for the long-dead Dobie, or that the mission would make Hooper, for once, a man not of thought but of action, the kind of son to be proud of. Maybe he needed to do penance in advance for the whoppers he'd be telling his parents tonight. Who knows? Maybe it just happened.

The wise feather consults the breeze; Hooper was nothing if

not a wise feather, and he licked a finger and held it up to the cosmos, waiting for a tickle, a whisper, a nudge. The gods obliged. He was groping in his backseat for a suitable gift/bribe, and when — poof! — he unearthed a cauliflower (it must have dropped out on the trip home from the grocery last weekend), it seemed an omen: If you find a coarse-lobed white cabbage in your car, then by all means visit the ape. Hooper, obedient to his auspices, cranked the car and aimed it toward Turvyland.

As quick as that — a pang of lunatic kindness, a cruel shove from the gods, and bingo . . . instant, life-altering blunder.

Chance played a role as well — had the park been open, Hooper would never have gone through with it. He'd have quit as usual. Maybe he was counting on that. It was, after all, an August Friday night, prime time for Ferris wheels and fresh-squeezed lemonade. He'd get to the park, discover a major impediment, shake his head, and say, "I tried, I really did." That might have been enough to appease his conscience — it didn't take much. But a group of angry locals had managed to get Turvyland shut down for a week on food-service violations. Worse, Hooper knew this already, though it surfaced into memory, dimly, only when he saw the bare flagpoles, the empty parking lot. Right, yes, he'd heard about this; but until now the knowledge had been just white noise, part of the constant background buzz of grievance to which Hooper paid no heed. God, everybody was pissed about something, and who had time to keep track?

The radio report (motive) plus the deserted lot (opportunity) put him in business. And in truth, the adventure hadn't started badly. He seemed to have a knack for the cloak-and-dagger (the benefit of a clandestine life — you get practice at deception). He slyly bypassed the main lot, which abuts a busy street, swung off the boulevard a few blocks later. He stashed his car at a funeral home, figuring they couldn't chance towing the wheels of the bereaved. Then he set off to find a back way into Turvyland.

This was easier than expected. Hooper trekked across an abandoned putt-putt course that had, in the glory days, capitalized on the park's overflow. Its fakey turf was now overrun by scrub — jack pine, elderberry, poison ivy, cat's-claw. Reclaimed by nature. Somebody had hauled off the windmill on one hole as a campy trophy or lawn ornament, and in its scar stood a cluster of yucca holding aloft a huge feather-duster bloom. Hooper hurried past. The back nine abutted Turvyland's rear fence, which was a litter-strewn sieve; the chain-link had been rolled up or cut in half a dozen places, and he squeezed through, being careful not to his snag his suit.

Inside, he was surprised to discover how dinky the park was: maybe twenty acres of sidewalks heaved up by roots, trash migrating with the wind, dented food trailers, stagnant mini-ponds traversed by footbridges that looked none too sturdy. At the far left perimeter was a clearing packed with rides, and the pissant menagerie was situated at the front, under a colonnade of live oaks. Hooper crept across Turvyland, dodging the wisps of paper that tumbled across his path. He had a kind of homing signal leading him on: the intermittent screak of the scarlet macaw that occupied Breaux's second-biggest cage.

This was Hooper's first venture into the park, but he had some idea of the setup. A few weeks ago he'd overheard an acquaintance — a guy named Croft — decrying the rotten conditions here. Croft was a volunteer docent at the city zoo, and a crusader of sorts; he'd played a role in getting the food inspectors out here. (Croft was also gay, and a looker. But he suffered, at least by reputation, the activist's typical malady: his overfed conscience had starved out any sense of humor.) Croft had told Hooper's friend Rick that there were, all told, a dozen animals, whatever elderly or injured discards Breaux could get on the cheap. Most were domestic critters he'd trapped, or hit with his car: a turkey too old and stringy for eating, an amputee armadillo, a goat who was short a horn (the master impresario tried, for a time, to bill it as a unicorn); and so on. There were a few oddities and exotics — the macaw, the albino otters, and of course Taffy — but they hadn't set Breaux back much either. Turvyland was one of a dying breed, the roadside attraction, and it was easy for him to acquire animals from his old competitors as they retired. He offered to take these screeching liabilities off people's hands, to save them feed and board-ing costs.

Hooper made his way down the gallery of trees. The pens were arranged in a rough circle around the one showy cage, Taffy's, and the chickenwire box that held the macaw. He reached the bird's hutch first, and it was enough to ignite even his sluggish sense of injustice. It was a six-foot square made of warped scrap lumber, wire, and industrial staples. Hooper looked in at the bird, which was still jabbering angrily. Its plumage was lusterless, worn, but with remnants of beauty intact; the bird looked like a regent down on her luck — sitting on a park bench toping out of a sack, but still wearing her ermine collar and fading velvet cape. Hooper tapped on the wire, cooed at his new friend. He spoke no jungle bird, but he meant something like, I'm with you, babe. I feel your pain.

The macaw seemed only now to notice him. It flailed its wings, shrieked, hurled itself at him. Hooper leaped back just as the bird crashed into the wire; it lay on the mossy floor of its hutch, stunned. Or maybe dead . . . had Hooper managed to kill another blameless creature? No, the bird was slowly reviving, regaining its bearings. It got up, tottered a few steps, then flew up to its dead-branch perch. It fixed a dazed, hateful stare at him.

So much for his Dr. Dolittle fantasy . . . and he hadn't even met Taffy yet. He could see her now, though, over the top of the macaw's quarters; roused from her torpor by the noise next door, he guessed. She was standing with each hand wrapped around a bar, like the falsely accused in a prison flick. Hooper collected himself and moved on toward his goal.

In the car he'd imagined a tender chat with Taffy, to let her know he was sorry she'd been mistreated. The point was to be something like, Not all humans are assholes. I'm here, eh? Me friend of monkey many years. But what did he really want from her? Absolution? Advice? Was he planning to spirit her home, wrap her in a blanket, and nurse her to ruddy good health so she could make her space mission and save us from the Russkies after all? Things had turned turbid on him again. He felt his high purpose evaporating. This break-in was starting to take on the familiar taint of a bad idea. What else was new? His was a life full of misguided whims pushed and pushed and pushed until they yielded, sometimes spectacularly, the irresistible secret at their core. The siren song of debacle: I know this is dumb, but why? Only one way to find out . . .

He wasn't prepared. A fillip of breeze carried the same nasty odor Dobie'd had years before, and Hooper felt the old fear and loathing shudder over him. Taffy had let the bars loose, backed off. She was poised on her knuckles and the balls of her feet, waiting to see what fresh torture this human had to offer.

She was such a different animal. She was huge, comparatively speaking; Dobie had weighed maybe ten pounds, but Taffy must be five feet tall, one-fifty. Heavier than Hooper. This was not a monkey one could wear on one's head. This was not a pet, not a prop for one's personal drama. And she looked — with her wrinkled features, watery eyes, and patches of grizzled hair — she looked so world-weary, so sad and smart, so old. It's a cliché, but so human.

Now was his moment. Do or die. Sink or swim. But what to say? Hooper half expected the same reception he got from the macaw down yonder, but the chimpanzee didn't fling herself at the bars, didn't hiss or bare her teeth. She sat there patiently, waiting for Hooper to reveal his reason for coming. He didn't know, couldn't tell. His mind had gone blank. He looked down for a second, and when he raised his eyes he saw that Taffy had turned her back to him, was splayed out near the bars. The light was beginning to fail, but there was no mistaking this shocking incarnadine flash. Hooper blinked at the vivid red of her genitalia, and Taffy swung her head sideways to gauge his response. Was she . . . rearpresenting? This was more forgiveness than Hooper had bargained for. Another lie exposed: he'd envisioned talk, not action. How did you explain to a wanton chimp that, in more ways than one, you're not that kind of guy? Hooper swallowed hard a few times, examined his shoes, the cage's concrete pedestal, the dying ring of Mexican heather surrounding it.

He snapped to attention when the first glob hit his forehead. What? What? Hooper started talking fast, bobbing and weaving, babbling reassurances, explaining himself. He wasn't really a monkey-killer, it hadn't happened but that once, and then it was the power company's fault, and half-suicide, and there'd been plenty of provocation, and . . .

But the more agitated Hooper got, the more frenziedly Taffy pelted him with her poop. She was flinging it hard, chattering all the while. She'd made a generous offer on behalf of her family and gender, and he'd rebuffed her, rejected them all. Forgiveness was never to be his. What kind of pervert was he?

It was at this point, as Hooper cowered before Taffy's cage, loudly baring his soul and dodging her crumbly shit-missiles, that the real commandos had arrived to save her.

4.

On his way home from school this afternoon, Hooper figured he'd buy a Johnny Mercer disc. He has so little in common with his parents these days that he's willing to stoop to ploys like this. The plan: he'd put on mutually agreeable music, Mom and Pop would bob their heads out of politeness or appreciation, and then — since they were enjoying it so much — he'd accidentally turn Johnny up too loud, choke the talk to a trickle. A quick jog through his sanitized apartment (which his father's never seen), a few drowned-out pleasantries, and his parents would plead exhaustion and retire to the hotel. The worst would then be past: tomorrow he'd give a campus tour (with emphasis on Huey Long's brazen frauds, which would strike Hooper's dad as heroic); they'd eat crawfish, try to wrap their country tongues around the phrase *Laissez le bon temps rouler,* then visit the Tabasco factory like good little tourists. By Sunday noon Hooper's parents would be safely on the road, and his elf candles and Tzabaco catalogs would be restored to prominence.

The hard part was tonight. The vision of his parents sitting on that couch, in that room, among the ghostly reverberations of Hooper's pleasure-cries . . . the idea of the small package in his bedroom closet that would contain every secret flamboyance of his new life. Unbearable. That cardboard carton would be a kind of Telltale Box, pulsing under the floorboards for as long as the elder Hoopers stayed. And the phone might ring at any moment: "Buona sera, Geppetto. How's about making me a real boy?" So Johnny had better be in good — make that loud — voice this evening.

It wasn't just fear of discovery, though. Not at all. Hooper felt awful about not confiding in his mother. She was a saint, loved him no matter what; she'd never abandon him. But sainthood had a drawback, too, its rigid rule of honesty. He could never ask her to help delude his father. Which left him in a tough spot.

The most uncomfortable thing to admit to himself, the most vexed and tangled aspect of all, was that he'd been battling pangs of dissatisfaction, even shame. Not about preferring men, certainly — his sexuality was what he wanted; it was his identity, his genetic destiny. No control over that. But . . . the way he'd been going about it? His vita nuova had started with an ecstatic burst of lust, and for a time that seemed to Hooper the point. Being gay was, after all, a "sexual preference"; what defined you was having sex, so the more you had, the gayer you were. Every erotic kick during the first few months had been deepened, redoubled, by the knowledge that he was finally celebrating who he was, who he is.

But lately the slap-and-tickle's lost its luster. Over the past few months he's embraced not only a string of men but also a life that gives him license, finally, to revel in the things he cares about most; and this turns out to be at least as important as the physical stuff. Hooper wouldn't go so far as to say he's happiest when devising a costume for Lazarus, the glorious gay masque in New Orleans; or sitting among friends and snorting over the vacuous speeches and fashion abortions of Oscar night; or trading Cole

Porter couplets over Bloody Marys on the porch at The Columns, the run-down hotel that played the whorehouse in *Pretty Baby* . . . but he's definitely happy at those times. What he's bought into is a ready-made world for exploring: these are stereotypes, but stereotypes he can tweak and use, take on or off as he chooses — swish today, butch tomorrow; Paris esthete now, Hindsville redneck later — to puzzle out who he is, in all his moods and incarnations. He's learning himself.

Hooper remembers, for example, how wonderful it was the first time he ate with friends at the Ho Chi Minh Grill, in the Quarter. The fare is grubby Thai food served on chipped plates, but it's whisked to the tables by gorgeous androgynes got up like Carmen Miranda. He watched one sashay across the room to take their order, meanwhile adjusting his cornucopia. Admit it: If confronted by a cross-dressing Ganymede toting a platter of *larb*, could you mumblingly order a Bud? You could not, do not. Instead you say something glib, racy, goofy: "My, what fine firm fruit you have. You look yummy enough to pit." You ask for a "Pimm's cup, super-extra Pimmy, darling." And then, amid the stained velvet curtains and tinkling mismatched glassware and bouzouki music (this place is velly eclectic) and the smooth, lovely boys with their falsies and pineapples, you begin to appreciate the extent to which being gay is about making your life a perpetual festival; it's a way of living at a higher emotional pitch than the drones and burghers and mudsticks can manage. It's all so clever and bubbly and bright. And, too — this matters if you're rich and white, a graduate of Vanderbilt, a wearer of silk bow ties — for once you're part of a living, breathing minority community. You're among the oppressed.

Which isn't to say that the sex doesn't matter, or isn't good — it is, *cher*, it is. But the most liberating thing about Hooper's transformation may be that he has, at last, an audience for his catty wit, has friends eager and able to engage in repartee about anything from Lotte Lenya to L L Cool J, Lincoln logs to L. L. Bean.

When Hooper's lust began to ebb, it raised ugly questions:

Could he have been wrong? Had this been, after all, just a bout of hedonism that would now pass? The answer to each of these was no — he was sure of it — but nevertheless he felt disconcerted, cranky. He grew hypersensitive to insults, slights, fishy glances. He found himself looking for chances to vent righteous indignation. And the less randy Hooper felt, the more ostentatiously he ogled.

His closest English Department friend, Anja, his lunch partner three times a week, was the first to complain. She's been picking at him of late for becoming a cliché, with his fifty-dollar avocado hair products and crisply pressed chinos and snatches of opera — and the way he interrupts her a dozen times, during the walk across campus to lunch, to leer at some "feshing youf." Her smiles at his lechery have grown fainter and fainter, and two weeks ago when he started rhapsodizing once again about a passing sprite, she lit into him.

"The poor thing doesn't know he's gay yet. But he is, darlin', he is," Hooper said.

"Martin," sighed Anja, rolling her eyes, "this is really tired. At first it seemed like innocent fun. You were a teenager again, drowning in hormones. It was kind of cute. But there's getting to be something creepy about it. You bitch about the Bible-bangers assuming you're on the make all the time . . . but hey, you're on the make all the time. I mean you personally. What makes that kid gay is that you have the hots for him. No more, no less."

"Well, well, true colors at last," Hooper answered. "I never figured you for a —"

"Come off it," said Anja. "I wouldn't like you being a hetero lounge lizard either. I thought it was about being differently sexual, not more so. And why put on a show for my sake? I know who you are; you suit me fine." She paused; her look turned affectionate, nervous. "Besides, I worry about you, Hoop."

This was perilously close to a subject Martin refused to talk about, think about. It called — without delay — for a lightsome dodge, a retreat. He summoned up his best Noël Coward. "No, no. I worry about you, Sopping Blanket. Being so dreary violates God's law, and one of these days you'll pay. Pre-verts always do. It's unnatural."

Anja's an enigma. Mild, quiet, prim. Dull by choice and not by nature; it's unfathomable. Hooper's new playmates think she's a waste, an unfun person from good-fun stock. Her bloodlines are impeccable: In the early 1970s, in the *Journal of Psychoactive Drugs,* Anja's mother published a scholarly treatise based on emergency-tent research at Grateful Dead and Led Zeppelin concerts held on consecutive weekends in San Francisco. Zep fans, she concluded, grooved on hallucinogens, while Deadheads stuck mainly to grass. Or maybe, she hedged, Deadheads — being of naturally sunny disposition and possessing greater pharmacological expertise, were just less prone to uncool freakouts and bad trips in public. Anja's father had postponed college for an eight-month stint as a hobo, and once, trying to relive the salad days, he led the family on an ill-fated camping vacation — Anja will say only "It wasn't Disney World" — that involved riding the rails of Appalachia, roughing it on abandoned sidings, cooking over oil drums.

Their daughter, flesh of their flesh, teaches idiot frosh how to write persuasive essays about the need for campus parking. Sometimes Hooper will see Anja in the coffee shop, reading some earnest drudge like Doris Lessing, and he'll have a trippy vision of her mother at Kezar, laughing with a bored orderly while "The Crunge" booms overhead. She has a pad on which to catalog concertgoers' impairments. She takes a last drag of the doobie they're sharing, asks, "You figure that purple-faced guy in the dashiki was speeding?" Letting this image fade, Hooper focuses in on Anja — no makeup, muted clothes, pilgrim shoes with buckles — drinking her unaugmented coffee. She has a habit, when the cup is empty, of soaking up any spillage on the saucer with a napkin, then softly tamping the cup-bottom dry. It doesn't compute. And yet she seems perfectly content, in her way.

Theirs is a weird friendship, but it's lasted. Despite the differences of personality, they genuinely like one another. He teases her about how boring she is; she makes him eat at McDonald's to get in touch with his grease-loving, middle-America side. "Got to get you some gravity, Hoop," she says. "I'll settle for the waistline kind."

Today, as they made their way from the Golden Arches back to their offices, Anja took on a solemn look. "Hoop," she said, "I'm sorry, but I can't help you tonight. I just wouldn't feel right about it." Hooper had asked if she'd drop by, maybe pretend in a low-key way that they're an item. She's the only woman he ever talks about, and his parents have assumed . . . But Hooper knew all along that she'd say no; masquerades weren't Anja's style. So he'd already constructed a cover story to account for her absence: tonight, alas, she has to be up at Angola, teaching death row inmates to write sonnets. She's so compassionate, he'll say, so devoted to the civilizing effects of education. He's proud of his Anja. Maybe for good measure he'll invent a study that says the condemned are better prepared for the Big Jolt if they've mastered rhyme schemes.

"I'm sorry," Anja repeated. She reached into her bookbag, handed Hooper a folded manuscript. "A present," she muttered. "From me. A little something I've been working on. You know, trying to dry the blanket a little. I'm thinking of becoming maybe a little amusing, now and then, but I don't want to embarrass myself. Let me know what you think. And please don't take it the wrong way . . ."

That last remark would have set him to furious reading on the spot, but there wasn't time. Hooper had three hours of student conferences scheduled, and by the time he and Anja trudged upstairs to the department, two early arrivals were huddled outside his door. When Hooper finally closed the door behind the last supplicant, settled into his chair, and reached into his drawer for the flask of bourbon, he spotted Anja's manuscript on the desktop. He checked his watch: five-thirty. The CD shop was open until seven, and that would leave time to eat a leisurely dinner, smoke a dessert joint, and hide all incriminating material at home. He uncrimped the pages and began to read, with steadily increasing amazement.

Hooper Gets a Perm

Adrift and abed, again. As Hooper watched the late-morning sun drift across the floor, he did a bit of stock-taking. Hooper, old boy, he told himself — he was prone, in taking stock, to the pompous: where better than in fancy to be fancy? — Hooper, old boy, what you need . . . what you need, for true, is a half-decent inner life. His face was puffy, his mouth dry, and his filmy teeth ached; he might feel rotten, but Hooper knew a truth when he thought one. The word *desideratum* popped into his head. Desideratum: an improved inner life. Hooper had a sudden flush of pride. How many of the hurt and hungover were marking the sun's creep across their blond floors and plotting new, better, deeper inner lives? How many had marshaled a five-syllable word to the cause? Hooper couldn't vouch for anyone else, but he for one was no ordinary lush. His reverie was interrupted by the sound of an awful bandsaw or fan belt or something in the kitchen; the noise gradually resolved itself into what Hooper could identify as a horrific imitation of Glynis Johns singing "Send in the Clowns." Wincing, he glanced over to see that last night's hugger-mugger of hastily shed clothes was undisturbed in its place by the door. Oh, Lord . . . another night of passion mislaid, of youth and money misspent, of pearls miscast before swine. And this morning's misgruntlement, missatisfaction, misgust. Old hat, all of it. Another pretty-boy in his kitchen, in the buff, squeezing citrus and singing Sondheim. Another little serving wench with sticky knuckles and bad taste; another hole that would need digging out of. The mind boggled; the mind boggled.

Hooper rolled over, ground fists into his itchy eyes. He could hear the clatter of breakfast trays as his consort — what was this one's name: Chap? Henryk? Leif? Testostero? — made ready to sweep him away via *petit dejeuner*. Hooper knew he would not, could not, resist. How to spurn a man who stole out of bed to make you breakfast? One who was resourceful enough to make a tarnished jigger serve for an egg cup, a lens cleaner for a cozy? Whose perfect moons

189

of fingernail held scraps of pulp from fruits he ruined just for you? And if the egg — a beautiful tan thing, coddled in its prim Victorian cup and cap — if the egg were echoed, just below the advancing tray, by two of its flawless brethren, and if he'd wrapped Hans (semi-erect, left-leaning, flopping with every step) with pungent slices of bacon . . . tell me the word *desideratum* wouldn't take on a new meaning for you, too.

When breakfast was past, the world seemed supernally bright, and Hooper was in no mood, anymore, for the petty agonies of contemplation. The inner life would have to wait. This was no time to begin an overhaul of the soul, not with the tang of bacon on his lips and the word *Sizzlean* tumbling delightfully through his mind. Not this morning. The inner life be damned, today, thought Hooper. Today I will get a perm.

He smiled at the idea, felt a tender hand on his neck. "The uncontamined life," said Hooper, "is not worth living."

"Mmmff," said Testostero.

The perm could wait till afternoon.

Hooper, a bit shaken, set down the pages, permitted himself a second belt of bourbon. So it had come to this: his life was such a joke that it moved even Anja to comedy. After all this time, she'd emerged from stodgy exile . . . to poke fun at him. Him, her friend. Ah, those rambunctious jabs and japes; that goddamned joie de vivre. What was with her? Frankly, he liked her better as a lump. This was like being dissed by Abraham Lincoln, back from the dead to torment you with vile pork fantasies; it was like being raked over the coals on Leno by the pope: "D'ja ever wonder about this Hooper clown?" asks the pontiff. "I mean, what's his deal?"

Most irksome of all was that Anja . . . well, she hadn't entirely missed the mark: Hooper, what you need, for true, is a half-decent inner life. Chap, Henryk, Testostero. She'd feel guilty about this. Tonight there would be an anxious call — to make sure he isn't hurt, to let him know she just wants to be a good friend, and lately he's seemed a little, uh, troubled.

He wasn't sure he'd put it quite that way. More like he's, uh, fucked. Fucked: Hooper felt a sudden flush of pride. How many hopeless cases were sitting behind closed doors, enjoying a furtive snort of sour mash? How many, just insulted by their best friends, were headed home to lie to the people they loved about the most important element of their lives? And how many would be able to marshal an obscene monosyllable to the cause?

Okay, Hooper warned himself. Enough drama-queen stuff. Eyes on the prize. Get the CD, go home, hoodwink the parents, live to lie another day. He slipped the story into his desk, drew a deep breath, and left.

5.

The commandos were just suddenly there. Hooper heard a loud throat-clearing, turned to find three ninjas in blackface. Two of them had taken the trouble to crouch. It wasn't clear whether they were doing so to menace him or to give themselves a chance to sidestep Taffy's stray tosses, but it didn't matter: the fusillade ceased.

"Are you deaf, buddy?" asked the one standing straight up. "Fred Astaire here" — he nodded to his right — "only fell down twice."

"Shut up," said Astaire, abandoning his crouch. "You'd think a rich asshole like Breaux would pay his light bill. This time of day, the footing is treacherous."

Homo erectus, who looked to be the leader, chuckled. "Tell you what. Here's the flashlight. Go look for the complaint box." For the moment they seemed uninterested in Hooper, whose first, irrational thought — upon being confronted by three Jolsonish thugs in the gathering darkness of Turvyland — was to hope they hadn't overheard him: someone could get the wrong impression, listening to a grown man amid a hail of dung asking a chimp to absolve him of blame for a passive-aggressive pet murder that probably never happened twenty years before.

Hooper checked behind him, where the third man had wandered. Taffy was quiet now, her attention riveted on the backpack full of fruit that ninja number three was showing her.

"Take care of the lock," ordered the leader, and Astaire produced a bolt cutter. Number one turned back to Hooper. "What were you doing to that chimpanzee? They don't usually fling crap. That's a gorilla behavior. You don't get off on pestering captive animals?"

"It was nothing," Hooper managed. "Really. Just a teensy misunderstanding. Private. You know." This sounded insane, even to him.

"Sure, buddy, sure. Takes all kinds. I especially liked that 'moral intelligence' bit. That's priceless material. Were all the booths at the cathedral full?"

Had Hooper really said that? He's teaching Flannery O'Connor this semester, and as he faced off with Taffy, he'd recalled the laughable plea for dignity that a one-armed cretin named Shiftlet makes in one story: I am a man, he proclaims, I have a moral intelligence. But had Hooper really spoken those words aloud? Jesus.

"You don't work for Breaux, eh? What are you doing here?"

He was afraid to confess to being a mere trespasser, someone who (his father was right) lacked enough conviction to kidnap a monkey in the name of justice. No, he was just a media-fueled looky-lou, a rubbernecker, an amateur. What had brought him here? And why did he want so desperately for these minstrel-show commandos not to think ill of him?

"I'm fond of monkeys," claimed Hooper. "Used to have a beauty named Dobie, a capuchin. I heard about Taffy's plight on the radio." Beauty? Plight?

"See? I fucking told you this guy was an NPR wonk," said the leader to Astaire. "Who else would just stand there getting pounded with turds and not even think to run? Who else would try to save her with a cute little soliloquy and a . . . hey, what the fuck is that thing, a volleyball?"

The last ninja was in the cage now, passing Taffy fruits one by one, like a nurse assisting in surgery. When Taffy got mad, Hooper had tried to skirt around the cage and shove the cauliflower through to distract her, but it had been too big. While sustaining heavy casualties, he'd finally managed to shear off a few florets and force it through the bars. The third man bent down to where Hooper's offering had rolled. There was only enough light left for Hooper to see his teeth, which flashed into a smirk. "Cauliflower," he reported.

"Collie-flower. What's that about, chief?"

Hooper did the best he could. "I thought Taffy needed some B complexes," he said. He had no idea what he was talking about, but the leader nodded.

"Good man," he said. "B complexes. You NPR people are fuckin' useless, all right, but you mean well." He reached into his ammo vest, pulled out a gun, waggled it casually. "Sorry, but you're going to have to step inside. Can't be helped."

Only then did Hooper realize what was happening. It had seemed comic-bookish up to now, like no one could get hurt. But these were rabid animal-rightsists, subject to all the wacko stringencies of fanaticism. They were men of ruthless purpose; they might kill him. How had he failed to see until now who was in control? Of course, of course: he was just a budding queer with a hypertrophied sense of sympathy, a residue of monkey remorse, an hour to kill. He was no champion of animals — for God's sake, there was Big Mac still on his breath from lunch. So who would free Taffy? Right — the folks wearing burnt cork on their faces and packing heat; the ones who came equipped with handcuffs and wire cutters rather than old guilt and cauliflowers.

Hooper has to say this of his captors: they didn't rough him up. They seemed embarrassed to leave him this way. Ninja number three even offered him an orange that Taffy'd passed up.

"I hate," Hooper stammered, "I hate to see a monkey suffer.

I told you. I'm fond of monkeys. Solidarity now!" He gave a thumbs-up. As a last-ditch effort to effect his release, this was pretty feeble, so he tried to up the ante. "I used to carry Dobie around on my head, until he got electrocuted."

This piqued some interest. "Electrocuted?" asked the leader.

Hooper hadn't meant to say so much, and he was smart enough not to burst into tears and confess, à la Jimmy Carter, that he'd killed the little bastard many times in his heart. "A sad day," he finished. "Monkeys and I are *muy simpáticos*."

Astaire stepped forward, unable to take any more. "Taffy," he said, "is not a monkey. She's an ape. Chimpanzees make tools; they practice medicine; they're far nobler creatures than us. They are not fucking monkeys." He clicked the cuffs a notch tighter and glared, his eyes a brilliant white against his charcoal face. He stood inches away, seeming to command an answer. He oozed a potent vegetarian stink. Hooper tried to look thoughtful. Yes, he understood, got the point; he knew what an ape was, hoped he hadn't offended.

The third man was holding hands with Taffy, who wore a bemused look. She was eating a plum.

Hooper raised his free hand to his underarm, tickled the fabric of his shirt. "Ooga-booga," he explained. "Right, sure. I like them, too."

The ape-men snorted contemptuously, then turned and led Taffy away. They were talking to her in normal tones and complete sentences, like a person: something about reparations, promising a war-crimes tribunal.

The leader stopped to slit open the macaw's hutch. "Later, NPR," he called over his shoulder. "Have a pleasant stay."

So they hadn't killed Hooper. On the other side of the ledger, though, were several items: They'd caught him in a word error, ridiculed his vegetable offering . . . and they'd cuffed him, possibly forever, to the worn tin bars of the cruelly small cage of Taffy of Turvyland.

6.

Nearly eleven now, and it's all over. Hooper's parents are rooting around his apartment, beginning to panic. In the morning either the cops or That Asshole Breaux will find him here, and he'll trade these handcuffs for another set. The phrase "black night of the soul" flits prettily through Hooper's head. Yes, indeed.

Until now he'd thought — didn't everyone? — that no spot on earth was so eerily romantic as an amusement park after hours. The luminous carousel stallions arrested in mid-snort; the funhouse ghouls that might leap to life at any moment; all that nonsense. It turns out to be just another grim, dumb spot where you're assailed by all your shitty worries . . . though admittedly his mood may be dampened a bit by circumstance.

Hooper could write a hell of an exposé about Taffy's living conditions. The pen is a twelve-foot circle, concrete tilted to a center drain that's fouled with hair, jujubes, a plastic comb, three fluorescent condoms. A clown's mask has been painted on the floor — the drain forms a wen on the bulbous nose. If patrolling this garish face, day after day, year after year — if that wasn't enough to drive Taffy mad or stupid, well, the paint's probably leaded, too. A mad bright clown, poison paint, and your only intellectual stimulus is That Asshole Breaux, a man who thought confessing to chimp torture would bring customers out in droves to eat soft-serve ice cream and have their weights guessed. No wonder Taffy was out of sorts.

Right now, though, Hooper's preeminent concern is his bladder, which is near exploding. He's been reluctant to void in here. Some of his mother's lessons die harder than others. Taking a whiz in the cage would be tacky — and piddle shyness is about the only thing separating him, now, from reversing eighty million years of evolution in three hours. There are practical issues as well. Pissing would probably set the remaining animals — the finger-eating goat, the swamp rats, the wild turkey, the maimed armadillo — to bellowing. If the sharp-nosed cops can tell his piss from Taffy's, they'll heap a public urination rap on top of everything else. And worst of all, he'd have to endure the smell all night.

But it's too late for delicacy. He gingerly unzips with his free hand, lets arc a mighty stream. God, it feels good. He makes a point of soaking the clown's terrible eyes: Take that, Chuckles! As he prepares to shake, he recalls his father's bizarre warning as Hooper stood, one long-ago Saturday, before the long metal trough at a Razorback football game: "Keep in mind, son — more than one wiggle is masturbation." Hooper's dad smilingly shook his hands dry and left; the men at the sink chortled; Hooper kept his eyes grimly on the goal, which was to lift his feeble pee over the high, rusted lip. He couldn't have been more than nine at the time, and he remembers being perplexed: Do some men have more than one wiggle? Master who?

He's reaching to close his zipper when — of course — he sees a shadow advancing from the trees. But even as a kid he knew not to panic under these circumstances, and this is no time for backsliding. He's been visited with enough indignities today, isn't about to add a mangled penis to his list of problems. Hooper feels a rush of inappropriate pride as he stuffs and zips: he's taken a few blows, but he's still a cool customer. He tries to coax some defiance into his voice. "Who's there?" he calls. "Who is it?"

The figure steps closer. "You're not Taffy," it says lightly. "You're Hooper."

Hooper has to think a moment before he places the face. It's Croft, the busybody who landed him here. Croft is (in Hooper's circle) an anomaly: sweet-tempered, earnest, careful, kind. He is a vegan, a high-church Episcopalian, an unstoppable do-gooder. He feeds the homeless, tends the infirm, docents the decent at the zoo. He is also handsome: olive skin, slim build, a fabulous sense of style. A few months ago, at the gay club near campus, Hooper — yes, Anja, okay, on the make — had asked Rick about the good-looking man at the next table. "That's Croft," said Rick, rolling his eyes. "Doesn't drink, smoke, or speak ill of anyone. Thinks cold cuts have feelings. Is said, in bed, to use the word *cuddlefest*. In short, a male lesbian. The world's least fun fag." Snide grins all around the table, and Hooper crossed him off the list. Since then he's spoken to Croft briefly a few times, eavesdropped on a conversation or two, noted with private satisfaction some of Croft's fastidious habits: starched collars, perfect creases, professional manicure.

Croft has made no further move toward the cage, said nothing. He's just standing there, fifteen feet away, reconnoitering. He doesn't begin flailing his arms or wailing for help, doesn't ask a barrage of excited questions: What are you doing in there? Where's Taffy? Should I fetch the authorities? He's cool, patient; he's approaching Hooper the way you would a nut who's perched on a high bridge and looking longingly at the chop below.

They stare at one another forever, it seems. It's Hooper who breaks the silence. "Listen . . . you wouldn't want to get me out of here, would you? It could be your good deed of the day." Does he have to be sarcastic even now?

Croft smiles, takes one step forward. "I'll give it a shot. Don't have my rescuing-smartasses-from-cages merit badge yet." He rattles the paper bag he's carrying. "Want some overripe fruit? That's how Taffy likes it."

Hooper demurs, rattles his chains against the bars. Hello? I have more pressing needs than eating a spotty banana? Everyone offers fruit, but no one seems to want to unchain him.

Still Croft is in no hurry. He puts his hands on his hips. Are those handcuffs? They are. Might there by any chance be a story here somewhere? Well, yes. Would Hooper mind? No, he supposes not: sing for his supper. He wants out soon, before anyone else gets here — it's like Grand Central tonight. But he's in no rush now to get home, face the music.

So he tells it, starting with his arrival at Turvyland, and Croft listens with a look of untroubled mirth. This calms Hooper some, makes it seem like he's telling a frisky anecdote rather than the tale of how his whole world went into the tank. "That's the deal," Hooper concludes. He's warmed to the task. "They stuck me in here and spirited away their monkey. Taken hostage by Amos and Andy, then traded even up for Bonzo."

"Taffy's an ape, actually," corrects Croft. "They're smart and gifted creatures: they use tools. Some say they even practice medicine." Hooper growls; he's heard this before. "Not that that matters much right now," Croft amends. "By the way, I don't get the joke. That was a joke? Who are Amos and Andy?" He cocks his head, smiles again. Unembarrassedly. Hooper is amazed to discover that this slowness-on-the-uptake — the kind of failure that earned Croft the undying scorn of Rick and company — doesn't faze his rescuer. For some reason it doesn't faze Hooper, either; in fact he finds it endearing, in a way. Croft goes on: "How come they brought cuffs, do you think?"

"Maybe they're rogue cops, or bondage boys," Hooper replies. "Maybe the PETA crazies are just well equipped these days. How should I know?"

Croft has advanced, in a creep as subtle as continental drift, to a spot alongside the cage. He sets down his sack, swings open the door, steps in. After a pause to let his eyes adjust, he picks his way nimbly through the minefield of Taffy's and Hooper's wastes. He takes the prisoner's hand, looks over his stained suit, his smudged face. Croft's fingers are strong, papery, warm; they seem to exude tranquillity. "These are just novelty cuffs," Croft assures him. "I can pop these off with a hairpin. It won't take a minute."

This isn't at all what Hooper expected: not a simp, not an idiot. Croft is still holding his hand, looking into his eyes, and Hooper feels an odd urge to warn him: Nothing there. Nobody home. He notes again how attractive this man is: the straight line of his jaw, the shadowy concavity above his lip. Then he sniffs the acrid tang of urine. He knows that Croft, a born nurse, a caregiver, a samaritan, would look past this petty humiliation without a thought, but he has to say something. "I'm sorry," he whispers. "I've been in here for hours. When you gotta go, you gotta go."

Croft laughs, says, "When you gotta glow, you gotta glow."

Hooper is amazed. That's from "Glow Worm," the Johnny Mercer song he loves most. "You a Mercer fan?" he asks.

The question sends Croft into an ecstasy of eloquence. He positively burbles. "Johnny, Hoagy Carmichael, the whole gang. Never been a songwriter better with an intricate rhyme than Johnny. He's the best. 'Thou aeronautical boll weevil/Illuminate yon woods primeval.'"

"Glow for the female of the specie/Turn on the AC and the DC," tries Hooper.

Croft comes right back. "See how the shadows deepen, darken/You and your chick should get to sparkin'." He grins.

They have something in common. Hooper has to bite his tongue to keep from making this a moronic announcement: We have something in common! We're not so different, you and I. We are men; we have a moral intelligence.

"It's going to be okay," says Croft, "it'll be fine." All at once he starts into "Glow Worm." His voice is rich, sweet, and he sings, in the dark and intimate stench of Taffy's cage, the most haunting version Hooper has ever heard, will ever hear. Meanwhile he produces a hairpin — from where? — and begins work on the manacled wrist. Hooper tries to take it all in. Is this boring? Can miracles be boring? He leans against the bars. Croft stoops below, freeing him, singing. Hooper can feel his rescuer's breath on his arm, hear the scratch of the pin, divine percussion. His chanteur, his picklock, his savior. It's weird to hear this song here, in the humid night air of Turvyland, after all those hundreds of times he listened to it back in Hindsville on his parents' giant console, with its cherrywood cabinet the size of a car.

The work goes slowly — or maybe quickly, since "Glow Worm" isn't over yet. Hooper feels great, the rest of the world be damned. This is a lush life. He has a flash, a vision: When his hands are loose, when the song is done, they'll step out of the cage together. Polite awkwardness at the door: you first, no you. He'll say, How do I ever thank you?

Croft then, shyly, Don't mention it.

Please, Hooper will beg — he'll beckon with the hand still aprickle from the cuff — Please. Trust me. You can trust me. Not another word spoken, or needed. He'll turn away, know without having to check that Croft is trailing him through the oaks, a stride or two behind.

Across town they'll enter the apartment arm in arm, and Croft will stop at the threshold, smiling at Hooper's stunned parents on the couch. Hooper, meanwhile, his clothes still rumpled and coated with Taffy's dung, will march straight to the CD player, put on this same gorgeous melody. "This is Croft," he'll declare in passing. "These are my parents." He'll turn to face the three of them, and by the time "Glow Worm" reaches its climax, they'll understand, they'll all have grasped the only message that matters now.

Johnny will sing it: "Little glow worm . . . Lead us all to love."

The Trichologist's Rug

Lauren has aged magnificently: she's more beautiful now than when she married him. These days she seems to the trichologist frighteningly more at ease than she used to be, smarter, wittier, sharper. Her skin is unmarred by pouches or spots; her stride still has its Prussian snap; her legs are as yet untouched by blue. Gravity is, unaccountably, still her friend — while the trichologist scrubs his yellowing teeth, having slipped into a shirt to hide his belly, his wife assays her willowy legs in the vanity, lotioning. She chuckles to herself; she and gravity conspire before that mirror like schoolgirls, and meanwhile his beltline drifts slowly, unstoppably down. For fourteen years the trichologist has been shrinking, caving in, eroding; Lauren has grown wise and wondrous and great with possibility. She's lovely . . . lovely, damn it all.

The trichologist likes bananas, eats them every day. Each morning he carries two to his lab in a paper sack. The sacks grow, over the course of weeks, as soft as chamois. Finally they tear, are replaced.

It vexes the trichologist that he, a *cheveux* scholar, a *pelo* professional, a prober of the shaggy perplexities of hair, should be balding. It's coming out in hanks, in hunks, in handfuls. In Lauren's new green convertible, his denuded scalp aches from the sun.

Lauren buys bananas at the open-air market on Glaber Avenue. She has some occult way of separating the wheat from the chaff, bananawise. She sniffs, prods, plumb-bobs, interrogates: scorning the lazy mobocracy of bunches, she clips especially promising specimens off their stems. Let others catch as catch can; Lauren buys her fruits one by one. The trichologist has never had to pare a bruise from his fruit, has never had to skirt a soft spot or a fruit fly. His wife has impeccable taste in bananas. Really she does.

Every day the trichologist's hairs — fine, flexible, keratinized filaments — grow less numerous. They clog his sink and tub drain, cling to his pillow, sully the leather in Lauren's new car. He collects the fallen warriors in his pockets, flushes them down the toilet when he amasses a clump. He works the growing wad of hair in his pocket like a worry stone.

The trichologist does not, of course, complain aloud about his sun-seared scalp. He bears up, does his grieving in private. He'd buy a cap, but caps are silly, a giveaway, just one step up from a toupee. Toupees are for the desperate, the vain, the stupid.

Early in their marriage, Lauren scratched the trichologist's head at night. She grew her fingernails long, strengthened them with egg whites and clear gelatin, raked them through his thick, dark hair until his scalp was on the verge of kindling — all the while relating the details of her day. He looks back at those times fondly now: a stimulated scalp, a wife who liked to tell him things.

The trichologist, like most men of his generation, has an anecdote about meeting his father-in-law. Fourteen years ago — at the time fresh from graduate school, a mere trichologist-in-waiting — he went to meet his wife's father. (Lauren's mother had been killed years before, in a cruise ship mishap. The trichologist has heard the story countless times, and he could boil it down for you to its three key words: Chambord, shuffleboard, overboard.)

The stump-tailed macaque is the only mammal other than *Homo sapiens* to exhibit male pattern baldness. The stump-tailed macaque lives at high altitude, in Asia, and may or may not be vain.

*   *   *

They had eloped, Lauren and the future trichologist, to a place called Haarklammer, a faux-alpine village in hilly Tennessee; at the chapel their blood-test results were scanned by a perky blond in a dirndl and braids; she was sucking on a clutch of pungent Swiss cough drops. "Got to keep the world safe from inbreds," she said cheerfully as she handed over the paperwork. "You'll find the J.O.P. in the Alpenglow chapel, second door on the left."

Lauren's father, Joe, was (and is) a barber. He spoke the lingo of 1950s admen. "What line you in, son?" Joe asked the trichologist, once they were all settled into chairs with glasses of bourbon on ice. The living room was furnished with vintage barber chairs bolted to the floor in a rough pentagon; Joe had set his a smidgen higher than the trichologist's. Atop the battered television at the center of their pentagon were a box of Doodads (stale) and a half-empty bottle of George Dickel.

"I'm in hair," mumbled the trichologist.

Joe looked at him skeptically, eyeing the uncallused fingers, the wire-rimmed glasses, the perfect posture. He reached around the back of his chair and cranked himself up a couple more inches. "You a scissors man?"

"He's a scientist, Pop," Lauren chimed in. "A hair scientist. A scholar."

The corners of her father's mouth crept up a bit, and he levered the chair into a slight recline. "Science my ass; it's *hair.* What kind of pissant science can you make out of hair?" They laughed then, all of them, out loud. For a long while.

Barbers' jokes get laughed at. Their wisecracks are backed with gold, are a currency traded with absolute confidence; barbers are used to an appreciative audience. Most of their witticisms are delivered, after all, while they're edging ears or razoring necks. Barbers punctuate their one-liners the way Catskills comedians do, but instead of a drum roll they give the air a few sprightly scissor-snips. Barbers' jokes are hostage situations; barbers' jokes get laughed at. Out loud. For a long while.

*　　　*　　　*

The jokes of fathers-in-law are also hostage situations, and so the trichologist laughed and laughed. "We've got a lot in common, us two," announced Joe the Scissors Man, cranking his chair down. "Here, let me show you my cuspidors; I got one in the shape of Ethel Merman's open mouth. And have you gotten a whiff of the new wintergreen talc? Come on, son. I'll have your boil-board smelling minty fresh in no time. You might could use a little trim, too. I don't know what idiot you let barber you last."

The trichologist doesn't chew his bananas; he presses the sweet flesh gently against the roof of his mouth, lets it soften and dissolve. Bananas, says the trichologist, are not to be gnashed. Gnashed, they cause the sour cud, the iron stool. The trichologist is nothing if not regular.

Back then, years ago, early in the marriage when his wife used to scratch his head and talk to him, they slept in a double bed. The lamp and the alarm clock were on the trichologist's side. Now, the hair-scholar business being what it is, they sleep on a mattress the size of an Olympic swimming pool; it's flanked by recessed halogen lights. At night Lauren and the trichologist read, silently, separated by vast, crisp reaches of white. Itches go unscratched, stories untold. The world changed, a little, when the trichologist's wife got her own light source.

Darwin's hypothesis: women are more alluring to men because their relative hairlessness makes the mons pubis stand out. It is a dark, tangled shock, an uncanny abyss into which any man would love to leap.

The trichologist's brother-in-law is a stunt pilot. The trichologist's brother-in-law spends his days flying upside down in an ancient, ill-made bathtub with canvas wings and a sewing-machine engine; the trichologist's brother-in-law has alimonies, evil brats, termites, live-in relatives, repossessed furniture, a second mortgage, a spastic colon, almost every source of anxiety available to a man; despite it all, the trichologist's brother-in-law has hair like an anchorman's, wavy and potent and plentiful. "Hey, Mr. Wizard," says the trichologist's brother-in-law one day at a barbecue. He — the in-law — is wearing an apron that says "A Good Slab of Meat Is a Friend Forever." "Maybe," he continues, "you need to drop that science bullshit and fetch some oil from the hoodoo man. You've got the toilet seat look working up there. Ouch, brother. I repeat: Ouch."

About the time Lauren got the convertible, she changed her hair. For years it was mousy, lank, graying a little; she drove a taupe Buick with a balky AM radio. One day the trichologist — preoccupied as always with his latest study of trace metals and color, of how to predict disease by reading strands of hair, of the arcane chemistry of baby-down — came home from the lab. He found his wife in the driveway, at the wheel of a jade-green convertible, in tennis whites, wearing lipstick of some lurid new shade. Her hair, so long that lovable, homely mop, had transformed itself into a smart auburn bob. "Back at eight," she called, gunning the engine. "Bananas on the counter, beer in the fridge. Have at, hair doctor. Ciao."

Or did she say "Herr Doktor"? It's hard to say, standing tongue-tied in her wake, watching. As she rounds the bend by the Wolfes' place, the trichologist watches for the reassuring wink of her brakes — but he sees only the narrow, sporty leer of the taillight. As he turns toward the house, he hears the sharp burst of an upshift.

Now and again, the trichologist goes after hours to Joe's Cuts to collect hair for his research. On those afternoons his father-in-law, now an ancient with waxy gobs of fur in his enormous ears, does not sweep. He sits in his barber's chair, pumps it (an ancient green Nardo, from St. Louis, a finned beaut from the golden age of populuxe) to its kingliest height, and watches the trichologist whisk the hair into a pile and transfer it into a garbage bag. Joe smokes a cigar, pages through a *Playboy* riddled with stubble. "Don't protect that bean, you gonna catch the big C," says the barber. "Is that sunburn, or did somebody try to bile you?"

Once, during sex, while the trichologist strained and worked, Lauren reached over to pluck a thicket of loose hairs from his brow. She frowned, with humiliating calmness, at the waxy strings in her hand. "Easy does it," she said.

The trichologist doesn't exactly *like* his father-in-law; how much affection can a bald man muster for a septuagenarian with black curls thick as a sheep's? But he does like the shop: all those liniments, pomades, oils, shears, striped sheets, spritzer bottles, strops, blades, bibs, bay rums, and the rest — a whole business, a crisp, bright, fragrant world devoted to the gramarye of hair. On his knees at Joe's Cuts, scooping up varitextured, varishaped hairs — hard cuticle, sweet cortex, flexible medulla — and stuffing them into his sack, the trichologist is as happy as he gets, these days. There may be something sad about that, he knows, but it's best not to dwell on such things. The trichologist is wise enough never to dwell.

Still, the trichologist keeps his mouth shut. One doesn't complain about a scorched scalp while sitting, in traffic, next to one's bronze and beautiful wife. One tries instead to entertain her with funny stories from the hair lab, tries to ignore the jumpy grunge-metal music emerging from the speaker system. One's unutterably lovely spouse is drumming on the steering wheel to the music, checking her lipstick in the rearview mirror; her rhythm is flawless. On the console one sees that this is something called "Trouser the Cow," performed by a group called the Blue Samsons. The lead singer's crop of hair is too rich to contemplate. In the photo on the CD case the bluest Samson straddles a Holstein with a porthole in its side, through which the cow's innards can be seen. On his outstretched hand is a cattle egret pretending to be a dove. In such a situation, one does the best one can to feel adequate. One's head aches doubly. One would buy a fancy driving cap or even a see-through cow of one's own, but who would be fooled? The haired, one knows, are not easily duped.

On specimen-gathering days the trichologist buys a soft drink before he leaves. Joe's machine dispenses those six-and-a-half-ounce Cokes made delicious by the faint tang of green glass, bottle cap, and memory. It's one of those automat-style drinkboxes: the trichologist feeds it a quarter and then — if destiny lets it be — he yanks the bottle from its cold tin collar like a sword from its stone. Our weary hair collector slugs it down, draws the sweaty bottle coolingly across his brow, clinks it into its wire rack. Then, giving the neck of his bag an expert wrist-twist, he hefts it over his shoulder and aims for the door. "'Preciate the hair," he calls to Joe, who is still perched high in his Nardo, swishing a whisk brush in front of his face like a fan. "*De nada*," says Joe. "My shop is your shop. My hair is your hair."

Sometimes, as he scoops clippings into his booty-sack, the trichologist ponders. There's something about being on one's knees amid a day's carnage of shorn hair that sets a man to pondering. Barber shops, thinks the trichologist, are still a man's world. Joe's — with its well-thumbed *Playboy* littered with cuttings from old men's eyebrows, with its autographed footballs, its Dr. Grabow Pipe Center, its collection of expired license plates, its hand-lettered "Spit out your chaw, Dammit" sign — Joe's shop is a throwback, and the trichologist is ashamed to realize that he feels nostalgic. He knows the world is different now, knows that's all to the good, but he remembers with a pained fondness how happy he used to feel when Jimmy Irick raked the broom across the back of his freshly shaven and powdered neck, how pleasant it was to hear stories about dove shoots and whorehouses and heroic punt returns. He supposes he's nostalgic about how free and sure he felt then, about how it felt to occupy a world that was built for you. The men in Jimmy's shop spoke so forcefully, so fearlessly.

Sometime during the trichologist's young adulthood, things changed — improved, he knows it, improved immeasurably — but by then men had been bred to imbecilic sureness for so long that they couldn't possibly adjust to life in the new world. The trichologist has been lost now for fourteen years, shrinking, diminishing, failing; his hair is betraying him, and he finds himself on the floor of Joe's with dishwashing gloves and a dustpan and a kitchen cinch-sack, trying, futilely, to stop it. Joe, atop his hydraulic throne, is the last emperor — his kingdom is paved not with gold but with greasy chunks of scalp waste, and he's old, and there's no putting it together again. The world has buckled, and the last long slough has begun, already. From now on there will be only falling: out, in, away. Under.

One day at the lab, taking a break from dipping black rats in pantothenic acid, the trichologist bites into a banana with a soft spot the size of a man's thumb, and he knows suddenly, knows absolutely: He has lost her.

A lesson: As one grows older, weariness and heredity lessen the secretion of pigment. At Irick's the hair on the floor came in a hundred colors. Watching Jimmy chivvy it into a pan was a reminder of the world's richness, of its youth. These days, at Joe's, the strands in the trichologist's dustpan are gray or tallowy yellow or the fraudulent black of shoe polish. Those vaguely pubic curls that stick to his gloves are eyebrow hairs grown wild. The trichologist has seen the candy-striped plank Joe once used to lift his young patrons to scissors level: it sits, flyspecked and warped, in a corner. The most recent *Boy's Life* in the magazine rack dates from 1974.

Lauren has two tortoiseshell cats. For years their shedding irritated the trichologist. It made him sneeze, and he had no need of hair in his home life. Now he doesn't complain. He even likes them, a little, his brethren in loss. They arch their backs for him, leave loose fur in his petting palm.

* * *

He can understand, he supposes, why Lauren has strayed. All those years living a separate, a lesser life; all those sullen years of duty to a contract she hadn't meant to enter; all those years she urged the trichologist to loosen up, have some fun, let down his hair. Now his hair has let him down. (Old joke. Not funny.)

The trichologist is a professional. He ought to be safe from panic. He can call his malady by its name: simple alopecia. He can unravel its etiology; he can cite statistics; he can shrug his shoulders at it, snort at the vanity of minoxidil users, hair-plug guinea pigs, comb-over buffoons. Pattern baldness — he knows all this, knows it cold — is widespread, largely hereditary, basically harmless. Women, too, carry the tendency, but the loss is triggered by testosterone: as a man gets older, his maleness comes to betray him.

Despite his knowledge, the trichologist can't help reading his baldness as a moral failing. The thinning hair reveals not only one's skull but one's weakness. The scalp is a pink, mottled, helpless thing. It's made of angles.

The trichologist feels like he's been stripped of mystery. His thoughts are inane, transparent. Any fool can read them: *I'm bald, I'm bald, I'm dying of bald. Does no one love me?*

Hair's breadth. Against the hair. Hair of the dog. Split hairs. Hairshirt. Hair of the dissembling color. Keep your hair on. Hair-raising. Hair-trigger. Hide nor hair. Just a hair away. Hair in the butter. All hair by the nose. More hair than wit. Got me by the short hairs. Hair today, gone tomorrow.

There comes a day when the trichologist buys a rug. He buys it off the rack; he buys it as a joke, really, or at least persuades himself that he's buying it as a joke. It even seems a funny joke for the time it takes to buy it. He and the clerk point and shrug and whisper and smirk — the same charade one sees at the 7-Eleven when a customer, having bought a bag of chips and an Icee to establish his normalcy, points at the porn rack, to a copy of something called *Deep Banana*.

"Do you want it in a bag, or will you be wearing it home?" asks the wig-store wag, smiling. In the car, the trichologist stuffs the stapled bag into his glovebox.

Lauren is lovely and ageless and lonely; the trichologist is balding fast. It comes as no surprise, then, when one morning he finds a bright red axillary hair glued to his deodorant stick. A strong hair, a shiny, healthy, young, potent, orange hair.

The trichologist's rug is made of genuine hair, of the spare hair of the strong. The toupee's strands are thick and lustrous. Now and again in a bathroom stall at the lab he tries it on, adjusts it, wishes it were really his. One day the superintendent calls the trichologist into his office. He wants the trichologist to keep in mind, he says gently, that there are surveillance cameras in the restrooms — the lab is conducting top-secret follicle experiments for the Feds, and, well, at any rate, one might want to avoid admiring one's toupee in the john.

From that day forward the security guards' smiles seem to have more than a measure of mirth. The trichologist takes his wig home, finds it a hideaway.

If you were to confront him, the trichologist could tell you that he's not really bald: no one is. Where once his hair grew dark and dense he now has tiny, colorless lanugo hairs. They're nearly invisible, they're downy and white and infantile, but he has as many as he's always had, if you'd care to count them. He'd like to find in this the solace of expertise. Trichology has let him down, let him down horribly. Isn't that what knowledge is for, after all, to protect you in some secret way from truths any fool can see?

There comes the day, the inevitable day: the trichologist's bananas are store-bought, speckled, mealy things, and they come, like trouble, in bunches; mocking tufts of hair have sprouted at the base of his spine, on his knuckles, on his upper arms; Lauren's beauty grows, implacable. The trichologist dreams of his wife's ruthless nails, of the way they used to cut furrows into his scalp through that dark and familiar thicket. He is hairless; Lauren is in love with a fire-headed man; tonight a well-meaning waiter asked the trichologist if his daughter would be drinking wine with her meal.

There was a time when the trichologist thought he would be a scholar of death, a thanatologist. He believed education had a talismanic power, thought a thoroughgoing knowledge of death could keep him alive longer. But he opted for hair, and now he is bald. It's all gone. He's bald and alone and a scholar of hair, laughed at by security guards, stunt pilots, barbers, redheads, wives; and his knowledge cannot save him. His has been a wasted life.

So this morning he steps into his closet, reaches to the highest shelf. He pulls down a two-tone bowling-ball satchel, unzips it. Inside is a bell-bottomed vase in a bed of excelsior. Inside the vase, sealed with tape, a parcel wrapped in brown paper. He removes the parcel, tugs away the swags of tape, unwraps.

Lauren is at the breakfast table, peeling an egg, when she hears her husband's heavy tread on the stairs. She doesn't say a word when she sees him pass, in his finest suit, shoulders straight, briefcase in hand, eyes damp but impassive. He doesn't look at her, and she doesn't say a word about the tatty thing splayed across the top of his head. She doesn't say anything, just plucks shards of shell without relent, without even the hint of a smile, until the door slams shut behind him: She is kind to him, in her way. One is kind to the bald.

Junior's — We Cap Hubs

Ray walked to Junior's in the dark. It was bone-cold. He hated the midnight shift — not so much because it was dangerous (it wasn't), but because there was nothing to do, no one to talk to, nothing on the tube except infomercials for woks and thighcisers and tooth bleaches. It was desolate, the graveyard shift; dawn was as far away as Marrakech, or the presidency — how to get there? Sure, naps were *part* of the answer, hubcap-counting, Danish, masturbation; but in the cramped office, in the vast night, amid his various crusts, Ray felt bad. His wool watch cap made his scalp itch. He had a rash in the shape of a maple leaf at the base of his spine. His teeth hurt, and his willie, and it seemed to him sometimes that there was no pleasure in the world.

Ray even resented his feeling of safety a little, coming as he had from the Lower West Side of the City. Newark was second-rate in every way, a pitiful shithole. Not as many people, and those few not as fierce or as savvy. Wasted space. Graffiti suburb-dull and all one color, a halfhearted black like filtered smoke. Shitty pickup basketball on courts where new nets might last for days, even weeks; they weren't even chain. Whores with complexions like Spam, legs like overstuffed duffels. Newark's pastries had fillings the color and consistency of spunk. There wasn't a decent frank or bialy or slice to be had in the whole town. Ray preferred danger, thanks . . . and good eats.

Even Newark's squalor was irreal, kind of Hollywoodish, like if you picked up a brickbat or a beer can off the street and took a bite out of it, it would turn out to be rock candy. A pit, Newark. A shithole. Second-rate. Not like New York. Even its name was just New York slurred and contracted.

But there was nothing to keep Ray in the city anymore, ever since Ruth had filched his stash of bills and run off with that dickhead Ned. Ray had seen it coming — at least the running-off part. He had watched Ruth, mornings, in the street below his window, holding the bastard lightly by the kidneys and murmuring into the gap at the neck of his overcoat as though Ned's throat were the dark mesh of a confessional. Her cheap, thick hose were askew when she came in, her eyes were rimmed with red; Ray just stared harder into the mirror and tried to take care with his razor. All he said to her was this: "I bought those hose. Those hose are mine to take off you." So Ruth let him, but didn't even pretend to like it.

Ned had upswept red hair and a nose like an eggplant; he wore paisley scarves with gold threads woven in; his Brit-fag coat reached the tops of his shoes; his pinkie nails were big as ice cream scoops. He habitually leaned on hydrants, and he wore a T-shirt that bore the legend, "Hitler's heart was *empty,* baby/the cupboard's only bare." Ned also had a habit of swabbing his ears in public, even carried around a mini-bottle of rubbing alcohol and a baggie full of Q-tips; when done, he inspected the cotton as closely as a chemist. A goddamn college boy, slumming — but a college boy *con drogas,* which was what mattered. Ray thought of the pink pockmarks he'd seen way up the insides of Ruth's thighs: needle tracks, Ned's telltale trail.

Ray ran over it in his mind, again. That faraway look of Ned's, one foot atop the hydrant, like some urban admiral at his bridge. Ruth's swollen eyes. The needle marks like footprints. And Ned's pecker would be even more like an eggplant than his nose, Ray assumed; size always mattered to Ruth. It all added up.

It added up to Ray being in this shithole Newark, at midnight, on his way to guard hubcaps.

Brown Avenue was, as always, black and empty. Every streetlight had had its eye put out by kids with rocks. There were glowing cigarette ends on nearly every stoop as Ray passed; they looked like runway lights or cat eyes or something else entirely. Bottles broke like voided hopes behind him. No fear, though —

these people were too tired to thieve, and anyway, what fool would wander around Newark at midnight with money on his hip?

Ray missed New York more than he missed Ruth. Home. The City. If he climbed the grimy trestle across the way from Junior's he could probably see it, see its lights, but why do that? Gestures were for buttheads, Ray knew; he for one was made of sterner stuff. *He* would just do his job and keep his mouth shut. Even so, he wished he could be downtown again, watching greasy rotisseries spin in dirty restaurant windows, hawking flimsy Taiwanese umbrellas during rainstorms, meeting Ruth at the Ear for drinks. But a job was a job, Ray reflected, a bitch was a bitch. This struck him as a profound thought, or at least a serviceable one. And he kept walking.

Ray stepped into the blinding light of Junior's compound. The compound — "like the Kennedys'," Junior curtly reminded anyone who slipped up and called it a "lot" — was a square enclosure of chickenwire about thirty feet long and eight feet high, wired top to bottom with a gleaming assortment of hubcaps. There were ten or twelve thousand hubcaps on the lot (Junior wasn't around at midnight, so Ray felt free), clotting doorways, filling wheelbarrows, heaped atop disemboweled appliances and La-Z-Boys and Chryslers.

But the fence held as many as would fit, hung like funeral wreaths, stacked like drawers in a mausoleum, bursting forth like blooms from a trellis. The fence was Junior's pride and joy. It was art, he had told Ray with something like a catch in his throat; then he had compared himself to that guy in Watts who made a totem pole out of rags and scrap and tin cans and had it knocked down by rioters (or was it politicians?) who couldn't tell art from blight. And Ray was, he had to admit, amazed by the wall of hubcaps. He liked chrome. It gleamed. The fence was pretty as hell, looked in the gloom of night like a mirage, like a storehouse for stars. You could see its glow three-quarters of a mile away . . . and Newark needed something like it — a claim, if not to fame, then to a certain respectability, a second-rate respectability to be sure, but you can't, Ray figured, make chicken salad out of chicken shit. The fucker *showed,* yes sir, the fucker let you know it was there at least.

Junior kept the lot open twenty-four hours a day just so he wouldn't have to hire security to protect his masterpiece. Which was, of course, the purest bullshit — Ray was security in everything but name. No one bought hubcaps in downtown Newark before eight in the morning. And if some poor asshole *did* get an insomniac impulse to buy wire-rims at three A.M., he'd be disappointed; at the beginning of the shift, Ray padlocked the gate with a chain thick as a dockworker's arm, and the door didn't swing open until Junior arrived in the morning.

Nonetheless, for reasons of either insurance or lunacy (no one seemed sure which), Junior insisted on calling Ray a salesman. He gave Ray glossy pamphlets on how to sell. He insisted that Ray wear polished shoes and keep some pomade and a sport coat in the trailer. He told Ray never to smoke outside the office, or to pace; it wouldn't do to have clients think Ray was too anxious to hook them up with a set of caps. Junior gave Ray speeches about the history, the glory, the sacred mission, of hubcap men. Hubcap Men. It would have been laughable, except that Junior had the kind of rock-crusher sincerity that powders all opposition. He believed more in Hubcaps than in God, or in love; there was always someplace to put them. Useful, simple, beautiful — what more could one ask? Capping hubs was Junior's life. The compound was a shrine.

Ray felt it best to play along. Every morning when Junior arrived to relieve him, Ray would shake his head glumly. "Nothing, not even a nibble — it's been a hell of a dry spell, boss," he'd say (or something like it), and Junior would clap him on the shoulder like a sympathetic dad. "They'll sell," Junior would assure him. "The world will always need hubcaps; they're like death, taxes, quim. Hang in there, son." Whenever Junior mentioned sex or booze, he winked; he was one of those people who wink. So he winked, standing (as always) way too close to Ray; he looked, up close, like a tugboat — earnest, ugly, blunt-prowed. Ray winced, slunk by, went home.

Ray's job was easy but boring. He had to make sure no one stole the hubcaps off the fence, and when the sun rose, it was his duty to switch off the lights. Junior had mounted two halogen Goliaths on tennis-court standards fifty feet tall. They lit the lot as brightly as God's grace, but with somewhat more of a hum. They were big. They were bright. Moths clotted around them in thick clouds. In the middle of the night, amid the black lonesome murk of Newark, Junior's Hubcap Compound glowed like Vegas.

Ray found Larry in the trailer, watching the end of *Mama's Family*. "Hysterical," pronounced Larry. "That Mama is plain hysterical."

"Mmm," answered Ray.

"The things she thinks up," continued Larry.

"Wacky," agreed Ray. "Ho ho ho."

Larry pulled the thirty-eight from his belt and leveled it at Ray. "Don't you smart me, New York. Say 'Mama is so funny I want to gnaw my own johnson off.' Say it, or I'll kill you right now."

"Fuck you," said Ray, plopping into the beanbag chair. The thin floor whined.

"Well okay, then," said Larry, grinning, and handed Ray the gun.

Ray stuck it in his coat pocket. "Want a Danish? I got the purple kind."

"My mama says they make Danish jelly out of cow balls, man. Eating that's like giving a heifer a hummer."

"Cows don't have balls, shit-for-brains."

"You calling my mama a liar?"

"Calling her a fool," Ray answered.

"Well okay, then," Larry repeated. "Fool she was, but honest as the day is long. Hasta." He chuckled. "And remember, Ray my boy" — he blew out his cheeks and gestured hugely —

217

"people need hubcaps like houses need roofs, like sundaes need cherries, peas pods, women pricks." This last was Larry and Ray's favorite among Junior's adages. It was funny, they thought. Their boss was a three-time loser at marriage himself, and Larry's girlfriend had run off to Washington State with some chain-smoking poet named DuBeaux who had jazzed up her sex life with an eight-volt battery and a strand of copper wire. Larry was a whiz in bed, to hear him tell it, but you couldn't very well expect him to compete with electricity.

And then there was that dipshit Ned. Fuck him.

When Ray looked up, Larry was gone. Ray trudged out to lock the gate. The keys were cold in his hand. His cod itched; could it be cooties? Just what he needed. Ray scratched. Relief. So . . . what to do? He weighed his options. The hookers would be out soon. That was the best bet. A couple snorts, Ray figured, maybe a little nap, then showtime. He snapped the lock shut, pocketed the keys, and picked his way back to the trailer through the metallic clutter.

One of Junior's giant lights was on a right-angled pole that jutted over the street to illuminate the front of the hubcap wall; prostitutes gathered in front of it late at night both because it was safe and because it provided a dramatic backdrop, like Times Square only more automotive. Ray liked to peer through a chink in the fence at the women, watch them adjust their fraying garters, spray their fruity breaths with mint. He liked to eavesdrop. The prostitutes were often cold, and tugged at their thin coats, reached under their skirts to rub their bare bright asses with shameless brown hands. There were only four or five who gathered at Junior's now. Part of it was winter. The rest was that business was bad; the action had moved to Hoboken, where the yuppies were.

Ray reached into the file cabinet and pulled out the bottle of Rebel Yell. He walked to the empty water cooler and plucked a paper cone from the bottom of the dispenser. He filled it, drank; filled it again. The metal dispenser was frigid. Only one way to keep warm on a night like this. He drained the second cup. Ray flipped on the television, found a salvation show; he liked to watch the evangelists' hair. He had a theory. It never failed — preachers whose hair moved meant what they said, and Ray wouldn't watch their shows (Ray didn't believe exactly, but you can't be too careful). This guy's hair, though, was a silver helmet; he was hawking sanctuary bricks at thirty-five bucks a shot. Ray licked flakes of Danish glaze from his fingers. He settled down on the battered couch. He fell asleep.

He awoke refreshed, squinted at the digital clock above the desk: 3:24. Hell of a nap. Ray pulled himself to a sitting position on the couch, ran his hand over the painful dimple a vinyl button had left beneath his mouth. He scrubbed his front teeth with his index finger, sniffed the finger, wiped it on his shirtfront. He shivered — fucking cold. Ray reached into the file cabinet and poured himself another cone of whiskey. Then he put on coat, cap, and gloves and stepped outside.

Ray could hear the whores as soon as he opened the door — their fretsaw voices, the clicks of their heels as they stamped to stay warm, the rattle of their backs against the fence when they laughed. He gloved his warming crotch, crept closer. There were a few pleasures left in the world after all.

His eavesdropping spot was invisible, protected by hubcaps in front and by the massive lopsided wreck of a refrigerator on one side. The fridge's door was open; its shelves were thickly crusted with windblown dirt and Ray's spoor. It was an Amana. The refrigerator listed to the left like a cripple; then again, so did Ray. This made for a nice arrangement. Snug, like a wife, or a crypt. Neat. Convenient.

The hiding place had one drawback; Ray couldn't see out very well. This made his furtive jerks somewhat more taxing on his imagination than they might otherwise have been; for erotic fuel, he had to make do with glints of sidewalk mica, snippets of raunchy shoptalk, a riot of perfumes, an occasional glimpse of flabby whoreshank through a gap in the curtain of hubcaps. Not much to go on. In large part, Ray was obliged to fly by his instruments. This was difficult, but Ray was up to the task. He strode across the lot, ready.

But then, as Ray planted his hand atop the fridge to guide himself into position, he heard another voice, a man's. Not, Ray judged by the command and ease in the voice, a customer. The boss? Ray had never seen the hookers with their pimp, not even once. He slid forward to see. The fence mesh was frigid as a blade against his cheek. Ray located the voice; in the lurid light he could see black wingtips, a few snowy snatches of pelt near the ground. Full length. Newark pimps still took their fashion cues from *Kojak*; no surprises there.

"So this fat white boy says he wants to go down on me," Ray heard one of the women say, "and he sticks out his tongue at me, and it's, Lord be my witness, as big as a ham. He can make the sumbitch *dance,* too. Got a rubber in one hand, pulls it on. Right on his tongue. Keeps talking the whole time. I ain't shitting you."

The man said something Ray couldn't make out, and there was laughter. It was a white man's voice. Young. Somebody leaned heavily against the fence. This startled Ray, and he stepped back onto a stray hubcap and fell.

Instantly, the man's voice boomed through the fence. "Who's there?"

Ray pulled himself to his feet. The light beat down on him. Colors swam in his eyes. He zipped up, careful not to pinch.

"Hey! You whacking off back there, Hubcap Man? There's no such thing as a free ride. You come, you owe. That's the free enterprise system, my man. You hearing me?"

Ray moved closer to the fence. How could the pimp have known? Had he heard the zipper? Ray could smell the man's hot breath. Chicken vindaloo, weed, gum rot — what was it psychic powers smelled like? Ray had read somewhere, he was sure. What was it? His mind was a blank.

"You open, cuz? Quit beating your meat and open up. Sign says twenty-four hours, seven days. Open up! I need me some hubcaps. I got to have some hubcaps. This a hubcap store or not?"

Ray hissed loudly, surprising himself.

"Hey!" shouted the man, and yanked on the fence. One of

the hubcaps flapped up and popped Ray in the nose. He groaned loudly. He bled like a tomato.

"I need some hubcaps for my ladies, to show them how much they mean to me," cooed the pimp. Laughing. Calm. "You got 'em to fit us, don't you, Pee Wee?"

There was a pause. Ray stepped close to the fence again, squeezed one eye shut. Then he saw it. A flash of cotton in the violent light. A blue-shafted Q-tip, working at a glossy ear. Six scant inches away. Ned.

Ray stepped back and yanked the gun out of his coat pocket. He fired wildly at the wiggling swab, heard the shot ricochet into the side of the fridge. He fired twice more, frantically, heard the scrabble of feet, muffled curses, the man's voice yelling, "What the fuck is wrong with you?" He heard the sympathetic murmur of the hubcaps along the fence, like a thousand tiny bells; the sound rippled around him like applause. This was his moment. Ray had Ned on the run. How long could it be before he conquered Ruth again, New York, his life?

"Ruth!" shouted Ray. "Ruth!" It was like a battle cry.

Ray stepped back and blew a few hubcaps off the fence with his last three shots. The metal discs were arrayed there like the carnival balloons kids hurl darts at; no need to aim. The gun was pure power. Ray couldn't miss.

When he had finished shooting, there was a hole in the hubcap chainmail the size of an ottoman. Ray stood near it, holding the gun limply at his side. He could see the hookers in the distance, retreating into the dark of Paley Avenue. Behind them, walking deliberately, was the man. He wore a garish Rasta stovepipe. He was still idly reaming his ear with the Q-tip. He looked nothing like Ned.

Ray walked back to the office. He opened the middle desk drawer, pulled out six bright bullets, reloaded. The bullets clicked prettily into place. His bag of Danish lay atop the desk. The pallid joys of pastry — Ray was beyond them now. He stepped back outside. The lights above were cruel, blinding. Ray swung the pistol up toward the one nearest the street and fired. Nothing. He aimed carefully, shot again. The light exploded. Ray spun to face the other, feeling somehow that it had sneaked behind him. There was a purple flash, a loud buzz, the tinkle of spent glass. Darkness.

This was the way Ray liked it. He thought of the spooked moths bumping one another overhead. Ray remembered an accident he had seen once on Ninth Avenue. A taxi had plowed through an intersection and into a panel truck. There were squeals, screams, the gnash of metal. And then, after the impact, almost as an afterthought, a lone hubcap had rolled away from the cab. Ray had watched the silver disc make a series of lazy circles in the middle of the avenue, smaller and smaller, until it started to wobble. But before it had the chance to fall, a little Oriental boy in a ratty green parka swooped across the street and snatched it up. The boy kept running, never looked back. His furry parka hood had bobbed behind him like a pigtail.

The darkness tasted sweet to Ray; he felt warm for the first time all night. Ruth didn't matter to him now. He wished Ned the best. Newark, too. Stepping proudly, heedlessly, crashing like a Hun across a vast steppe of junk, Ray made his way back to the trailer to wait for his relief. This was all there was, and it was, by God, it *was* enough. He might, he knew, never be this happy again.

Acknowledgments

I would like to express my gratitude to the editors of journals in which parts of this book originally appeared: Robert and Peg Boyers of *Salmagundi,* Jodee Rubins and Stephen Donadio of *New England Review,* Willard Spiegelman of *Southwest Review,* Peter Stine of *Witness,* Janet Wondra of *New Delta Review,* and Virgil Suarez and Richard Foerster of *Chelsea.*

Heartfelt thanks, too, to those friends who read and shaped these stories in manuscript, especially Dave Racine, Josh Russell (who generously let me filch from him the premise of "Kidnapped [A Romance]"), Wayne Wilson, Laura O'Connor, and Brock Clarke. Webster Younce, Doug Stewart, and Andrew Pope — vielen Dank.

I am deeply indebted to the wonderful people at Arcade, especially Dick and Jeannette Seaver, Darcy Falkenhagen, Greg Comer, Cal Barksdale, and Casey Ebro. Miranda Ottewell did an expert job copyediting.

An Individual Artist Fellowship from the Louisiana Division of the Arts was invaluable in helping me finish this book, as was the support of the Department of English & Comparative Literature at the University of Cincinnati.

Thanks, above all, to James Olney, the most generous friend imaginable; to my parents, Colette and Rufus Griffith; and — first, last, and always — to Nicola.

— Michael Griffith